THE FAME EQUATION

LISA WYSOCKY

Published by
Cool Titles
439 N. Canon Dr., Suite 200
Beverly Hills, CA 90210
www.cooltitles.com

The Library of Congress Cataloging-in-Publication Data Applied For

Lisa Wysocky—
The Fame Equation

p. cm
ISBN 978-1-935270-37-9
1. Mystery   2. Horses   3. Southern Fiction   I. Title
2015

Copyright 2015 by Lisa Wysocky
All Rights Reserved
including the right of reproduction in whole or in part in any form.

Printed in the United States of America

1 3 5 7 9 10 8 6 4 2

Book design by White Horse Enterprises, Inc.

For interviews or information regarding special discounts for bulk purchases,
please contact cindy@cooltitles.com

Distribution to the Trade: Pathway Book Service,
www.pathwaybook.com, pbs@pathwaybook.com, 1-800-345-6665
Also available via Ingram, and Baker & Taylor

Other Books by Lisa Wysocky

Fiction
The Opium Equation
The Magnum Equation

Nonfiction
The Power of Horses
Success Within
Front of the Class (with Brad Cohen)
My Horse, My Partner
Horse Country
Success Talks
Two Foot Fred (with Fred Gill)
Horseback
Walking on Eggshells (with Lyssa Chapman)
Hidden Girl (with Shyima Hall)
Therapy Horse Selection

DEDICATION

To therapy horses everywhere.
I've thanked you before in other books,
but thank you again. Your contributions
are invaluable.

CAST OF MAIN CHARACTERS

Cat Enright: A horse trainer who lives near Nashville, Tennessee. She is thirty, single (but in a relationship—she thinks), impulsive, vulnerable, and the owner of a small stable.

Jon Gardner: Cat's stable manager and right hand. No one, Cat included, knows his secrets.

Darcy Whitcomb: Eighteen-year-old teenager with a trust fund. She might be spoiled, but Cat loves her like family.

Agnes Temple: Eccentric woman of a certain age with short, spiky, electric blue hair. She owns two horses in Cat's barn.

Bubba Henley: Budding juvenile delinquent and eleven-year-old son of a neighboring horse trainer. He and Cat had become close earlier in the year.

Hill Henley: Bubba's father and fourth generation Tennessee Walking Horse trainer. He's about as sharp as a mashed potato.

Keith Carson: A neighbor and country music superstar. Cat has a secret crush on Keith and is thrilled that he chose her as his riding instructor.

Brent Giles: A tall, blond small animal veterinarian from Clarksville, and Cat's boyfriend. Cat thinks he's cute, but isn't sure she wants to take the relationship to the next level.

Martin Giles: Recently promoted former sheriff's deputy. Martin is now a full-fledged detective—and Brent's brother.

Melody Cross: Rising country music star who is Keith Carson's duet partner, and a close friend of Cat's.

Ruthie Cosgrove: Pastor of the Holy Church of the Mighty Happy.

Allen Harding: The church's financial advisor, and Ruthie's brother.

Emily Harding: Allen's wife. She also runs the church's therapeutic riding program.

Buffy Thorndyke: Reporter turned publicist, she works with Melody Cross.

Davis Young: Melody's manager.

Augie Freemont: Stocky, older man with a shaved head, goatee, and earring. He is the booking agent for both Keith and Melody.

Bill Vandiver: Melody's hair stylist.

The Potts Family: Mother Claudine, father Cletus, sister Brandyne, and brother Bodine are blood relatives of Raylene—which prompted her to change her name to Melody Cross.

Chas Chadwick: Head of Melody's record label.

Scott Donelson: Melody's entertainment lawyer.

Robert Griggs: A former student of Cat's who now works at the Mighty Happy Therapeutic Riding Center.

Annie Zinner:	A horse trainer from Oklahoma and a mother figure to Cat.
Tony Zinner:	Annie's husband and training partner. He and Jon Gardner have a past.
Gusher Black:	The owner of a new horse in Cat's barn.
Hank:	Cat's incorrigible Beagle-mix hound dog.
Sally Blue:	A (possibly) psychic, red roan Appaloosa mare owned by Agnes Temple.
Peter's Pride:	A tall, older black gelding owned by Darcy Whitcomb. Petey is a calming influence on Darcy, but he also likes to play.
Hillbilly Bob:	Bay, aged gelding owned by a local orthopedic surgeon. Cat swaps training fees for treatment of broken bones and other injuries, and has won several championships on Bob.
Glamour Girl:	A gorgeous, but silly, yearling filly owned by Mason Whitcomb, Darcy's dad.
Redgirl's Moon:	Tall and elegant, she is a chestnut mare owned by Agnes Temple. Reddi is a real go-getter and excels in English events.
Ringo's Jetstar	Former racehorse who is a new horse in Cat's barn.
Wheeler	Short, squat palomino gelding who may be moving to a new home.

The Holy Church of the Mighty Happy, and the Mighty Happy Therapeutic Riding Center

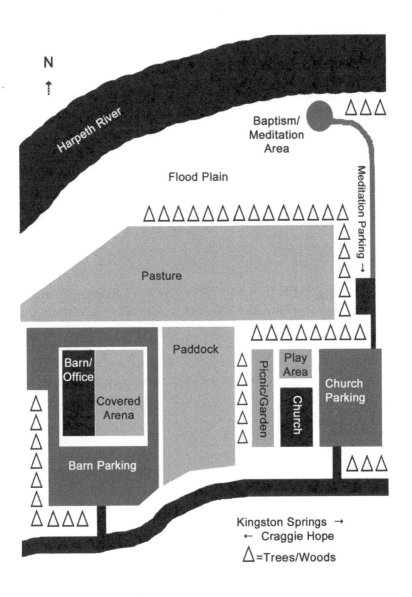

1

THE COWBOY AND THE LADY cantered across the grassy field, then turned toward a large video camera that perched on a set of portable tracks. The autumn reds and golds of the hillside trees were duplicated in the rider's clothes, and in the bright red roan and bay coats of the horses. As they neared the camera, the riders looked longingly at each other, then reached out to grab each other's hand.

It would have been quite romantic. Except the male rider, who was to the right, moved the reins from his left hand to his right so he could grasp the other rider's hand, and in the process dropped a rein. Of course the horse stepped on it and it broke. Both horses were being ridden in bitless bridles, so I wasn't concerned that the horse's mouth had been hurt, but I had kind of liked those reins.

The director, a rail thin fifty-ish man with dyed black, spiky hair who went by the name of Fitch, waved his arms around and everything came to a screeching halt. I wish someone had told me about Fitch's arm waving when I got my horses, Sally Blue and Hillbilly Bob, ready for this video shoot. Sally was okay with his windmill-like maneuvers, but Bob, normally a "steady Eddie," often looked at Fitch as if he was from Planet Crouton. And who knows? Maybe he was. I'd asked Fitch to tone down the arm waves a bit, explaining that we didn't need to get country music superstar Keith Carson dumped onto the ground, but Fitch just looked at me as if I was a pesky ant and made shooing motions with his hands. I'd been here all day and he had yet to speak one word to me.

As the video crew tweaked the position of the cameras and lights for yet another take, I looked longingly at the craft services truck that was set up near the back entrance of the steeplechase grounds at Nashville's Percy Warner Park. I sighed. Craft services had some amazing hot chocolate and I thought longingly of a cup, but I needed to replace the broken rein, find another way for Keith to reach his hand out, and see to my horses.

Well, technically, Bob and Sally weren't mine, even though I thought of them as family. Bob, a bay Appaloosa gelding with a bright white blanket and spots over his hips, belonged to an orthopedic surgeon who occasionally patched me up. Sally Blue was a young, red-roan Appaloosa mare who belonged to Agnes Temple. Think stout seventy-year-old cheerleader with short, spiky, bright blue hair and attention deficit disorder, and you had Agnes. In spite of that, Agnes was a dear friend.

Keith was riding Bob and I have to say the hunky singer looked darn good on a horse. He, his wife, Carole, and their large brood of kids, lived next door to me. I've had a not-so-secret crush on Keith as long as I can remember and when he asked me to give him riding lessons so he could look good in this video, my brain instantly turned to mush and for a few minutes there, I couldn't walk straight.

I quickly learned that Keith was a stickler for perfection. The trouble was, many cowboys ride with a split rein, which means the left and right reins are not tied together. This is so a cowboy can drop the end of the reins to the ground when he dismounts as a signal for the horse to ground tie, or stand "tied to the ground."

Keith wanted to be that cowboy and resisted every effort I made to get him to ride with a knot in his reins, or with a closed set of reins. Closed reins are made up of one long strap, and barrel racers use them all the time. Yet another idea was for Keith to hold the split reins in his right hand, but according to Keith, none of those options were "the cowboy way."

The obvious solution was for Keith to ride to the left of the blond girl. Then he could just reach out his right hand. But with the lay of the land, the surrounding hills, the ambient light, and a host of other technicalities that I had no interest in, Fitch wanted Keith to the right of the other horse and rider.

"Sorry about the rein," Keith said. "What is that, two broken reins now?"

"Three," I answered with a smile.

"I'll replace—"

"I know. We'll deal with it later. Fortunately, I have one other pair in the trailer. But Keith?" I made sure he was paying attention. "You *have* to knot these. They are the last pair I have with me and I heard Fitch tell his assistant that we are losing the light. Just keep your hand over the knot and no one will see it except during the quick moment when you transfer your reins. Besides," I finished, "no one will be looking at your hands. Your fans will be looking at your smiling face."

I knew I certainly would be.

The other rider, rising superstar Melody Cross, was on Sally Blue. By the time I finished with Keith, Buffy Thorndyke and Bill Vandiver, Melody's publicist and hair/makeup/wardrobe guy, had surrounded her. I'd known Buffy for a while. She used to be a reporter with the *Ashland City Times*, the local paper for the northern half of Cheatham County, where my stables were located. We were about fifteen miles west of Nashville, Tennessee, close enough to the city to be attractive to commuters, yet rural enough to house some interesting characters.

I had just met Bill today, although his reputation had preceded him by several months. Melody swore by his hair color and extension work and I had to admit that her hair always looked fabulous.

Melody was last year's Country Music Association New Artist of the Year. Her first three singles had gone number one and she was on a fast track to major stardom. I had met Melody a few months ago when she, at Keith's suggestion, also contacted me about riding lessons. Before she and I met, Melody had not only never been on a horse, she had never touched one. But, she was just as determined as Keith that she perform her own riding in the video, and also ride well. The horses and I found her to be kind, with a natural ability to understand equine body language. She progressed quickly.

What also moved fast was our friendship. Outside of my barn crew, a few other trainers, and the owners of my horses, I didn't have many friends. Noah Gregory was a friend from college who now managed horse shows, but I only saw him a few times a year when we were both at shows, and when we were both supremely busy. Keith's wife Carole and I were friends, but she had four kids, the oldest being around ten, so her time was limited.

Annie Zinner was like a second mother to me, mine having passed away when I was nine, but she lived in Oklahoma. Annie and her husband, Tony, were trainers who had a unique connection to my assistant and barn manager, Jon Gardner, who was also a friend. Then there was my live-in riding student Darcy. She had just turned eighteen and had a trust fund. While Annie was like a mother to me, I was like Darcy's second mom, hers being so busy marrying and divorcing minor European royalty and all.

But I didn't have a close BFF girlfriend until Melody and I clicked. Right from the start I found myself making trips to her little rental home in Pegram, a commuter town in the southern part of our county. Between recording sessions and tour dates, interviews and meetings, Melody often showed up at my barn with old-fashioned cake doughnuts and a thermos of hot chocolate, or on warmer days, iced chai lattes. I liked her, and I found that fact odd. My veterinarian boyfriend aside, I normally liked dogs and horses better than I liked people. But I liked Melody.

I liked gossiping with her, watching chick flick DVDs, and helping her eat her latest batch of homemade cookies. Cookie-eating aside, those other things were not activities I normally liked to do. I even liked helping Melody choose her wardrobe for her live performances and found that task wasn't so different from helping a riding student choose attire for the show ring.

The reason for the shoot today was the music video for Keith and Melody's new single, "Do Good." In the past few months I'd learned a lot from Melody about the music business. She and Keith were two hot stars on the same label, Southern Sky Records, and the powers that be had decided that teaming them up on a duet was a great way to maximize the label's brand.

The single was a catchy, feel good song written by Melody, Keith, and Melody's manager, Davis Young. Davis was a former guitar player in a band that had a few hits a decade or so ago. He was a little taller than medium height, had a lean body, and the requisite music industry goatee. His was a reddish brown. Rather than try to stage a comeback, he'd moved into management and had done well. I'd learned that it was not unusual in Nashville to have three or even four songwriters collaborate on a song, or, like Davis, for those songwriters to also have other music industry jobs.

In addition to Davis, who stood near the craft services truck drinking a mug of hot chocolate that should have had my name on it, Chas Chadwick, head of Southern Sky, was on the set. Chas was a dark, broody, preppy sort of fellow who looked to be in his mid-forties. He had spent most of the day standing just past the reach of Fitch's windmilling arms. I guess when your company is paying more than a hundred grand for a video, you want to be sure you get your money's worth.

Augie Freemont, a stocky, older man with a shaved head, goatee, and earring, was the booking agent for both Keith and Melody, and had come by during lunch. He was memorable also for the impressive double roll of fat on the back of his head. I've always wondered how that happens. I mean, who gets fat rolls on the back of their head? Augie wasn't thin, but he wasn't obese, either.

Scott Donelson, Melody's attorney, had popped onto the set earlier, but only stayed a few minutes. It was a show of support that was probably worth at least two billable hours to his client, plus mileage expenses of course.

The lights and cameras had supposedly been tweaked and Fitch was now waving his arms in a way that I assumed meant they were ready for the horses and riders. I gave a last swipe of baby oil to Bob's dark nose to make it glossy, and placed my fingers over Keith's left hand to encourage him to tighten his grip on the knot in his reins.

The riders jogged across the wide infield of the steeplechase grounds and I wondered, for what must have been the thousandth time that day, how the label or video company got permission to film here. Usually Metro Nashville guarded the grounds like a crown jewel and firmly encouraged hikers and other visitors who came to Percy Warner Park to stay off the steeplechase course.

The music cued and the song began to play. Although they were not recording audio in this scene, the music helped both the horses and the riders get into their roles. Keith and Melody turned Bob and Sally and they all began to canter, again, to a point near the moving video camera. The horses cantered in time to the music and at the appropriate spot Keith and Melody looked longingly at each other. Keith then transferred his reins into his right hand and reached out to enfold Melody's right hand in his left. Then the two stars cantered on, past the camera and presumably off into happily ever after.

"Cut!" Fitch yelled. "That's a wrap."

Numerous hugs and high fives were exchanged amongst the crew. You'd have thought they'd just won the lottery, and in their world, maybe they had. Keith and Melody handed the horses to me, and both stayed to help untack. Jon Gardner had been here most of the day. But, as the afternoon lengthened, good guy that he was, he felt a need to head back to our barn to feed the other horses in our care. Fortunately, he had driven over separately, in his rusty, dark blue sedan.

"Go," I said to Keith and Melody as soon as the horses' legs had been wrapped for trailering. "You have a party to get ready for."

The "wrap party" was a traditional festive event held after the close of any major music industry project. This one was being held at a therapeutic riding center in Kingston Springs, the southwestern-most town in Cheatham County. Melody was a member of the church that sponsored the riding center, The Holy Church of the Mighty Happy.

Melody had tried several times to get me to go services with her on Sunday mornings when she was in town, but either I was at a horse show, or just didn't feel the need to go. Catholic by birth, even though I did not attend mass regularly (okay, hardly ever) I was uncomfortable in the Southern Methodist church my boyfriend Brent went to, and assumed the same would apply with this congregation.

"Cat? You want a little touch up before we go to the wrap party?" Bill asked, a cordless hair straightener in his hand. "A little smoothing? Your curls are really . . . curly."

Bill was being tactful. My long hair looked like a dull brown rat's nest. A day of humid November breezes had turned my careful ponytail of this morning into a frizzy mess. Despite Bill's stellar reputation, I made a habit of avoiding hair salons. No one had ever made my hair look good, so I stopped wasting my money. Melody had been working on me, though. Maybe someday soon I would pay a visit to Bill's salon.

"Ah, not right now, Bill," I said. "But thanks. I have to get the horses home before I can head to the party. I'll see you there, though."

I loaded Bob, the heavier of the two horses, first. The only trailer I had was a six-horse diagonal haul, and I'd made a spot for him just in front of the first trailer axle. I asked Sally to go in next, but she resisted. That was odd behavior for her, but Sally sometimes acted very oddly. Instead of joining Bob, she craned her neck to the left, and whinnied at Keith, Melody, Davis, and Chas, who were talking about a hundred feet away.

"Bye, Sally," Melody called, waving at her favorite horse. "See you soon."

Sally looked at the group a moment longer, sighed, and stepped into the trailer.

After a quick wave of my own, I got into the cab of my truck and headed for River Road.

Cat's Horse Tip #1

"Horses see light and dark more intensely than humans, and may not want to get into a trailer because the interior is too bright or dark for the horse to see well."

2

MY FARM WAS LOCATED ON the south bank of the Cumberland River. It was twenty rolling acres of what used to be part of the massive Fairbanks Plantation, which was owned during the Civil War by a scoundrel named Col. Samuel Henley. I had learned a lot about Col. Sam earlier this year when my neighbor, a recent owner of the ancestral Henley home, got herself murdered.

I purchased my farm eight years ago, just after I graduated from Middle Tennessee State University with a degree in equine science. My beloved grandmother, who had raised me from the time I was nine, passed suddenly and I found more than eighty thousand dollars in cash stuffed under her mattress. I used every cent to buy my old farmhouse and accompanying old tobacco barn, and hung out my horse training shingle. I had been fortunate since then, racking up national wins on the Appaloosa horse show circuit just about every year, and I couldn't have done it without Jon Gardner.

Jon showed up on my doorstep roughly four years ago and moved into the apartment I had just renovated in the barn loft. He was an enigma, although I had learned something about his family a few months ago. Not much else about his past had come forth since then, but I gave thanks every day that he was on my team.

I had hoped to convince Jon to come to the wrap party with me, but as soon as we got Sally settled in her stall she sank her head deep into her water bucket and began to blow bubbles. Agnes was positive that Sally only did that if something big was about to happen (or had already happened). And indeed, in some people's minds, a case could be made that Sally might possibly be psychic. In this instance, maybe Sally understood that millions of people would soon see her on Country Music Television and other music video channels. That didn't explain the tie in to the water and bubbles, though.

Jon was more concerned with Sally's behavior than I was and decided to stay home to watch her. I also suspected that he just didn't want to go. Jon was a quiet watcher, an observer of people and animals, which is one reason he was so good with horses. Interacting with people, however, was another story. Jon was not a gregarious sort, and I had the feeling that a party filled with people he did not know was the last place he wanted to be.

Many in Nashville would jump at an invitation to a music industry wrap party, but after a phone call, I realized that in addition to Jon, my boyfriend Brent was not one of them. Brent was a small animal veterinarian in nearby Clarksville, Tennessee and was quite certain that he'd much rather balance his checkbook than go to the event.

Darcy, however, was another story. Darcy was a senior in high school, a student and friend who now lived with me. Her dad, Mason Whitcomb, was a Nashville magazine and Internet media publishing mogul who lived in the ritzy Green Hills area of Nashville. He often was too busy for his only child. Darcy's mother I have already mentioned. Both parents loved her dearly, but Darcy decided last summer that I was the one to give her the attention she needed. I actually didn't mind.

"Seriously?" she said, snapping a wad of pink bubblegum. "The wrap party is at a therapeutic riding center? Like maybe I can do my forty hours for my senior project there."

I tried not to get too involved in Darcy's school. Her dad tolerated the fact that she lived with me but that was about it. He also had two horses in my barn: Gigi, this year's national champion yearling filly, and Darcy's tall, dark Appaloosa gelding, Peter's Pride, who we all affectionately called Petey, so I didn't want to overstep my bounds. But, I did know that Darcy was supposed to have cleared her service project with her advisor last week.

In fact, the poor woman was so frustrated with Darcy that she had begun to make suggestions for volunteer hours. Darcy had deemed every suggestion "inappropriate." The woman's ideas had recently descended to such brainstorms as implementing an anti-litter campaign, building a bridge over a small stream at a local park, and horror of all horrors, singing songs to preschoolers.

None of those ideas even remotely fit Darcy. My favorite teen could often be superficial, but she was passionate about fairness and was a strong defender of justice. I could easily see her going into law or politics, or possibly even social work, although I didn't think her dad would support that effort. Not enough money or prestige. No, Darcy needed a service project that meant something, that would make a difference. Maybe volunteering at a therapeutic riding center would be it.

So, with a change into a clean pair of Wranglers and my least mud-stained Cat Enright Stables jacket, I gave a few quick swipes of my hairbrush and put on some lip gloss. Then Darcy and I headed out of my driveway, and took a series of rights and lefts on River Road, Sam's Creek Road, Hwy. 70, and Kingston Springs Road. We finally wound through the tiny town of Kingston Springs, and landed in front of the Mighty Happy Therapeutic Riding Center.

The parking lot was packed, so we followed the car ahead of us and pulled onto the grass to the left of the barn. Inside, two women dressed in dark gold sweatshirts with the logo of the riding center in black greeted us.

"We are mighty happy to see you," the older one said as the younger one handed us brochures about the center. "The party is in the covered arena. Just head down the aisle and take a right about half way down."

I loved snooping in other people's barns. Here, the floor was a gorgeous red brick. The first three twelve-foot sections of stalls on both sides of the wide aisle were fully enclosed with doors labeled FEED and TACK on the left, and VIEWING AREA and OFFICE on the right. We walked past those to find two rows of open concept stalls, five on each side. These open concept stalls had dividers between the stalls that were wood on the bottom four feet or so, then heavy mesh from there on up. The stall fronts were mesh all the way to the floor, including the stall doors. I thought the design was brilliant, as it fostered a herd environment and allowed the horses to see each other. Humans are predators, and horses are prey animals who feel safer in a herd. Each stall was also thickly bedded with fragrant wood chips and came furnished with a shiny silver automatic waterer.

We still had fully enclosed wooden stalls and a dirt floor at Cat Enright Stables, and I wished I could import the brick floor and open stalls to my place on River Road.

Three horses currently inhabited the stalls. The first was an inquisitive chestnut Haflinger pony with a white blaze and a thick, fluffy, flaxen mane and tail. The card on the front of the stall said he was a ten-year-old gelding and that his name was Noodle. The second horse, a narrow, dark brown Saddlebred/Quarter Horse cross of about fifteen hands, was eighteen years old and called Cinnamon. The final horse, Tinkerbelle, was a massive, gray Percheron/Thoroughbred cross.

Past the horse stalls, I saw room for hay and equipment storage, and to the right was an entrance to the covered arena, which was alight with festivities. In the arena, I took a moment to get my bearings. There, to our left and across the arena, tiny, blond Melody and tall, gorgeous Keith were besieged by hoards of reporters and flashing cameras. As always, my heart gave a little lurch when I saw Keith. My platonic crush was in full force, but it looked as if the country music media had a crush on him as well. Keith was currently talking to Chuck Dauphin, a respected reporter and disc jockey, but was surrounded by many other hopeful members of the media.

Next to one of a dozen or so tall gas heaters that were spaced around the arena, Carole was talking to a slim man of medium height whose back faced us. She waved to beckon us over. Before we got there, though, the man turned and smiled.

That was strange, because although I knew the man well, I can't ever recall seeing him smile. Robert Griggs was a former riding student, and earlier this year was in a class with Carole, Darcy, and Glenda Dupree, my movie star neighbor who had been killed.

"Robert! What are you doing here?" I asked.

Carole answered on his behalf. "Can you believe it? Robert works here, at the therapeutic riding center," she said. "He's the volunteer coordinator, farm manager, and chief poop scooper."

The last I heard, Robert was volunteering at a center in Franklin, about twenty miles from here.

"Part time," said Robert, still smiling. Robert was the kind of person who was wound up tight inside—or he used to be. I had never seen him so relaxed or friendly. "I'm still nursing at Vanderbilt three days a week, and then I'm mighty happy to be here the other three days. Sundays I'm over at the church."

I'd almost forgotten that this therapeutic riding center was "faith based."

"I'd love to catch up Cat," he said, "but I have to get horses ready for the presentation we're giving in a few minutes. Maybe you can come back another time, say on Friday? I think Fridays and weekends are open for you now that the show season is over?"

Robert was right. Jon, Darcy, and I had just returned from the world championships, and it was the first national event in a number of years where we had not competed. My team had done exceptionally well last summer at the national show, and also at a special all-breed invitational show in August. We needed a rest. So, we had gone with the goal of generating new business, and had picked up one major new horse and a few strong possibilities for the coming show season. Mission accomplished.

"I'd love to come on Friday," I said. "Actually, Darcy wanted to talk with someone about volunteering here. She needs hours for her senior service project." I glanced around, but Darcy had disappeared into the crowd. "She's here somewhere."

Just then I spotted her on the other side of the covered arena talking to Bill, who was examining her long strands of wavy, honey blond hair.

"Darcy's last period is a study hall," I said. "If it's related to her service project, I'm sure her advisor would be happy to let her skip it. Would three o'clock work?"

Robert grinned and stuck out his thin hand. "See you then," he said.

Wow, I never thought quiet, morose Robert even knew what a grin was, and here he was, giving a really good impression of one. I walked away grinning myself.

I headed toward the long tables of food hoping for hot chocolate, and maybe a chocolate éclair, but before I got there Melody dashed my way with an entire group of people in tow. I willed my stomach to stop rumbling.

"Cat, you've heard me talk about my friends from church," Melody said, "and here they are."

In a rush of names and introductions I eventually sorted out Ruthie Cosgrove, a short woman in her forties with a tiny waist and an unfortunate set of thighs. Despite her lank brown hair and frowsy appearance, Ruthie was the founder and pastor of the church and I could see why she had been so successful with it. There was something electric about her. Stage presence, Melody would have called it.

"How are you," I nodded politely at her.

"Mighty happy, Cat. Mighty happy. So glad to finally meet you."

I had a suspicion that all the talk about being mighty happy was going to get to me sooner or later. Oh, guess what? It already had.

Also in the group with their own confirmations of being mighty happy were Allen and Emily Harding, and their daughter Rowan. Allen, I gathered, was Pastor Ruthie's brother and the church's financial person. He was a proud, pompous fellow about six feet in height, barrel-chested with a full head of salt and pepper hair.

Emily, his wife, was the program director and lead instructor at the therapeutic riding center. Emily was a stunning biracial woman who looked thirty, but was probably a decade older. With Allen and Emily was their nine-year-old daughter, Rowan, a cute Asian girl in pigtails and glasses.

"We're big on adoption in this family," said Allen with the air of someone whose words were of great importance. I really hadn't meant to stare at the colorful family. I was just trying to sort everyone out. "Emily," he continued, "is of Mexican, Navajo, and African American descent and was adopted when she was three. Rowan is Chinese, and we adopted her when she was fourteen months. Ruthie and I grew up with our biological parents, and our ancestors all came from England, Ireland and Scotland—far as we can tell."

"I'm Irish myself," I said, trying to process what my brain clearly told me was too much information.

A volunteer arrived and whispered something into Emily's ear. "I must go," she said. "Our riders are ready to get on their horses. It was nice to meet you, Cat."

I nodded and looked toward the craft services table. Davis was there, mug in hand, next to a tall, silver container and a table sign that read in large bold letters HOT CHOCOLATE. Dang, by the time I got over there he would have drunk it all. I hurried to the carafe, grabbed a mug, and sure enough, the drops of luscious hot chocolate that dribbled out were only enough to fill a quarter of my cup. Sighing, I nodded at Davis, who was now talking to Augie, the booking agent.

I saw Darcy head to the food line and snuck in behind her. As we filled our plates the PA system came to life and I looked to the end of the arena. Ruthie stood on a small platform and as she began to speak, clips from Keith and Melody's video shoot began to play on two large screens near her. In addition to today's footage, there was some intense concert footage of Keith and Melody that I knew had been shot last week, as well as footage of people with disabilities riding and interacting with horses that I realized had been shot here, at the riding center.

"Thank you all for coming," Ruthie said. "We are so blessed to have Melody Cross as a trusted volunteer here at the Mighty Happy Therapeutic Riding Center and we are 'mighty happy' to host this wrap party for her and for Keith Carson."

Ruthie had the delivery of a person who warms up audiences for game shows, and soon had the crowd cheering and applauding.

"Our riding center, of course, is affiliated with The Holy Church of the Mighty Happy, which most of you passed just before arriving here," Ruthie continued. "I invite each of you to worship with us Wednesday and Saturday evenings, and Sunday mornings. If you'd like more information on our church or the center, our volunteers are all wearing gold sweatshirts tonight, so feel free to get to know them.

"And now we have a little treat. Many of you do not know what we do here, so we thought we'd take a few minutes to show you. Here are three of our riders, along with our lead instructor, the fabulous Emily Harding."

During Ruthie's speech, volunteers cleared people from the end of the arena, ushering them away from Ruthie and toward the tables of food. Now, a dozen or so volunteers held a long golden rope as a barricade between the people and the riders who had just entered the arena.

I have to admit the riders were impressive. An army veteran in combat attire rode Tinkerbelle, the Percheron/Throughbred cross, without the assistance of any volunteers. This, even though he was missing both of his legs below the knees. A young woman who, Ruthie explained in her continuing spiel, had cerebral palsy, rode Cinnamon with the help of three volunteers: a leader to lead the horse, and two sidewalkers, one on each side of the rider, with their arms draped across the rider's thighs. Apparently, before she started to ride, the young lady could not sit up on her own.

The last rider was a small boy with Down syndrome. He rode the Haflinger, Noodle, and only needed a leader. He made us all laugh with his infectious smile. He certainly was having a good time. The riders wove their way through a series of orange cones that were set in a line down one side of the arena, then stopped their horses at a mailbox, took out a letter and rode with it to a drop box on the other side of the arena. Then they did trunk strengthening exercises, followed by learning to turn by riding in a circle.

Throughout, Keith and Melody's single, "Do Good," was playing on a loop over the PA.

Do good
Do right
Do the thing that keeps love in sight
Do good
Tonight
Do your best to be the light

The presentation ended amid a mixture of laughter and tears and when the horses left the arena I found Melody standing next to me.

"Sorry I wasn't able to break away earlier. The reporters were very persistent tonight," she said with a smile.

"No problem," I said. "This is a great place. I see why you like coming here."

"I really love it," she said. "And you know what else I would love?"

"What's that?" I asked.

"If you would come over tomorrow and take your pick of the furniture I am not taking to the new house."

I had almost forgotten that Melody had bought a sprawling house not too far from here. She'd had a great year on tour, and Davis and Scott, her manager and attorney, encouraged her to spend some of the money on real estate.

"I'm closing on Thursday," she said. "Can you believe it? I am going to be a homeowner!"

I remembered how I felt when I closed on my farm. It was a mixture of excitement and promise—and fear that I would not be able to pay the mortgage. I didn't think Melody had to worry about that, though. I was pretty sure she was paying cash.

My furniture needs were fairly well met, however. When my grandmother died and I purchased the farm, I moved most of her things to the farmhouse. What I needed, I had bought over the past eight years. Jon, however, was another story. I hadn't been up to his loft in a while, but I thought he lived rustically. With only a minimum amount of cast-off furnishings up there when he moved in, I didn't think he had added much since then.

"Are you sure you don't want to donate the furniture to the riding center, or maybe to the church?" I asked.

"Positive. I give generously to them. I want to do something nice for you, and I am sure there must be something in my house that y'all might want or need."

"I'm sure I can find something," I smiled. "I'll see you tomorrow."

Cat's Horse Tip #2

"Riding a horse moves a rider's pelvis and hips in a way that is similar to a human gait. That's why riders who have physical disabilities can show improvement in mobility, flexibility, muscle strength, and balance."

3

"THOSE PEOPLE ARE WEIRD," DARCY said, popping her gum as she slouched in the passenger seat.

"How so?" I asked.

"Seriously? All that mighty happy crap isn't overkill?"

"Well, maybe a little," I said. "But, you have to admit, they did seem . . . mighty happy."

I felt Darcy roll her eyes in the darkness.

On some level, I understood the concept Pastor Ruthie promoted. If you tell yourself something long enough, eventually you begin to believe it. And what pastor, priest, or rabbi didn't want several dozen pews full of happy congregants? On the other hand, when some people repeated the "mighty happy" phrase, it seemed forced, even patronizing. I understood Darcy's point of view, too.

Darcy switched the radio from the classic country station WSM-AM to one that played a mixed format of music. Meghan Trainor was singing "All About That Bass."

My old green truck had developed a little hitch in its "git along," and hiccupped as we drove up the long hill on Sam's Creek Road. The truck was ten years old, had well over two hundred thousand miles on it, and would soon need to be replaced. I had Jon looking online, to get an idea what a newer used one would cost, and the prices were frightening. It had to be done, though. Pulling up to six world caliber horses in a trailer behind me, I could not risk a breakdown.

As Whitney Houston belted out the Dolly Parton classic, "I Will Always Love You," I recalled a time in Texas when an axle broke on my trailer. We limped into a tiny town and had to wait a full day for a new axle to arrive with no place other than the trailer to house the four horses we had with us.

Twice a day Jon and I unloaded the horses and walked them around the little town square, then fed and watered them next to the trailer. We tried tying the horses to the trailer, but there wasn't room at the repair shop, and when the horses got restless I was afraid that even with polo wraps that they'd bang their legs up pawing by the trailer. When the axle finally came in, mechanics jacked up the truck and trailer, with all the horses in it, about six feet in the air. My heart pounded in my throat the entire three hours it took to install the new part. Fortunately, the horses came through the ordeal in better shape than I did. It was a scenario I never wanted to repeat.

Now, back at the house, Darcy went to cram for a history test and Hank I went out to the barn. Hank is a howling, yowling part-beagle, part "who knows what" hound dog who showed up on my front porch about a year ago. He was a puppy then, so was maybe sixteen months old now. Since then he'd turned into a great barn dog who was protective of the horses, and me, on the road.

Tonight he had a long, narrow stick in his mouth and had to turn his head sideways to get in through the barn door. Hank usually preferred shorter, fatter sticks. We then walked companionably up our dirt aisle to check on Sally. She was dozing as we came up to her stall, but when she realized I was there, she dunked her head into the bucket again, and blew.

"Okay, I get it," I said rubbing the soft red hair on her forehead. "Something to do with water. Are we getting a flood? Will the pipes break in a cold snap? You want swimming therapy?"

Several places in the Kentucky-Tennessee area now offered spa services for horses. From standing on a vibrating plate to loosen muscles, to acupuncture, Reiki, and water therapy, many horses now received the same kind of physical therapy that people got. The vibrating plates had made a huge difference in quieting our yearling filly, Glamour Girl, whom we called Gigi, at a big show last summer. I would love to have one of those plates right here.

I gave Sally a final pat and looked in on the other horses. Darcy's tall dark gelding, Petey, was sprawled out flat on his side, snoring, and Reddi, the other horse owned by Sally's mom, Agnes Temple, was munching the last of her hay. Bob, and Wheeler, a palomino gelding who would soon be moving with his owner to another state, were dozing, and Gigi was walking in circles around her double stall. That horse had more energy than all the others put together.

Excited about the furniture Melody had offered, Hank and I trotted up the stairs to Jon's loft, and I knocked. Until earlier this year Jon and I had a great working relationship. But, Jon thought that finding two dead bodies within a matter of months had distracted me from the barn and the horses, and I have to admit that he was right. A lot of extra work had fallen on his shoulders as a result, and he did what he could, but sometimes the boss has to be there to make decisions. That would be me.

Jon was intensely private, and I had recently discovered that was part of his background. His privacy was why I rarely went up to his loft. But new furniture was a big deal and I wanted to get his ideas.

"Coming," Jon called. Then he kept talking. It sounded as if he was speaking to someone other than me, but his words were soft and indistinguishable. His voice grew louder, however, as he got closer to the door.

"Okay honey," I heard him say. "Love you, too."

I was flabbergasted. Love you, too? How could Jon have a girlfriend? He never went anywhere and often chose to work on his days off. Maybe once a month he disappeared down the driveway for the day, but he was always home by dinnertime. To make matters more confusing, even though I often begged him to come out with Darcy and me to lunch, dinner, or a movie, he rarely accompanied us. Now I hear him say, "Okay, honey. Love you, too?" What was that all about?

Jon ended the call as he opened the door.

"Cat?" he asked. "You okay? Your mouth is kind of hanging open."

"Ah, fine. I'm just fine." I said.

With anyone else I would have asked about the call, but with Jon it seemed inappropriate to inquire. Jon still had on the matching blue jeans, turtleneck, and warm, waterproof vest that he had worn to the video shoot, but he had removed his ball cap and boots. Short dark hair, high cheekbones, dark eyes, and a slender frame on a five-foot-nine inch body, Jon was probably around my age. Thirty.

"Um," I stammered, still flustered, "I have good news. I think."

"You think?" Jon smiled all the way up to his eyes. "Come in. Hank, you too, but leave your stick. Hurry, though. This standing in the doorway is letting in cold air."

Hank debated his options, obviously torn, but then he clamped down hard on his stick, turned, and trotted back down the stairs.

The loft was long and narrow with an open living room, dining alcove, and kitchen, with a small, three-quarter bath and bedroom at the far end. The whole place was only twelve by fifty-four, so it was a little over six hundred square feet. The roofline of the barn came to within five feet of the floor, which further reduced the space, but there were several skylights to let light in and the bedroom had a big window that looked into the covered arena. The furniture was as I had remembered.

"I've got a bit of news and thought it would be best to deliver it in person," I said.

"Sit down," he said pulling out a chair next to a small, white table that had been placed under a skylight. Years ago the little rectangular table had sat on my grandmother's front porch. Often, a yellow ceramic pitcher filled with flowers had been on top of it.

"You remember that Melody is closing on her new house on Thursday?" I asked.

"No, but go on." Jon's eyes were now intent on my face. I had his attention, at least.

"When I saw Melody tonight she mentioned that she had some furniture that she didn't want to take to the new house and offered it to us."

"To us?" Jon asked.

"Well, to me," I said, flustered. "I wasn't sure what you had in here or what you needed."

I looked around the small apartment and saw that Jon could probably use a new sofa and coffee table, and a new lounge chair, low bookshelves maybe, for storage, and some end tables. I looked toward the bedroom, but the door was closed.

Jon noticed the path my eyes had traveled.

"I'm fine with what I have, Cat," he said. "I don't need a thing."

"But if you had the option, maybe you would trade up?"

"Maybe," he said. But he looked doubtful.

"Why don't we do this. I don't want to force anything on you, but I can take pictures of what she has and text them to you. Then you can tell me if you are interested, or not."

"Sure," he said.

I also told Jon about finding Robert Griggs at the therapeutic riding center, and that Robert looked a little grayer at the temples but still had the long bangs that went almost to his eyes. Most important, though, Robert seemed calm and happy.

"Maybe you could come with us on Friday, to tour the center," I said. "I know Robert would like to see you, and they have done some interesting things in their barn."

A series of conflicting expressions danced across Jon's face, but I knew my comment about the interesting barn would hook him, and it did.

Finally, we discussed Sally.

"I'm not ready to admit that she's psychic," I said, "but every time she acts weird something bad happens."

"Agnes, however, is sure that her Sally Blue has psychic powers," Jon said, a quirk at the end of his mouth.

"Well, let's watch her closely. I want to be sure she isn't starting to colic."

Cat's Horse Tip #3

"Horses developed an intuitive nature because they are prey animals. To survive, a horse has to know the intention of every living thing within his or her proximity."

4

THE NEXT MORNING I WAVED Darcy off to school and joined Jon to check on Sally. She was on her back in the center of her stall, eyes closed, with all four feet up in the air.

"She looks dead," Jon deadpanned.

"Except that she is breathing quite steadily," I replied. "Plus, she keeps opening her right eye to look at us."

"There is that," he said.

"Maybe she's stretching her back."

"Maybe," said Jon.

"Okay," I sighed. "I'm off to look at Melody's furniture."

"I'll keep an eye on her. I'm sure it's nothing. She's just being Sally," he said.

On my way to my truck and through the tall hedge that divides our properties, I glimpsed Carole and her kids raking leaves in their front yard. Carole was pointing out the different shapes of the leaves, and the kids were calling out the names of the trees they came from. The Carsons could easily have shuttled their kids off with nannies, but both took a hands on approach to raising their offspring. The kids attended public school, and Carole made sure her children learned something from everything they did at home. Keith was involved, too—when he was home.

"Hey," I said, pulling a few hedge branches aside and glancing around, hoping for a glimpse of Keith. Unfortunately, he was nowhere to be seen.

"Hey," Carole said back. She gestured to the kids. "Teacher in-service day at school."

I nodded.

"Hi, Cat!" Kevin, Keith and Carole's second oldest, dropped his rake and ran over to show me a colorful leaf he had crammed into his pocket. He had the exuberance only a seven-year-old can have.

I admired the leaf, which had crumbled some inside Kevin's pocket, then called to Carole. "I'm heading to Melody's. Any words of advice for her? She's moving into her new house on Friday."

Carole stopped raking and smiled. "Go with the flow, that's all I have to offer."

Go with the flow seemed to be Carole's entire philosophy on life, and it wasn't necessarily a bad idea.

Melody was renting a cute yellow cottage in Pegram, up the hill from the new Dollar General. The home was gated and partially screened by shrubbery. Perfect for a rising young star. I'd been to her house a number of times, and today, I half expected it to be piled with boxes. Melody reminded me, however, that the movers would do all of that tomorrow.

We wandered around the small house and I took pictures of some of the furniture as Melody told me the history of a few pieces, including those she was taking with her to her new, gi-normous home in Kingston Springs.

"I bought that futon the first week I was in Nashville, even before I had a place to live," she said. "It folds up, and it fit in the back seat of my old Honda. A few nights, when I had nowhere to go, I pulled it out and slept in the woods."

Melody offered her trusty futon to me, and I was honored. I knew it would come in handy when either Jon or I had guests. Not that Jon, to my knowledge, had ever invited anyone other than Darcy or me to his loft, but hell could possibly freeze over someday.

Melody had come a long way in a short time, and I admired much about her. She had a good work ethic and she never, ever took her eyes off her goal of making a living singing country music. What made it all the more impressive was that Melody had come from almost nothing.

Like Dolly Parton, Melody moved to Nashville the day after she graduated from high school. But instead of a depressed town in East Tennessee, Melody hailed from Toad Suck, Arkansas. Toad Suck is an unincorporated community west of Conway, Arkansas in the central part of the state.

Melody once told me that when pop star Harold Jenkins changed his name back in the 1960s to become a country singer, he put his finger on a map and it landed on Conway, Arkansas, and Twitty, Texas. Thus, the legendary Conway Twitty was born. Melody hadn't used a map to change her birth name, but you have to admit that a name like Melody Cross is a bucket load of pigs better than Raylene Potts.

I'm not sure why Melody and I hit it off so well. She was short, blond, naïve, sweet, and talented. In other words, everything I am not. We did have alcoholism in common though, her mom and my dad.

We also shared not being raised by our parents. My maternal grandmother took me in from a rundown Chicago apartment after my mother died, and after my dad went off the deep end and started to drink. I was nine and she took me to her home in rural Bucksnort, Tennessee. My dad is still around, somewhere, but I rarely hear from him.

The little girl who would later become Melody Cross had been the youngest, by far, of the Potts children. Her mother, Claudine, had given birth to an older sister, Brandyne, at fifteen, and a brother, Bodine, a year or so later. Melody came along when her mother was thirty. And, yes, all three kids had the same father, who was now serving a long prison sentence for doing something Melody didn't want to talk about.

Claudine got tired of being a mom when her youngest was about six, so the future Melody Cross became a foster child. Melody spent most of her youth in the home of an older couple who attended a small Baptist church. I guess we both had small towns in common, too.

With Melody's help, I took photos of a coffee table that was hand made out of old barn wood, and two matching end tables. They would be big improvements over the battered tables Jon now had. There were also two lamps and some gently used pots and pans. Melody then helped me attach the photos to a text and we sent the lot off to Jon.

I swear, I am the most technologically challenged person on the planet. I must be missing a gene, because even though Darcy had shown me how to use my new iPhone a bazillion times, I never could remember how each feature worked.

Fingers crossed, I hoped Jon didn't think I was interfering with his private life. The furniture was free and I thought he needed it. I didn't want to commit to Melody though, until I heard back from him.

As it was a relatively warm November day, we decided to have iced tea on her shady back porch. Melody made sweet tea the real southern way, by boiling the sugar along with a pinch of baking soda and then steeping black pekoe tea before allowing the mixture to cool.

We settled in two large, white wicker rockers and, as usual, her peaceful view of the woods relaxed me. I had no back porch, and the back of my house faced my barn and parking area. My front porch did look over the pasture, but the road in front was busy, and during commute times the noise could be distracting. I had no complaints, however.

Melody had brought a notebook out with her and was busy writing in it. "I'm making a list of things I want the movers to hold for you and Jon," she said noticing my interest in what she was doing.

Was I that obvious?

"Um . . . thanks!"

"It's no trouble." She hitched her tiny bottom over in her chair so she could better address me. "Cat, your friendship means so much," she said. "Really. I am so glad we found each other and I hope we will be friends forever."

I've never done well with mushy stuff, even platonic mush.

"Me, too," I said, a fraction of a second too late. I saw something in Melody's eyes that looked suspiciously like disappointment. "You . . . you balance me out." I stammered. "I get too focused on the horses and my responsibilities, but you are a breath of fresh air in my life."

Was that a tear I felt sliding down my face? Couldn't be. Fortunately, I was saved from further embarrassment by the doorbell. Whew. I couldn't remember when I had been so relieved by an interruption.

Melody disappeared through the wooden porch door and walked through the house to the front while I composed myself. She returned a moment later with a tall, dark-haired girl she introduced as Kayla.

"Kayla works in Bill's salon," said Melody. "Keith and I have a radio interview at ten tomorrow morning on WSIX-FM, and I chipped my polish yesterday during the video shoot. People always expect me to look great, even on the radio."

Kayla nodded at me and began to set out a variety of nail clippers, brushes, emery boards, and polishes.

"Do you want a manicure, Cat?" Melody asked. "I'm sure Kayla has time to do us both."

I watched Kayla's body stiffen and I became quite sure she didn't have the time. And, when I looked at my nails I knew that while I could use some help in that department, they were pretty much a lost cause.

"Thanks, but no," I said, hoping for tact. "I'd just ruin them in the barn."

"But Kayla has all these cute decals," Melody said. "Look, here are some with fireworks, and these dark ones with the stars are cool, too."

If I had hesitated before, I was certain now. "Ah, no. But thanks."

I watched for twenty minutes or so with sincere interest, then Melody got a text and Kayla packed up. With a quick wave the manicurist was gone. I hadn't realized I had been clenching my fingers until they relaxed as soon as Kayla walked out the door.

"A text from Buffy," she said, waving her phone at me so I could see. I might have had a chance if she had held the phone still. "*HitFactor* wants to come on Friday to film me unpacking for a 'where are they now' special."

HitFactor had been Melody's ticket to fame. The show was an *American Idol* knock-off, and three years ago, Melody had won the most watched season. Since then, her shooting star had only gathered speed.

"You look like you don't want to do that," I said.

"It's not that I don't want to, but I hadn't planned to do any actual unpacking," she said. A delicate wrinkle appeared in her brow. "The movers were going to do that."

"Can you ask Buffy to offer them something else?" I suggested. "As your publicist, she could do that, couldn't she? Maybe Thanksgiving with Melody Cross? You can always have a pretend Thanksgiving a few weeks early so they can meet whatever production deadline they have."

"Perfect!" she said, her brow clearing as her fingers tapped her phone. "That's just one more reason you are so important to me," she said after the text had been sent. "You offer compromise and are the voice of reason in my crazy world."

I smiled, but thought my advice had been basic. At least it was basic in my world of horse training. If your horse has a different goal than you do, offer the horse something similar, then eventually move back to your original plan. Guess the strategy worked for people, too.

I looked at my watch. It was getting late and I had to get home. I gathered my bag and made leaving motions.

"You want to go to church with me tonight?" Melody asked.

"No, but I appreciate the offer." I stopped to look at her. "Soon, Melody. I promise that one day soon I will go to church with you."

She smiled, and then said, "Just think! At two o'clock tomorrow I will be signing the papers to my own home."

"Let me know if I can help you with anything. I just have to meet Darcy and Robert at the riding center at three on Friday. She's taking a tour and might volunteer there."

"Oh, Darcy will be a great addition. And, no worries about the move. The movers are coming to pack me up tomorrow afternoon, and my label is fronting me a night at Lowe's Vanderbilt Plaza as a housewarming gift. All I have to do is show up at my new house Friday morning to direct furniture placement."

I remembered loading and unloading my washer and dryer, along with the rest of my furniture, all by myself because I was too broke to hire anyone to help. But I didn't begrudge Melody any of her success or her luxuries because I knew that if I ever moved again, this time I'd have lots of friends to help.

I walked through Melody's little house one last time, then hugged my friend. And yes, I really did hope we'd be friends forever.

5

THE NEXT MORNING I SENT Darcy off to school then got on the phone to talk to Glenn and Jamie, co-hosts of the online radio program *Horses in the Morning*. I'd been a guest on the show quite a few times before, talking about horses and horse training, but today they wanted to talk about the video shoot, and what it was like to teach Keith Carson and Melody Cross to ride.

The show was always fun and informative, even if it was a bit early for my brain to be in full gear.

"Do you have the best job in the world, or what?" Glenn asked.

"I guess I do," I said. And honestly, if I'd told my ten-year-old self this is what I'd be doing when I was thirty, I would have been pretty excited.

"So what inside scoop can you give us about Keith and Melody?" Jamie asked. "Is Keith, like, bald under that cowboy hat or is Melody a really bad driver?"

"No, and no," I laughed. "But I can tell you that Melody makes great homemade cookies, and that Keith looks really good when he washes his boat in his swim trunks."

"Cat," Glenn told the listeners, "lives *next door* to Keith Carson. We're still waiting for her to invite us over."

"I want to watch the boat washing," said Jamie.

"Next spring," I lied. "I'll let you know when the boat comes out of storage."

The interview continued in that vein for another ten minutes or so. We even talked some about horses. Toward the end, Jenn, the show's producer, reminded us of the time, and I said my goodbyes. Then I joined Jon in the barn. Sally was peacefully munching her hay and turned a bored eye in my direction when I checked on her.

Jon had Petey cross tied in the aisle and I helped him undo the many straps and pull the gelding's blanket off. We each grabbed a brush and took one side of the horse. Petey had little visible dirt, but brushing is healthy for a horse's skin so we went at it as if he was covered with mud.

"Interview go okay?" he asked.

"Absolutely. They always make it easy," I said, teasing a few small tangles out of Petey's short mane. Then I changed the subject. "So, did you like any of the furniture? Melody really wants us to have it."

"Us," he asked, "or you?"

Petey raised his neck to indicate that he sensed tension. He also moved one ear toward each of us. A horse can move his ears independently of each other and there is an old cowboy saying that the position of the ear is the window to the horse's thoughts.

"Us—or me, or you," I said after purposely relaxing my body to let Petey know all was well. "The furniture has meaning to her from her early days in Nashville and she wanted it to go to someone who would appreciate that."

I felt Jon soften on Petey's left side. "I liked everything. Except the lamps," he said. "Not sure I need those." He was quiet as he brushed, then said, "What about what the furniture I have now? That was your grandmother's. Doesn't that have meaning, too?"

To be honest, I hadn't given that fact a thought and I took time to consider. "My grandmother," I said, now wiping my fingers through the long, silky strands of Petey's tail, "traded up whenever she had the opportunity. Yes, there were some things she was attached to, like the little white table you have. My grandfather built it for her. The headboard on my bed, her parents gave as a wedding present. But the little couch, the coffee table, and end tables? No.

"If she had known you, Jon, she would have said, 'My land boy! Give that stuff to a body that needs it and git yerself somethin' nice.'"

We both laughed and I realized that I had taken on my grandmother's tone and body posture.

"Okay," he said. "Tell Melody that *we* would be honored."

I pulled my phone out of my pocket and texted Melody while Jon pulled a surcingle, sidepull, and driving reins out of the tack room. We were working secretly with Petey, preparing him to pull a cart, as a surprise to Darcy. But, about the only time she wasn't here was when she was in school, so we used that time to work with him.

Driving should be an essential part of every young horse's education, but it often is overlooked. Early in the process, the horse is taught to drive without a cart, and that's the stage we were finishing with Petey. Driving from the ground also teaches horses to steer, stop, turn, back up, and even respond to voice commands and leg yields. Petey, of course, champion show horse that he was, knew how to do all that under saddle, but it was a little different giving him the cues on the ground.

Ground driving also was a good way for a human to establish leadership with a horse, as a lead or dominant mare will drive, or herd, a submissive horse forward from behind. In that way, ground driving meshes well with a horse's natural instinct to obey his herd leader.

Petey was an elegant mover, and would do well in next year's national level driving classes. Reddi, the other Appaloosa mare owned by Agnes, Sally Blue's owner, was too flighty, and Sally would have been willing, but she was too stocky. It would have been hard for her physically to achieve the beautiful, light floating trots needed from the top horses.

Over the past week Petey had become solid in his ground cues, and we were in the early stages of introducing the travois. This was a drag made of two eight-foot long four-by-four posts with room for the horse between them, with a cross bar of four feet in length at the end that dragged on the ground. Many Plains Indian tribes used a similar set up with a hide stretched between the poles behind the horse to carry crops and household goods. Today I drove Petey around our covered arena, while Jon took on the role of a horse pulling the travois.

Jon walked alongside Petey, and in front of and behind him, grasping the open end of the travois in his hands. The cross bar end dragged on the ground behind him. Horses who are driven often wear blinkers, but at this stage, I wanted Petey to see everything. He became a little wide eyed when the travois came close, so I stopped him and let Jon pull the thing toward and away, over and over until Petey relaxed. When the gelding lowered his head and began to lick his lips in acceptance, I decided that was enough for today.

As I led Petey back to the barn, he reached over and grabbed a portion of the lead rope and held it in his mouth. This might be considered disrespectful from another horse, but Petey just liked to lead himself. Just as I got Petey back in the cross ties my cell phone rang. For safety purposes, I have a "no cell" rule when working with the horses, but Jon was already undoing Petey's surcingle and reins, so I crossed the aisle and went to the tack room to get my phone. My heart gave an involuntary leap when I saw the call was from Keith Carson.

"Have you heard from Melody this morning?" Keith asked as soon as I answered.

"No, why?"

"She missed an interview we had on WSIX radio. It was an important interview. A really important interview and I was just wondering why she'd stand me up and embarrass me like this. Why she'd jeopardize our single. Why she wants to sabotage both her career and mine."

I'd never heard Keith so angry.

"Sorry to go off on you, Cat," he said, after taking an audible breath. "Carole told me you were at Melody's yesterday. Did she say anything while you were there? Give any reason why she might not show up this morning?"

I told him that, as far as I knew, Melody was looking forward to the interview, and that she even had her nails done so she could "look good on radio."

"Do you want me to call her?" I asked.

"No. Davis and Buffy have been calling her all morning. But will you let me know if you hear from her? Some young artists do stupid things unconsciously to derail their careers. It's a classic fear of success, but I didn't take Melody for someone who would do that."

Neither did I. All she'd ever wanted was to be a country star and she'd worked much harder than most for her success. Fear of success? Not Melody Cross.

As soon as I hung up, Buffy called, and that conversation was similar to the one I'd just had with Keith, with one exception.

"Some reporters might have made the connection between you and Melody at the wrap party. If anyone calls to ask about her," she said, "I'd appreciate you keeping quiet about her missing the interview. Especially if anyone from a national outlet calls: one of the networks, that sort of thing. We want to know what the situation is before we take a position."

Buffy would know all about that, as she used to be media. In fact, that's how Buffy and I met. She had been a local reporter who'd called me after Sally and I won our first world championship. Melody once told me that some of the best publicists had worked both sides of the media game.

"You're probably in the middle of something so I hate to ask," Buffy continued, "but I have a new client meeting that I cannot change and I was wondering if you could go over to Melody's house? Davis is in a lunch meeting or he would go, but someone should check to be sure she isn't sick or something. Maybe she fell and got hurt?"

Buffy said these last words as if she hoped that was the case.

"According to my paperwork, you are the person Melody asked me to call in case of an emergency and I know you have a key..."

"Of course," I told her. "Of course I'll go, and I'll call you as soon as I get there."

I hung up and filled Jon in. Instantly, our easy camaraderie of the morning was replaced with tension. "I know she's a friend," he said, looking at me, "a good friend, but don't get too wrapped up in her career."

I looked back at him, and rather than anger and fear that I was going to leave the bulk of the workload once again to him, I only saw concern.

"I'm just going to check on her. It's probably nothing. A sudden case of the flu. Or maybe she overslept and is embarrassed."

Just then Sally chose to produce so many bubbles in her water bucket that much of the water overflowed into her stall.

Inside my farmhouse I shook out my mouse brown curls, ran a brush over the worst of it, and re-fastened the mess into a ponytail. Then I dabbed on some lip gloss. It was much cooler today than it had been yesterday, so I grabbed my good winter jacket, the one without hay stuck in the lining and horse slobber all over the sleeves, and shrugged into it.

Agnes called my landline just as I was ready to go, and then Annie Zinner texted me with information about the horse she and Tony were going to drop off here on Sunday. Next, Darcy's school counselor called to okay the requested early dismissal on Friday so we could check out the riding center. She was quite chatty and by the time I had dealt with all of the calls and texts, forty-five minutes had passed.

When I finally opened my back door to leave, I found Keith standing there, his right arm elevated and his hand balled into a fist. He either was ready to punch me or knock on my door. I hoped for the knock.

"Now Melody has missed a lunch with our label head," he said, shoving both hands into the pocket of a handsome, black leather jacket. "Davis had to fake excuses, lie for Melody, and he was not happy."

Keith had an animal-like electricity to his anger.

"I'm headed to Melody's house now," I said. "Buffy asked me to go."

Keith nodded then shook his head from side to side. "I can't believe she did this."

"I'm sure she has good reason. I'll call you when I have news."

He nodded again, then squeezed through the hedge that separated our properties.

I went back into the kitchen for my cell, which I had left on the counter, and when I opened the back door to leave for the second time another man was there, also ready to either knock on the door or punch me, and with this man, it really could have been a punch.

Hill Henley had been the owner of what was left of the Henley Plantation and let's just say his gene pool could have used a little chlorine. His ancestral family home, Fairbanks, was a tall, pale, L-shaped structure located about a hundred yards east of my property line. It was the most prominent plantation home in the area during the Civil War. Hill, however, had let the antebellum mansion fall into ruin, and after he sold it he moved a flimsy single-wide onto the only twenty acres that he had left. There, he trained Tennessee Walking Horses, caroused, got drunk, and was an ineffectual single parent to his eleven-year-old son, Bubba, his wife having run off some years ago. Bubba was a local mischief-maker, but had, in a way, saved my life back in February, so I was partial to him.

A visit from Hill was never pleasant, especially now, as I needed to get to Melody's.

Hill took a grimy ball cap off his head to reveal long wisps of grimier hair. "I came askin' if Bubba can stay the weekend, from Friday after school to Sunday just before supper." Here in the South, many people called lunch dinner and dinner supper. Hill was one of those people.

I sighed and looked at my watch. Then I realized I wasn't quite as polite as I should have been. Until recently Hill would have left Bubba by himself while he was gone. Some months back I had asked Hill to let me know if he needed a place for Bubba to stay and here he was, hat in his hands, asking.

"Sure, Hill," I said as I forced my freshly-glossed lips into a smile. "I take it you don't plan to be around?" I would not have put it past Hill to drop Bubba off and then enjoy a quiet weekend at home.

"I got to head to Alabama and Miss'sippi. I got one client lookin' for a new horse and another who wants to send me two. Neither are what you might call kid people. Prob'ly not a good trip for Bubba to go on."

The parenting classes Hill had been court ordered to take might be doing some good. Bubba had gotten into so much trouble through Hill's neglect that a local juvenile judge had stepped in to re-direct Hill, rather than Bubba. The results in both had been positive.

"You did the right thing in asking me," I said. Then I remembered that Jon, Darcy, and I were touring the Mighty Happy center Friday afternoon. "I might need to pick him up after school, though. Jon, Darcy, and I have to be in Kingston Springs at three."

Hill told me that Bubba's social worker had made him add emergency contact names to Bubba's paperwork, names of people who had permission to pick Bubba up from school, and Carole and I were the two names he added. I wondered if Carole knew, as I certainly hadn't.

"I need you to sign this." Hill pulled a crumpled, letter-sized sheet of paper out of his pocket and handed it to me. "Then I got to get copies to Bubba's school and social worker."

I looked at the paper, and thought of the many other, mostly disgusting, things that could also have been in Hill's pocket, then gingerly took a corner of the page. At the top was a short paragraph that said Hill had spoken to me about keeping Bubba and I had agreed to do so. There were blank spaces to indicate the dates that I would be responsible for Bubba, and Hill had filled those in with a pen. From the uneven distribution of the writing, I gathered the pen had been trying to run out of ink. If the pen belonged to Hill, I couldn't blame it for wanting to die.

Nodding, I put the paper down on my kitchen table, pulled a pen out of my purse, and signed and dated the paper. I looked to see if a witness or a notary was needed, didn't see any indication that either was required, then handed the paper to Hill.

"Your horses?" I asked.

"My man, he'll come take care of 'em," Hill said. Hill often talked about his "man," who seemed to be one of several people hired to feed the animals and do odd jobs around his farm.

"Okay, then. I have to get to Pegram," I said, shooing him out the door. Then I turned to look at him. "I really do hope you find the horses you want," I said. "If you do well in your business, that will be good for Bubba."

Hill almost smiled before he put his grimy cap back on his grimy head and slithered between the fence rails that separated my property from his former home, Fairbanks.

More than an hour after Buffy called I finally found myself in my truck, headed toward Melody's house. I turned on the radio to find Razzy Bailey singing about his "9,999,999 Tears." It was about a fifteen-minute drive down Sam's Creek Road, then left on Hwy. 70 and through the little town of Pegram.

I was so sure that I'd find Melody at home—filled with embarrassment that she missed her morning appointments—that I almost stopped at Finch's Country Store for fried chicken and home fries. Everyone felt better after some of Finch's fried chicken. But, something urged me onward and I passed the tiny, wooden store without a glance.

When I pulled up to Melody's little yellow house the first thing I noticed was that her car was not there, and my heart sank into my stomach. I had been so sure that she would be home. I used my key to open the gate, and just as I got out of the car a dark BMW pulled in next to me and Davis got out.

"Hi," I said. "Buffy said you were in a meeting and asked me to come by to see if Melody was here. I take it you haven't heard anything."

Davis shook his head and we mounted the steps before knocking on the door. When Davis knocked again, louder this time, I called out Melody's name. The house resounded with silence.

"Her car's not here," I said, stating the obvious. "But I have a key."

Davis held up a key of his own, but I used mine to open the door, and we went inside. It looked much the same as it had the afternoon before, just without Melody. The movers had not yet arrived, and Melody's note to the movers about my furniture was on her kitchen table. Davis picked up the note, read it, and gave me a questioning glance. There was something in his look that bordered on hostile.

"My barn manager and I are supposed to pick up the furniture tomorrow, after the movers finish," I said with caution. "It was nice of Melody to give me things that meant something to her. She easily could have given them to someone else."

Davis nodded, and put the note back on the table. Then he shoved his hands into his pockets and walked through the rooms of the house. We both knew Melody wasn't there. There was no sense of her, and that was unsettling.

"Could Melody have gone to her family?" Davis asked, sliding into a chair. "She did that once before after a call from her mother. Claudine is . . . needy, or at least pretends to be."

"No. Well, I don't think so. All Melody ever said to me about her family was that she was done with their dysfunction and had decided to let them sink or swim on their own."

On the other hand, I thought, if a desperate call came in from one of them, would Melody have blown off an important interview and lunch? I shook my head. No. She might have found someone else to come to her family's aid, but she would not have put her career in jeopardy to do so. They had never been good to her.

"The house closing!" I said the words so loudly that I startled even myself. "Maybe she's at the closing. Maybe the time got moved up and she forgot to tell anyone."

Davis jumped up, cell phone in hand. "Do you know who her Realtor is?" he asked.

"No." My heart plummeted into my stomach. "She did her house hunting when I was busy with horse shows. But, if we look around maybe we can find a card, or some paperwork."

Despite a pretty thorough search, during which we found songwriting notebooks, an organized collection of gas and fast food receipts, and a stack of church bulletins, no indication of a Realtor or closing attorney was in sight. Probably, she had all of that with her in her car.

Davis called Scott Donelson, Melody's attorney, to see if he knew anything, but his assistant said Scott was in court. Davis didn't want to give too much away as the tabloids had spies everywhere, so he left a message for Scott to call him.

While he was on the phone I made a quick call to the church, finding their number in one of the bulletins.

"Why no," Ruthie said. "We haven't seen her today."

I was somewhat surprised that the pastor had picked up the phone herself.

"The, uh, address book in my phone isn't working," I said after a pointed look from Davis, "and I can't remember her number. I, uh, wanted to wish her luck with her new house."

Ruthie said she would pass the message on.

"I guess we can leave a note for her," I said after I hit the "end call" button on my phone.

"Sure," Davis said. "In case she hasn't gotten the four thousand texts and emails Buffy and Scott and Augie, and I, and even Keith, have sent her in the past few hours." Then he threw up his hands. "Sorry. I'm worried. I didn't mean to snap at you."

"It's okay," I said. "I'm worried, too."

And I was. The Melody Cross I knew wanted success so much that she would never have missed an interview. Not if she could help it.

Cat's Horse Tip #4

"Horses cannot vomit, because a valve that leads to the stomach prevents food from going back into the esophagus. This is one reason why tummy aches can be deadly to horses who overeat, or eat bad food."

6

AFTER RETURNING HOME, GETTING CAUGHT up on lots of paperwork, and tucking the horses in for the night, I spent the evening talking to Brent. If we didn't see each other, we often ended our days filling each other in on our recent activities over the phone.

Tonight Brent was in his clinic with a cat who had ingested some sort of poison. After doing all he could for the poor thing medically, he was now giving her emotional support. That was the kind of animal doc that Brent was.

I also called Melody numerous times, and even texted her and sent an email or two. Then I called the Lowe's, as I remembered she was supposed to spend the night there. A snooty receptionist insisted Melody wasn't there, even when I used the code name she sometimes used, Aria Bender. Then I sent Buffy a text to ask if she knew if Melody had checked in, or if she had closed on her house.

By the time I turned in at ten P.M. I had not heard from anyone and was so upset I couldn't drink my evening hot chocolate. Where was Melody? Had she been kidnapped? Mugged? Had an accident and driven into a ditch? We had many steep roads with no shoulders and deep drop offs in our area. I tossed and turned all night, wishing I had thought to get Davis's phone number. Maybe he had heard something.

The next morning I sent Darcy to school with the reminder that she needed to be at the riding center no later than three. Then Hank and I headed to the barn to work with Jon and Petey. Unless it was very hot or very cold, Hank usually slept in the barn. He often wandered up to the house after Jon fed him his breakfast, however, in hopes of some of my breakfast scraps. He usually got some, but they came from Darcy. I was a harder sell.

As soon as I walked into the barn Jon said, "What's wrong?"

People who work with horses together are dialed in to each other more than other co-workers might be. Because horses know more about people's emotional state than people often know about themselves, it is important to only try to teach a horse something when you are fully focused. Jon had sensed right away that I was distracted. Of course, the bags under my bloodshot eyes might also have tipped him off.

I filled Jon in, knowing he was the last person who would ever blab information about Melody to a member of the press.

After I stopped talking, Jon nodded. He wasn't a person who analyzed things; he was a "just the facts" kind of guy.

"You're a good friend, but you've done all you can do," he said. "Do you want to skip the session with Petey today?"

I considered. No. I didn't. I couldn't wait to see the expression on Darcy's face when we showed her Petey pulling a cart. I had bought a sleek, black wooden training cart with large, spoked wheels, and had it hidden under a tarp behind the barn. We needed to keep Petey moving forward.

"Give me a moment and I'll get my brain on track," I said.

By the end of the session we were able to hook Petey up to the travois and jiggle it, although we did not ask him to pull it around. Maybe tomorrow.

"I like this driving stuff," said Jon as we brushed all traces of harness marks from Petey's shiny coat. "Reminds me of my gramps."

The hand that held the brush I was using stopped itself in mid air. "Your gramps?" I asked.

"My grandpa. Gramps."

This was a rare opportunity to learn more about Jon and I knew I needed to tread carefully. "So how does driving Petey remind you of your, um, grandfather?"

"Gramps had this skinny, gray draft horse who pulled his plow. A few times I got to 'help' drive old Slim to the shed Gramps called a barn. I was six, maybe seven. Thought it was pretty neat."

"Where did all this take place?"

Jon looked at me as if I was a moron. Then he smiled. "Oklahoma."

He meant, I knew, the Cherokee Nation in eastern Oklahoma. In a strange turn of events, I had recently learned that

Jon was half Cherokee, as well as a mix of Norwegian and German. My question about location had really meant if the driving had taken place on tribal land or his grandfather's small acreage. Jon had interpreted the question differently and that's why people around the world misunderstood each other. Life was all about clear communication.

Love you, too. Jon's words when he ended his mysterious phone call jumped into my brain. Who was he communicating with then? Before I had time to ponder that thought, Hank dropped his stick and let off a beagle howl loud enough to curl my toes. Then the barn door opened and Keith Carson stepped through.

I gave a worried glance to Jon who nodded and continued to finish up with Petey. Somehow I found myself running down the aisle toward Keith. The words, "Do you have news about Melody" were on my lips, but Keith's angry voice jumped in first.

"Have you heard from her?" he asked.

I shook my head. "No."

"We're supposed to fly out at noon for the first leg of our tour. The production trucks are already in Louisville and her sound check is at four."

Holy moly. I had forgotten the Louisville concert was tonight. Agnes lived in Louisville and Melody had arranged with Davis to put her on the VIP guest list. If Melody did not show up, Agnes would drive everyone bonkers asking why. I looked at my watch. It was already after ten, but Keith was probably flying out of the small, private John C. Tune airport in West Nashville, which was a little over twenty minutes from here, rather than the commercial international airport on the east side of town.

"What happens if Melody doesn't show up?" I asked, my voice a lot smaller than I wanted it to be.

"We'll make an announcement, say she's got food poisoning or something," he said, hooking his fingers through a board on Bob's stall front. Bob woke up from his nap and came over to brush his nose against Keith's fingers. Bob was not a mouthy horse so I did not worry that Keith might lose a guitar-picking finger.

"Augie booked the date and just now called some songwriters I've co-written with to fill in," he said. "One of them is Brad Paisley. The audience will think it's a special night, and for them it will be. But, we have Columbus, Ohio tomorrow night, and St. Louis on Sunday. If Melody doesn't make herself front and center soon, we might have to cancel the tour."

Melody had taught me enough to know that a cancelled tour could mean millions in losses for the artists, record label, agent, manager, promoter, and venue, and more than one probable lawsuit. Keith looked like he was about to cry and I reached up to grab his shoulders.

"She will show up," I said, looking him in the eye. "This is not like her. There has to be a reason, a good reason."

Keith nodded, then steeled himself and nodded again. "You've got my number," he said. "If you hear from her . . ."

"I'll call or text you. And you'll do the same?"

He nodded again before he turned to catch his plane.

"Hey, Keith," I called after him. "I hate to bring this up now, but remember that Sally Blue's owner, Agnes Temple, lives in Louisville and has a backstage pass for tonight."

Keith looked perplexed for an instant, then smiled. "Is she the one who gushes? The one with bright blue hair who says her horse is psychic?"

"That's her."

"Ah. Thanks for the reminder. I might introduce her to Brad. He's got a guitar I've been hoping he'll sell me. He might give it to me real quick if I tell him I can make Agnes go away. Thanks, Cat. Your Agnes is going to be the highlight of my night."

After Jon and I picked up Bubba at Cheatham Middle School, the three of us met Darcy at the Mighty Happy Therapeutic Riding Center promptly at three. Robert greeted us, and ushered us right into the barn. Jon's eyes widened at the red brick floor and the open concept stalls, and he gave a slow nod of approval.

"Our volunteers undergo training in safety, horse behavior, various disabilities, and our program procedures," Robert said to Darcy as we stood by the arena gate and watched a lesson get started. "The mounting process can be tense, especially when we have riders with severe disabilities," he continued. "Getting an unbalanced rider on a horse can turn into an accident if everyone, including the horse, is not well trained."

I looked at Darcy. She wasn't a touchy-feely kind of person and I thought the close, physical contact the volunteers had with the riders might make her uncomfortable. But, her sharp eyes were scanning the scene, and I could almost see her brain taking it all in. Forget the bored expression on her face and the annoying snap of her bubblegum. Darcy was into this. I think we had a service project!

"What's wrong with that little boy?" she asked, nodding at a small child on a brown and white pony.

"He looks mighty happy, doesn't he?" said Robert. "And there's nothing wrong with him. He's perfect in his own way. His brain just processes things differently than yours or mine. See, they're playing a counting game."

We watched as the little boy threw one large, soft, stuffed dice and watched it tumble to the arena surface.

"Dillon, how many dots face the ceiling?" Emily, who was teaching the lesson, asked.

Dillon sat on his pony and smiled.

"How many dots?" Emily prompted again.

Slowly, Dillon took one hand from his reins, examined his fist intently, and then shot his arm up high above his head with four fingers showing. Then he laughed so hard I thought he was going to fall off his horse. He might have, too, if a volunteer who was standing next to him hadn't steadied him.

"Yes, Dillon. Four dots! You are a wonderful counter!" said Emily. "Now, you are going to ask Spanky to walk four steps, and then ask him to stop. Do you remember how to ask Spanky to walk on?"

Dillon considered this, as the volunteer who was leading Spanky started to ask the pony to walk. Emily shook her head and the volunteer stopped the pony.

"Dillon, how do you ask Spanky to walk on?"

This time Dillon bumped his ankles against the pony's side and Spanky began to walk forward.

"One," Emily counted as she held up one finger. "Two." Another of her fingers popped up. "Three . . . four and . . ." Emily waited for Dillon to show her that he knew how to stop his pony. When he began to pull back on his reins, she said, "And whoa." Then everyone on the team gave Dillon a high five.

"In addition to counting, Emily is working with Dillon on two step directions," said Robert. "She asked him to one, walk four steps, and two, stop. Dillon makes sounds, but is otherwise non-verbal. He is one mighty happy kid, though."

"The lady walking next to Dillon looks like she is, ah . . . mighty happy . . . too," said Darcy.

"Sandy Sweet is a sidewalker. We have supportive sidewalkers, who help the rider stay on the horse, and interactive sidewalkers, who interact with the rider to help them interpret the instructor's instructions. Dillon has good balance, but needs help in knowing what to do, so Sandy serves mostly an interactive role in this lesson."

Darcy nodded. "So what does Melody Cross do when she is here?"

"Just about everything!" Robert said. "She helps in the office and cleans stalls and tack. Usually she is a sidewalker, though. She likes being in lessons."

"Bubba," I asked, "What do you think?" Like Darcy, Bubba had been taking it all in. There was a lot to absorb.

"How old do you have to be to come here?" he asked.

"Four to ride in a lesson, sixteen to be a sidewalker or lead a horse in a lesson, and . . . how old are you now, Bubba?"

"Just turned eleven."

"And *eleven*, to help out in the barn," said Robert.

Thank you, I mouthed. Then I turned to Bubba. "Do you think you might want to help out sometimes?"

"If'n my dad lets me," he said, rubbing his toe into the arena footing.

I'd talk to Hill, I thought. Maybe Bubba could come out with Darcy—if Hill didn't get all riled up about it. He could be stubborn enough to argue with a stop sign.

We left the gate area and walked back into the barn where we almost bumped into Allen and Ruthie, who were coming out of the viewing room. They must have been watching the lesson, too.

"Sirens," said Ruthie, and we all stopped to listen. They were some distance away.

"I've been hearing them off and on all afternoon," Allen said to her. To us, he expounded, because that's what pompous people like Allen did. "The Harpeth River runs along the back of our property, and a lot of canoers and kayakers use the river. Once in a while one of them gets in trouble and the rescue squad has to fish them out. From the sirens, I think they are near Hwy. 70, which is about three miles away by road, but as the river flows it's about a mile away. As the crow flies, much less than that."

I looked at my watch. It was time to head back to feed. Before we left, Darcy committed to attending a volunteer orientation the following Tuesday night. I thought I might go with her, and maybe take Bubba, too. Who knows, maybe Melody and I could sidewalk in the same lessons. That might be fun.

Thinking of Melody, I checked my phone to see if I'd had calls or texts about or from her. Nothing. This was definitely not a case where no news was good news. Where was she?

Just as we were deciding who would ride in the truck and who would ride with Darcy, Martin Giles drove in and eased his way out of a discrete dark blue Chevy. Martin is Cheatham County's newest young detective—and my boyfriend's younger brother. If it hadn't been for Martin's belief in me when my movie star neighbor was murdered, I might be sitting in a jail cell right now, so he was one of my favorite people. Martin must have seen my truck and stopped by to say hi.

"Well, look who's here. It's always good to see you Miz Cat," Martin said with a casual two-fingered salute. "And Darcy. Jon. Bubba, you're keepin' good company with these people. Glad to see you outside of juvenile court." These last words Martin said with ominous authority.

I nudged Bubba. "Nice to see you," he mumbled to his shoes. Bubba was just learning to act like he had some raising.

Ruthie and Allen drifted up as Martin looked at the clipboard in his hand. "I wish this was a social call. But it's not. Jon," he said as he looked at Bubba, "how 'bout you an' the boy get Miz Cat's truck warmed up for her. It's getting' a might chilly in this late afternoon air." Then Martin moved his gaze to me.

I knew right then that my best friend, Melody Cross, was dead.

Cat's Horse Tip #5

"A therapeutic riding lesson focuses on a combination of riding skills, therapeutic goals, and the relationship between horse and rider."

7

Jon, Bubba, Darcy, Martin, Brent and I gathered around the big, scarred wooden table in my kitchen. It had been in my grandmother's kitchen for many years and had seen a lot of dinners, but no dinner had been as sad as this one. I was shattered by Melody's death and filled with questions, but Brent and Martin, whose shifts had both just ended, insisted that we eat first.

Somehow, I managed to make everyone some hot chocolate, and several large, gooey pizzas magically appeared. I leaned into Brent's solid frame as I picked at a slice of vegetable supreme, his arm around my shoulder. Brent was a good man. He and Martin shared a tall, stocky build and thick, blond hair, but Martin's protruding ears and jutting chin, typical characteristics of the Giles clan, were more prominent.

Brent wasn't perfect, but then, neither was I. He didn't like it when I was out of town at horse shows, which was frequently the case in spring, summer, and fall. I knew I could be moody, and I wasn't the best cook. In fact, I didn't cook at all, unless you counted hot chocolate as a food group, as I did. Unfortunately, Mama Giles saw my lack of prowess in the kitchen as a major flaw, and often mentioned it to her boys.

Why was I even thinking of Mama Giles when my best friend was dead? Horses sometimes distracted themselves from things they didn't want to acknowledge. Maybe that's what I was doing, but thinking about Melody would not bring her back. When it looked as if everyone else was finishing up with the pizza, I turned to Martin, then remembered Bubba.

"I know what y'all are thinking," Bubba said. He was the only one still eating. Bubba was chubby, but a recent growth spurt kept him from being fat. His dark hair fell over his blue eyes as he looked around the room. "Y'all are gonna talk 'bout Melody gettin' herself kilt and I'm a kid and shouldn't be hearin' bad stuff." He popped a pepperoni into his mouth and swallowed it without chewing. "But remember that I've already seen and heard a bunch of bad stuff. I was kidnapped and I know all 'bout what happened to Glenda. Ever'body does."

Glenda Dupree had been the movie star neighbor who lived in Fairbanks, next door to my farm. Bubba and Hill lived on the other side of her, and Bubba probably did know all of the grizzly details of her murder.

"B'sides, if you shuttle me off to another room, I'll just listen anyways," he said. "And if I can't hear it now, then I'll be learnin' 'bout it soon e-nuff."

I looked at Brent and Martin. Both shrugged in acceptance, but I hoped Martin would be tactful with his words.

"Here's what I can say," Martin finally said. "A call came in from a cell phone at one forty-six this afternoon. The caller, an unidentified male, said there was a body in the Harpeth River. The approximate location was three hundred yards before the river flows under the Hwy. 70 bridge, just before it makes a bend. We dispatched emergency services and near the location the caller mentioned, we found the body of a young, blond woman. From the series of red and blue stars tattooed across her right shoulder, we tentatively identified her as Melody Cross."

My heart sank. Up to now I had been holding out hope that the body that had been found was someone other than Melody. But those stars had been photographed hundreds of times. Almost everyone on the planet would recognize them. I turned to Brent as the tears I had been holding back finally ran down my cheeks.

"Beyond that we don't know much for certain," Martin continued. "I can speculate that the cause of death was drowning, but can't confirm that yet. How she got into the river, or where, we don't know. The sheriff has assigned the case to me and I guarantee we'll find the person who did this."

I snuffled and turned to see the misery on everyone's faces. Even Bubba looked sad. Darcy looked so miserable that I disentangled myself from Brent and went to hug her.

"There is one more detail." We all stared at Martin as he said, "Melody didn't have any clothes on."

Half an hour later Darcy, Brent, and Bubba went to the living room to play Go Fish. I knew the game would be a distraction for Bubba, but it upset me that they would play something so shallow at a time like this. Jon had left a while ago to check on the horses. Even though I was upset, I was glad Bubba had left the room, as I had questions to ask Martin that I didn't want Bubba to hear.

"Your best guess, Martin, and don't pull any punches for me. Was Melody murdered?"

His gaze across my kitchen was wise beyond his years. He was twenty-seven, although his doughy cheeks made him look younger. "Don't know, Miz Cat. Don't know. The medical examiner in Nashville will look at her soon. Tonight maybe."

"But why was she in the river without any clothes? Actually, why was she in the river at all? It's November. It's not like she was going for a swim."

Martin reached over to clasp my hand. "I don't know the answers right now, but I imagine we'll find out in good time. I wish I could make this all go away, but I can't. Now, I've got to git going. I promised Mama I'd stop by the store and bring her some milk."

Despite my grief I almost snorted. Mama Giles did a good job of keeping her grown-up boys mashed down tight under her thumb. "Mama" was healthy, worked a full time job and was in her middle sixties. She jogged, played tennis, and a year ago hiked fifty miles of the Appalachian Trail. It would be different if she asked Martin to bring her the milk as a favor, or if Martin, as a good son, had offered. My guess was that Mama Giles had pulled the "poor widowed me" card and wheedled the grocery run out of Martin. She probably didn't even need the milk.

Martin said his goodbyes and I went into the living room where a hearty game of poker was now going on.

Brent saw the look on my face and jumped in before I could get there. "Bubba was just teaching us a new game, weren't you Bubba?"

Bubba was teaching Brent and Darcy to play poker? This entire day had made me feel as if I had fallen down the rabbit hole right along with Alice, and landed upside down. My mind couldn't keep up with it all. I did, however, hone in on the fact that they were using marshmallows instead of poker chips. My marshmallows! My special gourmet, *handcrafted* marshmallows. These were shaped like gingerbread men and were one of the secret ingredients in my signature hot chocolate. Plus, they were expensive—as marshmallows go.

It was all too much. I grabbed my coat and headed to the barn. Jon was nowhere to be found, so I assumed he had gone up to his apartment. I walked down the aisle and smiled at Gigi, who bounded up to meet me. I patted Wheeler's wide, yellow head and watched the geldings, Bob and Petey, nap in their stalls.

Sally's stall was at the end of the barn and I could see a piece of paper tacked to it.

SHE WAS LIKE THIS WHEN I CAME OUT. VITAL SIGNS NORMAL. THINK SHE IS BEING PSYCHIC? WILL CHECK ON HER ABOUT MIDNIGHT.
JON

I peered into Sally's stall to see her looking as forlorn as a young mare could look. She was on the ground, feet tucked under her like a cat. Her head hung, her ears flopped, and her eyes looked as if she had taken on the pain of the entire world. I opened the stall door and slid inside.

"What's up big girl?" I asked. Sally flicked an ear in my direction, the only indication that she was aware I was there. I sank to the floor and hugged her face, Sally's warm breath softly blowing into the crook of my elbow.

We stayed like that for what seemed an hour or more, but was probably only about five minutes. Eventually I scooted away from her, and rested my back against the stall wall. It was never safe to be sitting on the ground when a horse was near, but tonight I didn't care. It was just too much effort to stand up. My iPhone buzzed in my pocket. Nine PM. It was a reminder Darcy had programmed into my phone to get the next day's TO DO list together, but I didn't have the energy. My best friend was dead. Nothing else mattered.

Idly, I wondered what story concert goers in Louisville had been told about Melody's absence. Did they even know? Davis and Scott, Chas, Augie, and Buffy, did they know their artist was gone? And Keith? Did he know? I sighed. I had promised to call or text if I heard anything, but Keith would be about ready to go on stage. It was an hour later in Louisville. Ten PM.

I debated. If I didn't send a text and Keith found out that I knew something, he'd be disappointed. Sighing, I picked up my phone and opened my message app.

I HAVE NEWS OF MELODY. NOT GOOD. TOUCH BASE WHEN YOU CAN.

Seconds later he texted me back.

DAVIS JUST CALLED. SHOCKED & DEVASTATED. NOT ANNOUNCING NEWS TONIGHT AS PER DAVIS & CHAS (LABEL) REQUEST. GOTTA GO.

I sat in Sally's stall for another hour. Sally hung her head the entire time.

By the time I got up the next morning, the news had broken. I had texts from Buffy, Davis, and Keith, and Agnes had called three times. I called Agnes back first, knowing that she'd call three more times within the next half hour if I didn't.

"Cat, darling!" Agnes effervesced. "How are you? Lars and I had such a fabulous time at Keith's concert last night, and then we wake up to this torturous news. Torturous! And Melody was your friend! I am so sorry, my dearest, dearest Cat."

I loved Agnes, but maybe not so much this early in the morning. A little of Agnes went a long way, and I wondered how Lars could stay focused around her. Lars was Agnes's tall, young, dark and very fit, assistant and driver. Some time ago several state troopers in Kentucky had appealed to a certain judge to take Agnes's drivers license away. The judge readily complied. Now Lars was a fixture in Agnes's life and was a (somewhat) steadying influence. Although at seventy, I had a feeling that Agnes was who she was, and not much about her could be steadied.

"I still can't believe that Melody is gone," I said, sitting on my bed. "I hadn't known her that long, but it was as if we were long lost sisters . . . Agnes, I don't know what to do."

"Now, now, dear. You go on being wonderful you! That's what she would want, isn't it?"

Agnes was right. Melody would not want sadness. She would want her friends to celebrate her life. Still, it was hard to lose someone I cared so much about.

"I have an idea!" Agnes's voice sang through the phone. I'd almost forgotten she was there. "Maybe we can stage a séance. Sally can lead it. Or . . . too many people there at once might confuse Sally. Maybe just a private reading. I bet my big, beautiful Sally Blue can get in touch with Melody on the other side. Hmmm. I wonder if horses can be taught to deal tarot cards. Cat dear? Do you think you can teach Sally to shuffle a deck of cards?"

"Maybe scatter them by blowing on them hard," I replied. Then I caught myself. Was I really having this conversation? I smiled in spite of myself. Maybe Agnes was having me on.

"Agnes, you've really cheered me up. Thanks so much . . . Agnes? Are you still there?"

"Oh yes, dear. I had you on mute, as I was asking Lars to order Sally a deck of tarot cards. Large print I think, don't you?"

Okay. Maybe Agnes wasn't having me on. What in the world was I going to do with a deck of large print tarot cards?

After we hung up I spoke with Davis, who had news that he delivered without much emotion. "You'll hear about it soon," he said, "but it does look as if Melody was murdered."

The news hit me like a punch to the stomach. "Murdered?" That was the only word I could manage.

"We don't know who yet," he said, "or the where, or the why, or exactly when. The how looks like she drowned, but there are marks on her neck that suggest she was held under water."

"She was the nicest, sweetest person anyone could ever know." I felt my Irish temper building up and made an effort to dampen it back down. I have a teensy anger management issue that sometimes gets the best of me. "Who," I asked after a calming breath, "would want to kill her?"

"I don't know. I just don't know." He sounded both distant and distracted.

My phone dinged and I read a text from Buffy that said there was going to be a press conference soon, in front of the Cheatham County Courthouse. Did I want to go? Yes, but I was too much on edge and didn't trust myself not to make a scene. I felt like throwing up. But I didn't. Instead, I ended the call with Davis, focused my anger, and started to plan.

Cat's Horse Tip #6

"Horses spend from four to fifteen hours a day in standing rest, and from a few minutes to several hours lying down. Horses only need about two and a half hours of sleep each day, most of which happens in short intervals of about fifteen minutes."

8

BEFORE I DID ANYTHING I needed to take care of some horse business, so I called my dear friend Annie Zinner. Tomorrow was the day she and her husband Tony were delivering a horse to us.

I had lobbied Gusher Black, the horse's owner, at the recent world championships and was quite excited that the horse was coming to my barn. I had first met Gusher at a world championship show a few years back. Jon and I were sitting in the stands one morning and made positive comments about a yearling filly. Turned out she just happened to belong to the guy sitting behind us.

Gusher and I talked at each major show from then on. He was a short, stout man who'd made it big in the oil business on his own. He had an ego that he could barely contain under his ten-gallon hat, and was the kind of man who'd settle for nothing less than the best. Despite all that, he was likeable. Agnes flirted with him shamelessly and I think had hopes that Gusher could become husband number four. Even though he was a good fifteen years younger than Agnes, he flirted shamelessly back, so shamelessly that I knew I'd see a screen door on a submarine long before I'd see a marriage between those two.

This particular horse of Gusher's was a coming five-year-old gelding who had won his halter class at the world championships as a weanling, then won his silver medallion this year in racing. The four areas of competition—performance, halter, distance trail, and racing—made up the Appaloosa Horse Club's medallion system. Only a handful of horses in history had won a medallion in each category and Gusher planned to make his horse the next one.

As part of his plan, the horse had to win a national or world championship performance class, or be the top horse in the nation in terms of points for a given class. Gusher thought the Southeast was a less intense place to bring his horse along and earn points, than the tough Texas and Oklahoma circuit. I was thrilled to get the new addition, but knew I also had to deliver.

"We're fixing to get an early start, should be in about five," Annie said, interrupting my thoughts. "Don't make dinner now, I'm bringing something special."

I smiled. Annie was a great cook and I, for one, could use a good meal. We'd all been running on pizza, hot chocolate, and stress since Melody disappeared.

In the barn, Jon and I decided to give Petey a day off to process his lessons from earlier in the week. Besides, it was Saturday, and although Darcy planned to spend the day with her dad, she could pop into the barn at any time. No way was I going to spoil her surprise.

Jon decided to pull Gigi out of her double stall. Gigi belonged to Mason Whitcomb, Darcy's dad, and had won several national and world championship titles already. "Glamour Girl" was a total space cadet, so we were giving her some time off from the show ring. Jon wanted to teach her to drive. She wasn't yet two years of age, and even though many young horses did well being driven, I hadn't been sure Gigi would be one of them.

Gigi, however, had surprised me. Of course, she adored Jon and thought the sun and moon rose and set in him. Me, she more or less tolerated. I was glad that Jon was so interested in driving, as he had no interest in riding. It wasn't that he couldn't ride, it just wasn't his thing.

Today, Jon put a sidepull and a surcingle on Gigi and was trying to get her directional with the long reins. They were doing well, even though I could see that Gigi was bothered by the surcingle. Basically, it was a wide strap that wrapped around her back and belly. It also had large metal rings on it to slide reins through. Wearing a surcingle was also a good way for a horse to get used to the cinch or girth on a saddle.

The session did not last long, mostly because Gigi has the attention span of a flea. Jon may be right, I mused. If Gigi had something to think about, maybe she'd be a little less bouncy in her stall. I always worried that she'd bang into something and hurt herself, even though we had tacked heavy gym mats to her walls.

By ten o'clock I had returned to the house. Darcy and Bubba hadn't stirred so I bounced them out of bed and got them going. I called a few clients while the two squabbled over what was left of the Alpha-Bits and milk. My breakfast had consisted of the rest of last night's pizza, so at least I'd saved them from battling over that.

After Darcy left for her dad's, Jon and Bubba went out to fix a few broken fence boards. Gigi was the culprit, of course. But, by the time I got back out to the barn, Jon was teaching Bubba to ground drive Bob. I smiled. It was good for Bob to be doing something, as his owner recently retired him from the show ring. Bob was a wonderfully consistent western and English pleasure gelding. Walk, trot, and lope around the ring nice and pretty until all the other horses bobbled a step or made some other grievous mistake. Bob was too concerned about his performance to ever commit a bobble, so he won. A lot.

But, Bob had done all he could in the show ring, and Doc Williams didn't want to campaign him anymore, so the horse's future was in limbo. Doc didn't want to sell him, so we had to find a good solution. One just hadn't popped up in front of my face yet. I loved Bob, but my trainer's finances didn't allow me to convert a horse who had been a source of income for me to one I had to pay for.

I had been restless all morning. Without understanding why, I waved at Jon and Bubba, and told them I had errands to run. Then I hopped in the truck and headed for Melody's as I listened to Garth Brooks sing about "the thang they call rodeo."

I almost couldn't get to Melody's house, though, as the narrow lane was packed with cars. By the time I got to her front gate I could see dozens of fans milling around, along with a few news trucks. WSMV, our NBC affiliate, as was there, as was WKRN, Nashville's ABC station. Their satellite dishes had been raised high, so they were probably transmitting. I made a mental note to avoid them.

The front of Melody's fence had been covered with cut flowers, stuffed animals, and posters. The sight brought tears to my eyes but I refused to let them fall. My previous anger simmered back to the surface and I vowed that whoever did this to her would see justice. Melody deserved that. I wiggled my truck into a spot just past Melody's house and saw Buffy pull into a spot three spaces ahead.

"I'm so glad to see you," she said, grabbing my arm. "Will you help me pick out burial clothes? Melody's family is coming in from Arkansas and Davis thought it would be good if we had most of the arrangements in place before they got here. We haven't seen a copy of her will, but he believes he is her executor."

We squeezed through the crowd and worked our way to Melody's front gate, which Davis and I had locked on Thursday when we left. So much had happened since then, it seemed a year ago, rather than just a few days.

I started to pull out my key, but Buffy already had one. "Davis," was all she said. I nodded. As soon as she started to unlock the gate, fans and media alike realized we must be people who knew something, and they rushed in. The crowd was suffocating and I began to get knocked around. I looked around wildly for an escape. Before full panic set in though, Buffy pushed me through the gate and rammed it closed. A beefy guy with a Duck Dynasty beard and a florid face began to yell at us, and the rest of the crowd joined in. Through the melee, I saw a microphone floating on a long pole held high in the air. Then I spotted a man with a network video camera in the crook of a tree across the little street.

My mouth flapped open, but for once words would not come out.

"Ignore them," Buffy said, pulling me around the corner of Melody's house and onto the back porch. "Will this key open the back door, too?" she asked.

I didn't know. I was still breathing too hard and was too shaken up to know much of anything. I could easily have been trampled.

Buffy stuck the key into the slot, and when she turned it, Melody's back door eased open. A flood of relief enveloped me and we rushed inside. Buffy locked the door and slid the dead bolt, and we both hurried to close the blinds in all the rooms. Then we collapsed onto the sofa. Actually, I was a little surprised that the sofa was still there. Maybe the movers could not get in last Thursday if Melody was not there to open the door for them.

"That was intense," she said.

"I didn't expect all those people to be here," I said. "I just came over because I didn't know what else to do."

"Looks like a lot of fans had the same idea," she said, mashing her finger into her phone. Before I knew it she was talking with a Cheatham County police dispatcher. "Mavis? Buffy Thorndyke." She was quiet for a moment, listening. "I'm glad to hear that," she said finally. "Have you seen the end of your squash, then?"

I listened as Buffy and Mavis first talked about gardening, then Mavis's Thanksgiving plans. It wasn't until the crowd started to sing the chorus to "Do Good," that Buffy switched gears.

"Listen, Mavis, I'm here at Melody Cross's house . . . I know. So tragic. Yes, the house is in Pegram and . . . That's right. That's the address. Mavis, there's a huge crowd out on the road in front of her house. A couple of news vans, too. Can you send someone over to do crowd control? I don't want to head out of here until the fans have settled down a bit."

Buffy finally hung up. "Mavis Hawkins is married to a cousin of my mother's maid's neighbor," she explained.

Of course she was.

Buffy stood and I followed her into Melody's spare bedroom, which she had used as a closet. Country music stars needed a lot of clothes, and Melody had all of hers organized by color and fabric. Lightweight blue over here, heavyweight blue on the other side of the room.

"Pink was her favorite color," I said, fingering a stunning sleeveless v-neck that was made out of a fabric that looked as if it could float.

"Then pink it is."

We quickly found a knee-length pink dress that was covered with faded yellow and gold butterflies. Tall white and gold cowgirl boots and a pink headband completed the outfit.

"What about . . . underwear?" I asked.

Buffy and I looked at each other, stricken at first, and then we bubbled into laughter. Grief sure had my emotions running all over the place. We rummaged through a few drawers, came up with a set of undergarments and added them to the pile. I hoped Melody would have approved of our selections.

We found a small canvas tote, folded the clothes, and put them in. Then Buffy cautiously peeked through a blind in one of the front rooms.

"Police just got here. We might want to wait until some of the fans leave," she said. "Are you in a hurry?"

I shook my head, and looked around the room wishing that Melody was sitting here with me instead of Buffy. Nothing against Buffy, of course. I just missed my friend.

Buffy had grown up in Belle Meade, Nashville's old money neighborhood. She was pleasant enough, even when she had been a newspaper reporter, but we didn't have much in common. Right now, I felt sure I'd never have another close friend like Melody.

Before I could get too maudlin, Buffy asked, "Have you met her family?"

I had not, but when I was with her Melody didn't have much good to say. "My brother couldn't punch his way out of a wet paper bag," she'd once said. Another time she said of her mother, "She thinks the sun comes up just to hear her crow."

"They can be overly dramatic," Buffy said. "Davis hopes they will be respectful, but that media circus outside the window? That's nothing compared to what her mother, Claudine, will stir up. I'm afraid they will turn everything about Melody into tabloid trash."

"Can't you stop them?" I asked.

"I'm a publicist, not a miracle worker," Buffy answered with a wry smile.

We were quiet for a while, then I asked the question that had been kicking around inside my head all day. "Who . . . do you have any idea who—"

"Who killed Melody?" she asked. "It could be one of those fans out there. Or, it could be someone we know. Someone she met on the road, maybe. Or Brandyne. That's Melody's crazy, jealous sister. It could even be me . . . or you."

I didn't like the speculative look on Buffy's face when she said that.

Before I could give her words too much thought there was a knock on the front door. Buffy and I both jumped before we heard, "Ladies? Mavis sent me over. You still in there?"

"That you, Bobby Lee?" Buffy asked. "Go around to the back door, hun."

Turned out Bobby Lee was a tall, thin, thirtyish fellow who would have had a shock of bright red hair, had his buzz cut not stripped him nearly bald. He was also Mavis's grandson and used to mow Buffy's lawn. After Bobby Lee explained that he was assigned to escort us through the now thinning crowd, Buffy asked for a lesser presence from him. "I don't want photos of us, or anyone, coming out of Melody's house under police escort."

Bobby Lee nodded his understanding, in a way that reminded me of Martin. In a department of several dozen, as Cheatham County had, they probably knew each other. I'd have to ask my favorite detective about ol' Bobby Lee. Our new law enforcement friend went back out and shooed away a few more fans. He then organized the remainders into an orderly line across the lane from Melody's fence. When we came out they all started to rush toward us and clamored for information, but when Bobby Lee told everyone to back off and hush up, they did.

I locked the gate with my key. Then Buffy's words came back to me. *It could even be me . . . or you.* Had Buffy killed Melody? Or, did she really think I had? By the time I got into my truck, key still in hand, I was shaking. Too much stress did that to me. I tried some deep breathing exercises to relax, but they didn't help much.

On my way home, Carole called. "The kids and I are going to my mother's for a while," she said. "Keith's label suggested we go, as the label has received two death threats this afternoon." Carole's voice broke. "Someone wants to kill Keith."

9

My heart thudded so hard inside my chest that I almost drove off the road. Keith? No way. He had to stay safe. Carole and the kids needed him. I was glad they were going to stay with her mom, who lived in a small town near Indianapolis.

Carole told me the label had added extra security and that the tour would go on. The promoters liked the idea of the songwriters, so at each concert there would be one or two as opening acts. Some artists had even asked to perform. That would make each event different, and very special for the fans. Keith had also worked up a Melody Cross tribute for his show. All that was the business of show business. The show must go on, no matter how much the entertainer hurt inside.

By the time I got home I was so distraught that I thought I might hyperventilate. Then Hank came trotting up and wedged himself and the short stick he was carrying through the kitchen door along with me. I closed the door and sank to the floor, Hank in my arms. He snuffled my face, but soon sat quietly, as if he knew that was exactly what I needed.

Get a grip, I thought. At this moment I was filled with so much energy and anger that I wanted to beat my head into the wall and pound my fists into the floor. I did neither. Instead, I gave a couple of good, deep Irish sighs, heaved Hank off my lap, got myself up from the floor, and got on with my day.

I was just finishing a restorative cup of hot chocolate (and if there was a wee smidge of brandy in there, I'm sure I don't remember putting it in) when Bubba rumbled in from the barn.

"Jon an' I got all the chores done, 'cept for fixin' a stall for that new horse," he said cheerfully. "What's his name again?"

The registered name of the new horse was Ringo's Jetstar. "I think they call him Ringo, but I'm not sure," I said. "If Annie and Tony don't know, I'll call the owner."

The horse was supposed to arrive with a completed questionnaire filled out by his former groom. I sometimes asked the owner to do it, but most often the person who actually cared for the horse needed to fill it out. Basic information such as feed schedule and veterinarian and farrier contacts were asked, as were questions about stable name, quirks, likes and dislikes, etcetera. I also asked that any new horse come to me with all of his medical records. I hoped the horse came with everything I needed, as I liked to make new arrivals as comfortable as possible by offering a similar environment to the one they had just left.

I desperately needed this horse. Wheeler, the squat palomino, was owned by a little girl who rode with me last summer. But they had moved away and Wheeler would soon be leaving us. Sally Blue would be four the next show season, her last year in the junior performance classes.

Reddi (Red Girl's Moon) was going to be bred in the spring. She was athletic in the English classes, but could be excitable. Agnes had the idea of breeding her to a warmblood, a quieter sport horse type, and that was actually one of Agnes's better ideas. There was a lot still to work out, like which stallion, and whether or not Reddi would gestate and foal here, or at a breeding farm closer to Agnes in Louisville. But for sure, Reddi would not be in my show string come spring.

Agnes was currently "communing" with her three dead husbands about all of this. After they had "spoken" I was sure Agnes would tell me what they all had to say. If I haven't mentioned it before, Agnes carried a purse the size of Montana so she could bring along some of the ashes of her dearly departeds wherever she went. She has trouble letting go.

Jon, Mason Whitcomb, and I had not yet made a decision about showing Gigi next year. That usually was a collaborative process between trainer and owner. I still thought she needed time to grow up. She needed to be a horse for a while. Petey took up a stall, but he was Darcy's project. Bob was being retired, so the only horses I currently had to show for next season were Sally Blue and Ringo, if that indeed was his name.

A trainer cannot make a living on two horses. I also gave riding lessons (on occasion) to Keith and Carole Carson's kids and did some consulting, but I needed two or three more high profile horses, and possibly a youth kid or two, to haul down the road to next years' shows. At eighteen, Darcy had finished her last year in the youth classes and would move to non-pro next year. It was early days yet, so I wasn't too worried. The season had just ended a few weeks ago and I was making calls and putting out feelers, so the right horses and riders should come around soon.

Bubba and I went out to prepare a stall for the new horse. I debated where to put him. There was a spot on the end, across the aisle from Sally. He could look outside a lot there. Or, I could sandwich him between Petey and the feed stall. Petey was a calming influence who engaged well with other horses. I ended up going with the end stall. This horse was coming off the track. He was used to being stalled in a shed row type stall where he could see outside.

I wished once again that we had open concept stalls like they had at the Mighty Happy center. The more that stalled horses could see each other, the more "herd-like" they felt. Horses are herd animals so I tried to cater to their instincts by regular, small group turnout. My horses got more of that in the winter than in summer, as summer sun could bleach out shiny show coats, and show horses who were turned out often ended up with scrapes and other dings on their perfect bodies. It was a balancing act.

Bubba made several trips with a large wheelbarrow filled with shavings, while I filled two water buckets and dropped a mass of hay on the floor. We used to have mangers, but a horse's natural position for eating is with their head down at ground level, so Jon took them out. We kept the shavings away from the hay as best we could.

After we were done, we went back to the house and I settled Bubba with a Harry Potter book. At eleven, Bubba was in remedial classes. When I found out he was into all things Hogwarts, we watched the first movie together, and then I bought him the book. I'm sure he thought it was the lamest gift ever, but when Darcy and I kept hinting at events that took place in the book that weren't in the movie, he cracked the book open. It was slow going for Bubba, but he was now about a third of the way through and seemed to be enjoying it.

Across the room I settled in a big easy chair, opened my laptop, and clicked over to Google. Then I went to the news section and typed in "Melody Cross." As the last technological holdout of my generation, I felt as behind the game online as Bubba did in school.

I grew up in the small Tennessee town of Bucksnort and my grandmother didn't have Internet. Really, I can't remember knowing anyone who did. When I went to college at Middle Tennessee State University, it was my first foray into technology and I already felt so behind the game that my stubborn Irishness made me not want to join in.

Darcy had been helping me, though, with my new smart phone, and with our stable website. Surprising even myself, I was catching on, although I thought of it all more as a necessary evil than as something fun.

Now, I looked at hundreds of news stories about Melody's death. I picked one at random, a story from *The Tennessean*, Nashville's biggest newspaper.

"Country Star Murdered," screamed the headline. I started to read:

> *Rising country music star Melody Cross was found dead Friday afternoon in the Harpeth River, just south of the Hwy. 70 bridge in Kingston Springs. An unidentified male called 911 to report a body in the river. The caller had a "no contract" disposable cell phone, which does not allow law enforcement personnel to trace the user of the phone. This man is not currently a suspect, however, investigators in Cheatham County would*

like to talk with him. If anyone has any information on this unidentified man, please contact the sheriff's office.

The medical examiner's report put the cause of death as drowning. An autopsy also discovered marks on the victim's neck that indicate she was held underwater prior to her death. Due to the cold temperature of the water, the victim's estimated time of death ranges from midnight Wednesday night, to mid-morning on Thursday.

Melody Cross was signed to the Southern Sky label and was the reigning New Artist of the Year for the Country Music Association. Her debut album launched three number one hits, and her second album, scheduled for release December 1, is currently in the number one country album slot on Amazon.com. Her current single, a duet with country superstar Keith Carson titled "Do Good," is the top single on the Billboard Country Airplay *chart.*

An Arkansas native, Cross was known for her kindness to her fans, and when the news of her death broke, hundreds of them gathered at her home west of Nashville. Masses of wreaths, flowers, letters, and other mementos were left along the fence next to her property.

Cross was also a volunteer at the Mighty Happy Therapeutic Riding Center in Kingston Springs, Tennessee. Calls to her representatives were not returned, and funeral arrangements have not yet been announced.

As I read, my insides felt like they were turning into a big black hole, especially when I saw the photos of the fans and the fence. Who would want to kill a beautiful soul like Melody?

I didn't want to read any more, but felt I had to. I needed to absorb every scrap of information. As her friend, I hoped a trivial fact would jump out at me and I could put two and two together in a way that no one else could. I slogged on.

Every site I went to had varying details of what *The Tennessean* had, but TMZ was the worst. TMZ had a photo of Buffy and me walking down the short drive of Melody's house. The caption read: THE PLOT THICKENS. ON SATURDAY AFTERNOON, PUBLICIST BUFFY THORNDYKE AND AN UNIDENTIFIED WOMAN LEFT THE HOME OF MURDERED COUNTRY MUSIC STAR MELODY CROSS WITH A MYSTERIOUS SATCHEL.

A mysterious satchel? Come on. It was a canvas tote filled with burial clothes. At least I was not identified by name. Although, I wondered how long that would last. Then I clicked on a link to the *Enquirer* and saw it. Melody's mother, Claudine Potts, had sold her story. That hadn't taken long. The tabloid was teasing online readers about their upcoming exclusive with Melody's family. In addition to Claudine, Melody's sister Brandyne would be interviewed, as would their brother Bodine, who was in prison. A picture of Claudine and Brandyne accompanied the tease. In it, Claudine had her nose so high in the air it was a wonder she hadn't drowned in a rainstorm, and Brandyne's hair was so messy it looked like it had caught on fire and somebody put it out with a brick.

I sighed and closed my laptop. My web surfing had taken up the better part of an hour and I hadn't learned anything new. Not about Melody's murder anyway. I did have my suspicions about her family and the sliminess of tabloid reporters confirmed, though.

Bubba was still reading, so I headed toward the kitchen. Another restorative hot chocolate was needed.

Much later, I called Brent. "Do you want to go to church tomorrow?"

"Uh . . . sure. I guess so."

Whether he was confused or hesitant, I wasn't surprised. Neither of us were regular church goers, and together, we'd only gone to services a few times. Catholic for me and Brent was Southern Methodist. My horse show travel schedule made regular church attendance difficult eight months out of the year, but I sometimes went to the Cowboy Church services they had at some of the horse shows. Okay. Twice. I'd gone twice.

Mama Giles had beaten church attendance into her kids so hard that as soon as the boys were old enough, they ran as far away as they could from it. Brent and Martin's sister Alison, though, stuck with it. She, of course, was a great cook, and at thirty was happily married with two kid—and another on the way.

I had nothing against church, and in fact, my faith was very strong. Maybe after I got married and learned to cook like Alison, church would come back to me.

"I thought we could try a new church," I said. Before, we had gone to his home church, and also to a local Catholic church.

"Let me guess," Brent said. "You think we should go to Sunday services at the Holy Church of the Mighty Happy."

I hated that he could read me so well. "Are you in?" I asked.

"I'm certainly not going to let you experience that for the first time by yourself. Just tell me when to pick you up."

10

BRENT, BUBBA, AND I SAT in one of the rear pews. Not the very last pew, but a pew far enough back that we could make a hasty exit without interrupting much, but not look like we were going to bolt at the first opportunity.

I hadn't been sure about bringing Bubba. Taking a child to a religious service without parental consent probably wasn't a good thing. But I knew that Hill and Bubba didn't go to a specific church. I had seen them over the years at various neighborhood weddings and funerals, so Bubba had been to church at least a few times, but I wasn't sure what Hill would think about me bringing Bubba to this particular church.

To complicate matters, Bubba hadn't wanted to come. It wasn't as if I could pick him up and throw him into the truck, as I had done a few times when he was in elementary school.

It wasn't until I told Bubba why I wanted to go, that I wanted to gather information to learn more about the people Melody knew, that he changed his mind.

"You mean I could be like a spy?" he asked.

Whatever worked. "Just like a spy, Bubba. I need your good eyes and ears to see and hear things I might miss. Melody spent a lot of time at the church and knew just about everyone there. We might pick up on something that could solve the case."

We might learn something good from the sermon, too, but I thought if I mentioned that it would kill the deal. A girl should always know when to stop her mouth from ruining her life, as my grandma used to say.

Bubba held a red windbreaker in his hands. He looked as if he was ready to put it on, then said, "I'm not sure if'n my dad would want me to go."

I looked at my watch. Brent was waiting in the driveway and we'd have to hustle to catch the first part of the service. "How about I deal with that when your dad picks you up later today? That sound okay?"

Bubba thought about it, then nodded his head. "I want to help you help Miz Melody. She was a nice lady."

Yes, she was.

At the church, I hadn't known what to expect. After we parked we got the traditional "mighty happy" greeting at the door. Inside, the church looked like most other small, nondenominational churches I had been in over the years. Light colored wooden pews. Tan tile floor with a carpet running down the center and side aisles. There was a spot for a small choir or band up front to the left, and a pulpit to the right. This church also had a second floor balcony that was accessed by a stairwell to the right of the small lobby. Another set of stairs, these on the left, led downward.

Several parents led young children downward and I thought they might have children's Bible classes going on during the service. I hoped so. The only thing worse than being stuck next to a screaming baby in church was being stuck next to one on an airplane.

Turns out we had plenty of time. We got there at least five minutes before the ten-thirty service was to start. The makings of a folk band were unpacking instruments in the choir area up front. Two acoustic guitars, a mandolin, and a flute, with one microphone between them all. Two other microphones were set up nearby for vocalists. They each tuned up and played a few notes, then, without any obvious signal, they broke into a lively hymn that I didn't recognize. Then Ruthie appeared from a door behind the pulpit.

I was surprised to see her wearing a flowing, brilliant green robe. I'm not sure what I had expected her to wear, but this wasn't it. She walked front and center, raised her arms and shouted, "How are you all this fine Sunday morning?"

The entire congregation raised their arms and in reply, shouted, "We're mighty happy!"

Eyes wide, Bubba turned to me and stage whispered, "This ain't anythin' like them other churches I been to."

"Me either," I whispered back.

The band did a little number, and then there was another song where the congregation got up and clapped and stomped their mighty happiness loud enough that everyone up in heaven was sure to hear about it. I was on the aisle and saw Robert four rows from the front on the opposite side of the center aisle. He looked . . . happy. Allen, Emily, and their daughter,

Rowan, were sitting in front of Robert. They looked happy, too. I was beginning to understand why Melody had liked to come here.

Two children that I had seen at the riding center sat across the aisle from me, one in a pew in front of the other. The little boy with Down syndrome who rode the Haflinger, Noodle, during the demonstration at the wrap party was one of them. He grinned with his entire body, wiggled his fingers at me, then clasped his hands and brought them to his heart. Oh boy. I almost had a moment there, but if I was to learn more about Melody's life, and thus her death, I needed to stay uninvolved. I hoped they'd all stick around after the service, though, as I wanted to talk with as many people as possible.

My attention drifted back to Ruthie, who had just started to speak. I have to say, she was as electric in the pulpit as she had been when she spoke at the wrap party. Brent slung his right arm across the back of the pew behind Bubba, who was between us. His fingers nudged my shoulder and I turned to look at him.

"Charismatic," he said, with a nod toward Ruthie. I agreed.

Without being specific, Ruthie began to speak about loss. I, and probably everyone else in the room, realized she was speaking about Melody, but she did not mention her by name.

"Think of a life well lived," Ruthie said. Rather than stay behind the pulpit, she walked across the front of the church as if she had been born there. "Now use that thought to empower yourself to live just as well, to make a difference, to help others, to fulfill all that God wants you to be."

Her passionate words incited much whooping and hollering among the congregation. Who would have imagined that drab, dumpy Ruthie could inspire such passion? The service was turning out to be part concert, part Southern revival, part black spiritual, and part theatre.

Carole once told me that some entertainers were always on, while others kept their "it" factor turned off until they hit the stage. Keith was always turned on. He was always vibrant and engaging, and drew everyone from the mail clerk at the post office to his kids' teachers to him. Ruthie was apparently of the other variety. She contained her energy until she needed it, then it exploded out of her. After the service, in a receiving line at the front of the church, Ruthie's eyes were shining. I wondered how long she could keep the bright light turned on.

"Cat, I am mighty happy to see you here today," Ruthie said as she grasped my hand in both of hers. I introduced Brent and Bubba, who both suddenly became shy and mumbled their hellos.

It was too bad, I thought, that Darcy and Jon weren't here. I would have loved their thoughts about the service and the people. But, when I asked Jon he gave me one of his looks and I knew, without him saying a word, that the answer was not only no, but that there would be no discussion about it. Darcy had planned to go, but when it came time for her to get up, she threw a pillow at me and told me to go away. Guess her day with her dad had been a mite exhausting.

People were drifting to a door behind where the band had played, and our little party began to follow. On the other side was a large, sunny room that looked over a garden and a playground that were bordered on two sides by evergreen trees.

Bubba tugged on my jacket. "Can I go around now, an' be like a spy?" he asked quietly.

"You go," I said. "But be nice to people and don't look like you're spying."

I listened to myself. Was I really encouraging an eleven-year-old boy to listen in on other people's conversations? Guess I was. I was glad I didn't have kids. This parenting stuff was a lot harder than it looked. Probably, I should back off on my criticism of Hill. On second thought, maybe not.

While Ruthie had not mentioned Melody by name in her sermon, it was clear by the conversations I listened in on that my friend was on everyone's mind. Across the board it sounded as if Melody had been well liked, and I heard words such as sweet, kind, dedicated, talented, and genuine. There were even a few tears.

Melody would have been touched. She had been going to the Holy Church of the Mighty Happy since she first came to town, long before she became a star, and it was apparent that she had real friends here.

I did, however, hear contradictory opinions of Ruthie. Most seemed to feel that she was just what their church needed in a leader, but others felt she was pushy. Even the nay-sayers, though, seemed committed to the church and the accompanying programs, including the therapeutic riding center. They knew they were making a difference.

As I kept an eye on Bubba, Brent and I were welcomed by many of the adults.

"Thank you. We're just church shopping," I repeated over and over. Some members were far pushier than Ruthie ever could be and put on a lot of pressure for us to come back. It was just that kind of pressure that made me want to stay away. Far, far away.

After our fill of lemonade and some amazing cookies and brownies, Brent and I rounded up Bubba and eased our way out the door. I could tell that Bubba was bursting with news, and as soon as the car doors were closed he let loose with a stream of unrelated tidbits.

"That Allen guy? He's not all that nice to his wife, Miz Emily. People say she's a good ridin' teacher, though. Miz Emily home schools Rowan. Rowan's okay for a girl, but she's studyin' all these things I never heard of. Astro-nomy, I think is one. And archaeology. Is that where you dig up dead people?"

"Sort of," I said. "It's the study of how people lived many years ago. Like in ancient times."

Bubba went on as if he hadn't heard me. "People said Miz Melody was a good sidewalker. I want to do that when I get old enough, an' lead horses in lessons, too. An' I talked with a kid named Jared. He's eleven, just like me. His brother's the one with the squinty eyes who smiles all the time. Coops is nine. He rides at the center."

"Jared's brother's name is Coops?" I asked.

"Maybe short for Cooper," Brent murmured.

That made sense.

"Jared's dad is an elder and is always goin' to meetings and stuff," said Bubba. "An' when his dad comes home Jared says he's always madder than a wet hen." Bubba added that he'd overheard some people who wanted to repave the parking lot, but others said they needed to raise the money first, before they repaved. Bubba had also heard a discussion about filming the service and either broadcasting it, or offering it for sale via DVD or online download.

"Sounds like a typical group of church people to me," Brent said as we turned into my driveway. "Lots of different people, personalities, and opinions."

Later that afternoon, after I'd kissed Brent goodbye, my friends Tony and Annie Zinner arrived with Ringo and their Jack Russell terrier, Mickey. I hugged them all with genuine affection, then Mickey ran off to have a friendly butt-sniffing reunion with Hank. Tony opened the back door of their big, gooseneck trailer, as Annie lowered the hydraulic loading ramp. I liked that their trailer, like mine, was a diagonal haul. If you turned a horse loose in a trailer, he'd stand diagonally, rather than face forward, as it was easier for him to brace for hills, turns, starts, and stops.

Ringo unloaded easily, and looked around without too much excitement. He was a big, bay near leopard gelding, which is to say that his head, neck, and upper legs were a rich, glossy brown; and his lower legs, forelock, mane, and tail a silky black.

The rest of his body was bright white with rich brown spots scattered throughout. Ringo's spots ranged in size from about the size of a silver dollar, to the imprint a coffee mug might make on a wooden surface. His spots were round-ish, but some were teardrop in shape, while others were more irregular. One spot on his hip looked like a miniature replica of the state of Texas. I wondered if his Houston-based owner knew it was there.

One concern I had actually involved Ringo's color. While it was stunning, any horse with this many spots was called "loud." Loud horses often had trouble placing as well as they should in the show ring, and this was for several reasons. Some judges preferred a more subdued color pattern. Color was not supposed to matter in the judging process, but it was hard to dampen the subconscious effect. The other reason is that it sometimes was hard to tell if the horse was moving evenly and soundly. All that color, which was different from side to side, hip to hip, and leg to leg, could confuse even the most experienced eye.

Ringo was so perfect in every other way, though, that he could have been stallion quality. But Gusher wasn't in the horse game for the money stud fees might bring. Gusher had gelded Ringo as a weanling, so he could win the weanling gelding class at the world championships. And he did. A successful race career was now going to be followed by a successful show career, and after Ringo won a national or world championship performance class, I knew Gusher would send him to a distance trainer so he could succeed there, too.

It would be nice to be part of a story like that. But first, I needed to get Ringo settled. Jon appeared from the barn to give Annie a warm hug, and Tony an awkward handshake. Last summer I found out that Tony and Jon had a long history, and that Jon had a problem with the connection. I looked at the two and hoped they could someday find common ground.

Collectively, we got Ringo tucked in. Sally Blue, who had been morose since Melody first went missing, even perked up some. Earlier in the day she had been lying flat out with one front leg straight out and the other bent at the knee to form a cross. Or as Jon said, an X. X marks the spot. But what spot? Maybe she knew a spotted horse was headed her way. Sally also had her back legs crossed in the same manner. She must have thought Ringo as handsome as I did, as she got up, shook the shavings off her body, then stuck her head out to inspect the newcomer.

Tony parked the trailer and cleaned it out, as Jon, Annie, and I brought bags and suitcases into the house. The Zinners were only going to stay few days, but they'd brought food and photo albums in addition to their luggage.

There was a problem, however. I only had one guest bedroom, which also doubled as an office. Bubba had used it Friday and Saturday and was supposed to have gone home when Hill picked him up at four o'clock this afternoon. But Hill had yet to show up.

"Maybe one of the horses wouldn't load and your dad is running late," I said to Bubba. Nothing was for certain when you hauled horses.

"He might've had him a flat," Bubba replied. "One a them trailer tires has had a bubble in it for a month of Sundays."

Only Hill Henley would attempt to pick up horses with a trailer that had a bad tire. In the same vein, I often thought Hill couldn't find water if he fell out of a boat. But, it takes all kinds. Bubba's things were packed up and one more for dinner would not be a problem. I called Hill's cell phone, but it went to voice mail, so I left a message. Good for him. I wouldn't pick up when I was driving either. Maybe he'd call when he got closer.

Annie's surprise dinner was a huge pan of tender pot roast, baked corn and potatoes, buttery sliced carrots, the best Southern biscuits that could ever melt in your mouth, and sweet potato pie. She'd cooked it all the day before and kept it cold on the long drive from Oklahoma to Tennessee. We heated it all up and dug in, setting small bowls of samples on the floor for Hank and Mickey.

Darcy even appeared. "Math homework," was all she said, her bubblegum of the day a bright green. Math was not Darcy's best subject. That we had not heard screams of frustration from her room, or textbooks being thrown at the wall, said a lot. The studying must have gone well.

I had met Annie and Tony some years ago when, by chance, they happened to be stalled next to me at several major horse shows. We struck up a friendship and they had become like parents to me. Tony and Annie conditioned and showed halter horses, horses that were judged on their build and conformation, as well as showing western and English pleasure horses. Tall and blond, Annie was in her fifties and looked like the truck stop waitress she once was. Tony was short, round, bespectacled, and gray, but these high school sweethearts had stayed madly in love for more than thirty years.

Would Brent and I still be together thirty years from now? To me, a long-term relationship is like eating with chopsticks. It looks easy until you try it. I still wasn't sure I was up for the try with Brent, or with anyone else.

Cat's Horse Tip #7

"In addition to a spotted coat pattern, most Appaloosa horses also have vertically striped hooves, a white sclera around the eye, and mottled (or finely spotted) skin around the eyes and lips."

11

HILL NEVER SHOWED UP. I bedded Bubba down on the couch in the living room and called Hill what must have been a bazillion times. I also called him a few other things that probably shouldn't be repeated here.

I set my alarm early, but apparently not early enough for Bubba to catch the school bus. I hustled him into the truck and drove as fast as I could to the school, keeping a lookout for patrol cars. I did not need to get a ticket, although I had sweet talked my way out of the last one. It helped when you dated the brother of a detective.

Bubba ran inside, and I debated going in after him to talk to someone in the school office. I settled on a phone call. I did not want to get too involved and the distance a phone call provided was within my comfort zone. If I had gone in, someone might have roped me into helping with arts and crafts or some other equally hideous activity that I didn't have time for.

On my drive home, I called the school office and was routed to the school secretary. I explained the situation, and that Hill probably had trouble with a horse on the way home. The battery on his phone could be dead. But he should be home by the time the bus dropped Bubba off. I hoped.

In reality, I had a bad feeling about Hill. He'd gone off before and left Bubba home alone for days. This time I figured he'd just left Bubba home with me.

As soon as I ended the call my cell rang. I normally use the cell for my convenience rather than for that of other people, meaning I called out more than I answered, but this call was from Carole, so I picked up.

"Have you heard?" she asked. There was a frantic tone to her voice.

"Heard what?" I wondered if this was news I needed to pull over for. I didn't want to be shocked so badly that I drove off the road.

"Saturday night," Carole stopped to gather herself. "Saturday night . . . Keith's monitor blew up on stage. Not a big thing, and it didn't cause a fire or anything. Just some smoke and, of course, the monitor stopped working."

As she spoke, Carole's words gathered steam and they now flowed in a pace that matched her frantic tone. I tried to remember what a stage monitor was and thought it was the little black box that sat in front of an artist or musician. Possibly, it allowed them to hear themselves and the band better.

"Then Sunday afternoon," Carole continued, "a set of lights almost fell on Keith during sound check. Well, they didn't actually crash to the ground, but they were hanging by one end right there above him. This is after the death threats the label received. Someone really is trying to kill Keith."

Carole started to cry and even through the cell connection I could feel how terrified she was. I wasn't sure what she needed from me, though. Reassurance? Indignation? Commiseration? I settled for practicality.

"Where are you, Carole? Still at your mom's?"

"Yes." She sounded so fragile that my heart broke for her.

"So you and the kids are safe," I said. "Now let's think about this. This does not have to be related to whatever kook sent the threats to the label. Monitors blow up sometimes, don't they?"

The only response I got was the sound of Carole blowing her nose.

"Carole? Don't monitors sometimes blow up?"

"Sometimes," she admitted.

"And banks of lights occasionally fall. They're not supposed to, but they do sometimes don't they?" I asked.

"Sometimes," she said. Her voice was quiet.

"And the tour has brought on extra security. Does Keith have security at home?"

"He does now," she said. It was the first time I had heard any backbone in her voice. "We hired a firm. A different firm than the tour did. Cat, I don't trust anyone. What if the murderer is someone on Keith's team? What if it's someone at the label?"

"You need to call Detective Giles. Call Martin. Because it happened outside of Cheatham County, outside of Tennessee, he might not have heard about this."

"But it was all over TMZ," Carole exclaimed. "The tabloids are bad enough, but now we have to have this horrible gossip site online, and now they even have their own television show."

I knew she was frightened, so I tried to be patient. "I haven't had time to log onto the TMZ site and Martin may not have had either." A smile almost came to my lips. Like many others in the entertainment business, her world revolved around TMZ, as well as more reputable industry news sources such as Country Music Television, *Billboard, Country Weekly*, and even E! Online. Carole didn't understand that the rest of us had other fish to fry.

After a pause, Carole said, "I'll do that. I'll call Martin right now. Thanks, Cat."

And with that, she was gone.

I had no time to wonder if someone was after Keith. Back at the farm I rushed into the house to change for Melody's funeral. Her funeral. A part of me still could not believe this was really happening. I pulled my curly mane into a low ponytail and secured it with a silver barrette. Then I found my one pair of dress pants, a dark charcoal gray, and paired it with a cream colored blouse and a long, black knit vest. With the addition of some lipstick and small amount of waterproof mascara, I was ready to go.

I met Darcy, Jon, Annie, and Tony in the kitchen. Darcy had taken the day off from school. Annie and Tony did not have to go with us, but they insisted and I was glad to have their support. I wished Brent could have come, but he was on duty at the clinic. This would not be an easy day, and his solid presence would have made it easier.

Melody had been found Friday afternoon and this was Monday morning, so the funeral had been put together quickly. Buffy told me yesterday that Davis wanted it that way, to minimize the dysfunctional family's involvement. The service today was only for family, close friends, Melody's church and riding center friends, and her music industry family. Buffy said a public celebration of life would be held later, possibly at the Ryman Auditorium in Nashville, and a special concert for fans was being planned for the CMA Music Festival next June.

After Jon bedded Mickey and Hank down in the tack room, Tony offered to drive, so Jon, Darcy, and I piled into the back seat of their big Ford truck. Annie rode shotgun. Other than the giving of directions, we were mostly silent on the ride to the church. We saw the first satellite news truck a block or so before we got there. A number of others were lined up next to it. All of the local network vans were there, as well as a CMT truck, and several trucks that were unidentified.

Closer to the church, however, past some barricades, the road was free of media. Buffy had told me my name would be on a list, and we quickly cleared the checkpoint, which was before we got to the church driveway. A Mighty Happy volunteer then directed us to a parking space to the left of the riding center. I was glad we were a little early. It looked as if the little church would be packed.

Inside, we were directed to a seat in the middle of the church to the left of the center aisle. I had wanted to sit toward the rear, so I could see everybody, but then realized that all of the key players would be sitting in the middle or front pews. The action, so to speak, would be a little closer to me here. I wasn't sure what I might discover about Melody's death at her funeral, but I planned to keep my eyes peeled and ears open.

Robert was sitting one row in front and farther to our left, and he nodded as we sat. Allen and Emily were there, across the aisle and a few rows closer to the front. I also spotted Davis and Buffy in the third row. Augie Freemont, Melody's booking agent, was sitting with Chas Chadwick, head of the Southern Sky label. In what I hoped was not an obvious move, I turned around to better drape my coat across the back of the pew, and in the process scanned the back of the church. Scott Donelson, the attorney, sat several rows directly behind us. Bill Vandiver sat next to him.

Many of the volunteers and riders I had met during previous trips to the riding center and church also were there, including the sidewalker, Sandy. I knew Melody would be amazed that so many had shown up to send her off to the afterlife, but she would also want people to rejoice, rather than mourn her. Easier said than done.

I checked my watch. Ten fifty-five. The funeral was supposed to start at eleven with a reception immediately after. I had asked about a visitation, but Buffy said Davis had nixed that idea. "The family," she had added in an ominous tone.

Speaking of family, right on cue, they began to head down the aisle. At least I gathered that the small group was Melody's family due to the solicitous church usher escort, and the caterwauling that came from the two women. When they passed by our pew, however, even though both held handkerchiefs to their faces, I did not see any tears on the face of the younger woman, and her mascara looked as if it had been applied with a spatula.

The man in the orange jumpsuit and handcuffs I assumed was Melody's brother, Bodine. If that wasn't enough of a clue, the two men on either side of him wore the uniforms of prison guards, and were armed.

Claudine Potts, Melody's mother, was a tiny woman who looked to be about seventy, although I knew she was in her middle fifties. She was a bottle blond who could have used a little less of the bottle, as her shoulder length hair was thin and brittle. Her grief, however, looked to be genuine.

Melody's sister Brandyne was in her late thirties. She was doing her share of dry-eyed wailing, and after they sat, I heard her tell her mother to hush up. Brandyne was taller than her mother and Melody, but not tall. Maybe five-foot-four, that was after factoring in the height of her stilettos. She wore a tight, short, leopard print dress that was cut lower than it needed to be. Her hot pink heels and purse matched the pink stripes in her hair.

In contrast, Claudine wore a sedate navy pantsuit that was a size too big. Bodine, as I mentioned, wore prison orange. He was the tallest of the three and seemed equal in height to Brandyne in heels. No sign of Melody's dad. His reason for being locked up in prison must be more serious than Bodine's.

There was a pause in the air, a stillness of expectancy after Melody's family and the prison guards settled themselves. I half expected Ruthie to descend on wires from the ceiling, but the only one to make an entrance was Keith, who strode down the aisle at the last minute. Dressed entirely in black, from boots and jeans to t-shirt and suede leather suit jacket, Keith was accompanied by two tall, burly men. One I recognized as a band member, the other must be one of his new security guards. Surreptitiously, I adjusted my coat again and saw two other tall, burly men standing at parade rest at the back of the church. I also spotted Martin Giles sitting in a back pew.

Ruthie arrived then, not from the ceiling, but through the door behind the pulpit. When she spoke, I realized again what a commanding presence she could be. She had the gift of gab, as my Irish father would say.

During the service it was hard for me to concentrate. All I could think about was whether or not Melody's murderer was in the room. Could it be possible, as Carole indicated, that the killer was someone on Melody or Keith's team? Was it a "mighty happy" person from her church family or the riding center? Or, as I thought, was it a crazed fan or a person from her past?

I didn't realize I was crying until Annie handed me a Kleenex, and when I felt an arm around my shoulders I realized it was Jon's. I hesitated, and then leaned into him, unreasonably glad for his comfort. My best friend was gone and it was time for me to mourn.

At the reception, the Potts family held court, supported by Ruthie. Brandyne kept looking around the room, as if to pose for a hidden camera that might capture her image. Claudine wailed throughout, and Bodine had the grace to look embarrassed, whether by his sister and mother, or his own circumstances, I couldn't say.

"TMZ has a long angle lens and will be shooting pictures and video of people exiting the church," Buffy murmured beside me. "There's also a helicopter circling overhead. Just wanted you to know."

"Buffy," I called as she walked away. When I had her attention I lowered my voice. "I know you're trying to keep the media away, to ensure the respect that Melody deserves."

She nodded as she eyed the crowd.

"But don't reporters sometimes turn up things police can't?" I asked. "You worked for a newspaper. Don't reporters sometimes inadvertently take a photo that shows a glance between two people, or some other clue that can help solve the case?"

"Sometimes," she agreed. "But the reporters have to be good—and they have to be honorable enough to turn over anything that might mean something to the police. I'm not sure that lot out there has either qualification."

She left to talk to Keith and I headed toward the food.

"Hungry?" Tony asked, coming up behind me. "The food looks great."

It did. Verna Mae's, a mom and pop restaurant in Bellevue, a commuter city between Kingston Springs and Nashville, had catered, and Verna's home cooking always made my mouth water. For a year or so, Darcy and I had a standing Wednesday night dinner date at Verna Mae's. It was mostly so I could catch up with her, ask about her schoolwork and boyfriends, that kind of thing. But since she moved in, we didn't feel the need. After all, we saw each other every day. But I had missed Verna Mae's.

I smiled and nodded at two of Verna's humongous granddaughters, who lumbered behind the serving table. They were almost as big as their muumuu-clad grandmother, who didn't seem to be present. The girls obviously made good work of their grandmother's turnip green salads, vinegar slaw, sweet potato casseroles, hot biscuits, buttery grits, fried catfish, melt in your mouth barbecue, and chess and key lime pies.

There was all that and more here, and even though I put tiny amounts of almost everything on my plate, it was heaping by the time I picked up my sweet tea, and Tony and I headed to sit with Jon, Darcy, and Annie.

"Good food," Tony said, digging in.

"Like get this," said Darcy between bites of a carob and sweet potato cookie. "I heard Pastor Ruthie say that the record label paid for the whole thing."

"They did." Keith set his tea down first, then sat to my right and across from Darcy. Jon was across from me, Annie to my left and Tony was across from her. Under normal circumstances my heart would do little flippy-flops if Keith was this close to me, but today it kept right on beating its usual slow, steady rhythm.

"Well, the label paid for the reception," Keith said, taking a sip of his tea. He must be practicing Artist Manners 101: the unwritten rule that stated no artist shall ever eat anything in public. Wouldn't want a piece of broccoli or egg salad to be photographed hanging between the pearly whites. Also would not want a photo of a celebrity, mouth wide open, waiting to chomp down on a sandwich. I looked around the room. No cameras here as far as I could tell, but Keith apparently wasn't taking any chances. Either that or the Artist Rules were so ingrained that it didn't occur to him that he could eat.

"Davis is taking care of the rest of the expenses out of Melody's accounts," said Buffy plopping down next to Keith. "Melody had life insurance, so I guess the estate will get reimbursed when that comes through." She looked around the table. "I can't believe we're even having this conversation. This is so depressing."

Just then Brandyne Potts came over, Claudine and Bodine in tow. "Which of y'all was my sister's friend?" she asked.

Buffy jumped up, ready to head off trouble. "We all were, Brandyne," Buffy said. "But Cat and Melody had been close friends for some time now."

Buffy nodded at me, and I wiped my hands on a paper napkin and stood up to introduce myself. In her hot pink heels, Brandyne was eye to eye with me. I was so busy looking at all her makeup that I didn't notice her reach back with her right hand until her purse clubbed me on the side of my head. Before I knew it, Brandyne was all over me.

"You didn't keep her safe!" she shouted as she went for my hair. "What kind of no account friend are you?"

It happened so fast that all I had were impressions. Claudine began to wail again. Keith put his arms around my waist and tried to drag me away from Brandyne, but her hands were wrapped in my hair. Maybe I needed that salon appointment with Bill after all. A shorter cut might have helped here.

I saw Davis, Augie, and Chas out of the corner of my eye. Davis comforted Claudine, who screeched Brandyne's name over and over. The security guards pulled Bodine away from the fray, then Bodine wrenched himself free and rushed to his sister. Next thing I knew he had put his cuffed hands over her head and shoulders and wrapped the link between his handcuffs across the front of Brandyne's throat. It worked. She let go of my hair to try to pull the handcuffs away.

Next thing I knew, Keith and I were in the center of a circle of tall men made up of Martin, and Keith's security team. They hustled Keith and me to the other side of the room, and somehow, Keith's arms remained around me. Bodine and his guards left, presumably to head back to prison, and Brandyne collapsed into a chair, Ruthie by her side. What had just happened?

"You okay?" Buffy asked, hurrying over.

I touched the side of my head where Brandyne's purse had made contact. Fortunately for me, she traveled light so I didn't think there would be any lasting damage. The circle of tall men around Keith and me dissolved, and Martin said, "Miz Cat? Do you want to press charges? Miz Potts gave you a big wallop, so you're entitled."

I looked across the room at Brandyne, who still looked like she wanted to knock me into next week. Then I shook my head.

"She's not worth it, Martin." When he raised his eyebrows I added. "Let's just chalk it up to funeral tension and let it go." Besides, if I filed charges the tabloids were sure to find out, and I didn't want any trash talk surrounding our goodbyes to Melody.

By this time church ushers were picking up cups and plates, and directing people out the door. When it was just our group and what remained of the Potts family, Buffy assessed us and said, "Here's how this is going to work. Tony, Jon, and Darcy will ride home with Keith in Keith's truck." They all nodded. "Keith, you do not need to be seen at the burial, but we will make a statement for you this afternoon about your friendship with Melody. Davis or I will text it to you and your publicist for an okay before we send it." Keith nodded.

"Now, to avoid further scandal," Buffy shot a look at Brandyne who was getting to her feet with Ruthie's help, "Annie and Cat will go to the burial and stand next to the Potts family. Mrs. Potts," she said to Claudine, "does that meet with your approval?"

"Yes, honey," said Claudine, extracting herself from Davis and wiping her eyes at the same time. "Yes, that will be fine." She, too, shot a look at Brandyne.

With the manner of a Marine Corps drill sergeant, Buffy had Keith's group leave the church first, followed a minute later by our group of Brandyne, Claudine, Annie, and me. Buffy and the rest of Melody's team were last, and walked somberly out the door with Ruthie.

When we hit the sidewalk, Claudine raised a trembling hand and waved at no one in particular. Was she, too, looking for camera time? Brandyne perked up then, and looked around. She must have seen the glint of a lens in a tree across the way, as she put on her best bereavement face as she looked in that direction.

"Don't think this is over," she hissed as we walked. "I am definitely not done with you."

I had no idea what it was about me that set her off. But, if I hadn't loved Melody so much, I would have taken my own purse and decked Brandyne right then, smack dab in front of all the hidden cameras and tele-photo lenses. And just so you know, I don't travel all that light.

Cat's Horse Tip #8

"Across the globe, there are more than four hundred different breeds of horses."

12

The cemetery for the Holy Church of the Mighty Happy was a mile or so away, on the other side of town on top of Pinnacle Hill. The land where the church and riding center were located, next to the Harpeth River, was low, so the church could not get approval for a cemetery there.

It was a pretty place, I thought. While I did not know if Melody had ever visited the cemetery, it was a place she would have liked. It was a small acreage, and there were less than a dozen graves. Allen saw me looking at the dates on the gravestones.

"You must remember that we are a very young church," he said. "And as congregations go, ours is not large."

I nodded, suddenly overcome by the fact that this would be Melody's final resting place.

Annie held out a hand and together we walked the few feet to the gravesite. I might have drawn comfort from Ruthie's words, had I been able to hear them over the wailing of Claudine and Brandyne. It seemed as if they were trying to out-do each other. One would stop to catch a breath and the other would jump right in. The noise was deafening and, I thought, a tad contrived.

In due time, Melody's casket was lowered into the ground along with a big piece of my heart. Annie and I took a final look, and then walked back to her truck. Along the way we were joined by Robert Griggs. When he took riding lessons from me he had a way of walking up silently, and startling me unintentionally in the process. He still had that ability.

"She was too young, Robert," I said. "Too young to die."

"Maybe so," Robert said, "but—"

I looked at him and whatever he was going to say he swallowed back up. I thought he might say something to the effect of "the Lord knows best," or "she's in a better place." Both of those statements might be true, but I did not want to hear anything along those lines right now.

Instead, Robert said, "Just a reminder about our new volunteer orientation Tuesday night, that's tomorrow. Bubba can come, too. I know we can keep him busy in the barn. There is always something to do. The orientation is from six to eight-thirty and you'd all, well, you'd all be welcome additions."

I wanted to come to support Darcy, but would have to talk to Hill. I still wasn't sure he would okay Bubba volunteering. It would be good for Bubba, I thought, but there was school to think of, and transportation.

On the ride home I was glad to be a passenger in Annie's truck, as I wasn't up to driving.

"Sad day," said Annie.

I nodded but had no words. Annie tried again. "I'm sure the police will find the culprit soon enough."

"They have to," the words exploded out of me, startling us both. I do admit that my Irish temper sometimes gets the best of me.

"They will," Annie said with certainty. "Melody ran with an eclectic group of people, from the church, to the riding center, to her career. My money, though, is on the career side. Music is a big business and you never know what she saw someone do, or who saw her as a threat. Interesting looks, though."

"Looks? I don't follow."

"Between Buffy and your neighbor."

"Keith? Between Buffy and Keith?"

"Big time. Didn't you see?"

To be honest, I hadn't. It hadn't even occurred to me to look for something like that.

"It was like they were warning each other with their eyes to not say or not do something. It was very odd. That's why I noticed it."

Keith and Buffy? I let Annie's thoughts digest for a few minutes. I had no idea what a mysterious look between the two could mean, but if Annie said she saw it, I had no doubt that it occurred.

We ended up behind Bubba's school bus the last mile or so. Annie stopped at the top of my drive so we could see Bubba get off the bus at the end of his driveway. He spotted us, waved, then ran down the long dirt drive to the single-wide trailer he and Hill lived in. A few minutes later, Bubba banged on my kitchen door.

"My dad, he ain't home yet," said Bubba when I let him in.

Annie and I exchanged a look. She was well aware of the situation, as I had vented to her about Hill many times over the phone. I picked up my cell and dialed Hill's number, only to get his voice mail.

"Why don't you and I go over to your house, and look for clues that will tell us when he might be back," I said after I left yet another message for Hill. Bubba was eleven, and I knew I was at the tail end of enticing him through spy games, but today it worked.

"I like figurin' stuff out like I did when we caught that scum-bag that kilt Glenda."

Bubba hadn't exactly caught the killer. I hadn't either. But Bubba had helped both of us get out of a life or death situation, and for that I was grateful.

"Ya wanna come, Miz Annie?" Bubba asked.

I gave my head an almost imperceptible shake.

"No, you two go on," she said. "I'll head to the barn to see what Jon and Tony are up to. I think Darcy might be out there as well."

Bubba and I slipped between the boards of the fence that divided my property from Fairbanks. We crossed the wide Fairbanks strip of lawn, then crawled between the boards on the other side.

Hill had chosen to decorate his trailer in early Confederate flag. They were everywhere, even on the ceiling. The result was dark rooms, highlighted by the pungent smell of stale fast food, cigarettes, and mold. I'd only been in the house once before, and I hadn't been invited. Bubba had been missing so I had taken it upon myself to see if he was home.

Today I was just as angry as I had been during my visit (okay, break in) earlier this year. Bubba should not have to live in such deplorable conditions. I was torn between being furious with Hill for being one brick short of a pile, and worried that something terrible had happened to him.

I started by opening drawers in a desk in the living room. At two bedrooms, the house was too small to have a separate office. There was an office of sorts in the barn, but Hill had two Dobermans running loose in there and they didn't seem to like me much.

"What are we lookin' for?" Bubba asked, opening and closing drawers without checking the contents.

"Mail from anyone in Mississippi or Alabama. Notes your dad might have written in the past few days. Maybe an address book."

"Won't be no address book," said Bubba. "My dad, he keeps ever'thing in his phone now. Keeps people from stealin' his private information."

People like me, I thought. I knew better than to ask about numbers for family members. What family Hill and Bubba had left hadn't spoken to them in years. Even if I had a number to call I doubted the person on the other end would be of any help.

We searched next in the kitchen and finally in Hill's bedroom. I stifled my urge to say "eeewww" every time I touched something in Hill's room. Finally, I put my hands on my hips, tousled Bubba's dark hair and said, "C'mon kiddo. We've got barn chores to do, then I bet Annie will have a nice dinner fixed for us."

After that I'd try to help Bubba with his homework, if he had any. I might also put a discreet call in to Martin, just to give him a heads up about Hill. Before we left we walked up to Hill's barn. I thought Hill's "man" might be there to see to the horses. The dogs kept us out of the barn, but I wrote a note asking the man to contact me, and wedged it into the outer frame of the office door on the side of the barn.

Back in my barn, Annie, Tony, Jon, and Darcy stood outside Sally Blue's stall.

"She's been lying like that lately," said Jon. "Our massage therapist said it was a good shoulder stretch. Maybe that's what she's doing."

I peeked inside to find Sally lying with her front legs straight out, but crossed again just below the knee with the hoof of her top leg pointing toward her tail.

Annie, who had recently been convinced that Sally was psychic, said, "X marks the spot?"

"We already thought of that," I said. "Maybe we need to concentrate on her pointed toes and look for a murderous ballerina."

"Or a figure skater," said Tony.

"A high diver!" said Bubba.

"No way. Don't you see?" said Darcy. "She's making a cross in honor of Melody. Melody Cross."

I loved each of these people so much. Melody should be here, too. The thought burst from my brain. Then a lump formed in my throat and the pleasant moment was gone.

Tony and Jon had already fed the horses their evening grain, but we all made sure the horses had enough hay and water, and that the stalls were picked clean. Both dogs helped by running circles around the wheelbarrow when Jon used it to get shavings. Then we went to admire Ringo, who seemed to be adjusting well to his new home.

"When will you start working with him?" Tony asked.

I looked at Jon. "We'll give him another day, then do a full evaluation on him on Wednesday," I said.

A thorough horse evaluation could take an hour or two, and covered everything from a gait analysis to flexibility tests to figuring out what the horse already knew and where the gaps in his education were. I sure hoped this horse was everything his owner promised. Right now, the rest of my career was riding on him.

Cat's Horse Tip #9

"To spot a rear leg lameness, look to see if the movement of the horse is rhythmic and even across the top of the hips, rather than looking at the legs."

13

It was getting to be my regular routine. Get up at the crack of early, get Darcy off to school, then get Bubba on his way. When had I turned into a soccer mom? I didn't even have any kids. I couldn't say that I disliked the schedule, but it was totally unexpected.

This morning I also had to say goodbye to Annie and Tony. I could never ask for better friends and I have to say I felt a teeny bit guilty about Ringo. Then the voice of reason stepped in and reminded me that Ringo's owner could have chosen Tony and Annie to train his horse—but Gusher Black hadn't. He had chosen me. I now just needed to deliver. No pressure there. None at all.

I hugged my friends, and Jon even came out to shake Tony's hand. Was it possibly that this short visit had put their relationship on slightly less rocky ground? That would be nice. After pulling a reluctant Hank out of their back seat, hugging Mickey, and then sending the Zinners down the drive, Hank, Jon, and I headed for the barn. Jon and I had not had time the past few days to work with Petey, and needed to resume his driving lessons. Christmas was inching closer every day and I was determined that Petey would give Darcy the surprise of her life.

Today we were able to pull the cart alongside Petey and also behind him without him trying to turn his head or body around to confront the cart. It was more validation that horses do process information if you let them sit and think about things for a day or so.

After patting Petey, allowing him to lead himself back to the barn aisle, and giving him lots of love for a job well done, Jon turned him out into a paddock with Wheeler and Reddi. Only then did I get Sally Blue out of her stall. I groomed her while Jon refreshed Petey's stall, and hers. Then we turned Sally out into the front pasture with Gigi and Bob, and let Ringo stretch his legs in the covered arena.

While Ringo explored the arena, Jon and I stood near the arena gate. After a few false starts, I asked Jon the question I had been mulling over all morning.

"How did your visit with Tony go?"

"Okay," he said after a moment. "Some awkward moments. Not as many as I expected. We'll probably always have some of that."

We watched Ringo paw, drop, and roll in the center of the arena, and I was glad to see that he rolled all the way over on his back from left to right, then reversed the process. A horse who could only roll from one side onto the center of his back and not flop over onto the other side, often had a sore back, hip, or pelvis.

"Mind if I ask you something?" Jon asked.

Gee, Jon was getting quite personal these days. Our previous years of existence as trainer and assistant had pretty much been limited to the job. I was so used to Jon as a private person that his reaching out felt odd.

"What's on your mind?" I said.

"Do you ever wish you had a better relationship with your dad?"

"My dad? We don't even have a relationship."

"I know." Jon gave a rueful smile. "But do you ever wish you did?"

I considered that. My dad was a charming Irishman with sparkling green eyes and bright red hair. He had loved my mother so much that when she died the only way he could cope was to look at the bottom of a bottle of whisky. When I was nine, he left me alone so often in a Chicago slum that child protective services rescued me and reunited me with my grandmother in Tennessee. That might be why I got so mad at Hill Henley and his treatment of Bubba, because I had once been a neglected child myself. Only a psychiatrist could help me sort that out and I currently didn't have the time, energy, or desire to go that route.

Since then, my dad called me once every few years. I occasionally got a birthday or Christmas card from him, and I'd seen him four times. He even showed up for both my high school and my college graduation. Well, he was two days late on the college one, but he made the effort. Once, he came to my farm. I had last seen him two years ago at a horse show in Oklahoma City. From what I could tell, he bounced around from one farm labor job to another, one racetrack to the next, and every bar in between. Did I wish I had a better relationship with him?

"I wish he didn't drink," I said. Then I picked up a broom and started to sweep the aisle.

Hill came home just after noon. I saw him pull in with his trailer and gave him half an hour to unload and get the horses situated. Then I hoofed it on over to his place and pounded on the barn door. Forget the Dobermans. After I got through, Hill might wish they had laid into him instead of me.

As usual, Hill's timing was unfortunate. If Jon had not just asked me about my dad and brought up a boat load of mixed feelings, I might not have been so hard on Hill. As it was, it wasn't pretty.

"—and if you ever had one, single, bright idea, it must have been beginner's luck," I shouted. "And Hill? You clean up that mess you call a house, today, or I am going to call the child welfare people." I was so worked up I realized that I sounded like Brandyne Potts.

"What you been doin' in my house?" he asked, his voice dangerously low. I needed to be careful, as Hill was holding a pitchfork. It was a plastic one, but I still didn't want to see it too closely. Even plastic tines could poke out an eye.

"Your son *invited* me," I yelled, waving my arms like Fitch. "He wanted help looking for a card, or a letter, or a phone number where he could reach you because you weren't answering your stupid phone." I wondered if people could hear me across the river. I hoped not. The Cumberland ran behind both of our farms and was wide enough and deep enough for barge travel. But I knew that sound carried over water.

I lowered my voice. "Your son cares about you. Why? I have no idea, but he does, even though you're about as useful as an ashtray on a motorcycle. You had better stand up, and be deserving of his care."

"Or what, missy?" said Hill. His eyes were black and I could feel the menace ooze out of him. "Or. What?"

"You just clean up your house and take care of Bubba. Take *good* care."

Before I knew it, I had turned and was striding away. I wanted to look back, to see if Hill's pitchfork was going to slam into the back of my head, but I resisted the urge. It would have spoiled my exit.

I was just crawling through my own fence when my cell rang. My instincts were to let it go to voice mail. It was probably Hill ready to throw more threats at me, but I looked at the screen to find it was Keith.

"I just got a copy of the roughs from the video shoot," Keith said as soon as I answered. "The sheriff's office got a copy, too, but I got the camera guys to send a full set over to me. Want come over to the house to watch with me?"

Did I? Absolutely.

"Bring Jon, if you can," said Keith. "He was there for most of the shoot. He might see something that we miss."

"What are we looking for?" I asked.

"An odd look, a conversation, facial expressions. Anything out of the ordinary."

"Got it. We'll be right over."

Despite my friendship with Carole, I hadn't had many invites to the Carson home. A party or two, and a few coffees with Carole when the older kids were at school was about it. Our schedules were completely different, and frankly, all those kids together made me want to stuff them into a closet. Not that I would ever do that . . . well, probably not.

Jon was a harder sell than I thought.

"I've got calls to make, feed and lumber and shavings to order, and I was going to get that new insulation wrapped around the water pipes in the barn today. If you haven't noticed, it's November. Winter is on the way."

Winter was a relative term here in Middle Tennessee. A typical January week might include six degrees and snow followed by sixty degrees and sun. Next up: a gray, windy twenty-eight with freezing rain, sleet, and ice.

"But it's for Melody," I said. "You might notice something in the raw footage that Keith and I miss. You were there. You could help."

Jon couldn't say no after that, so we walked over to the Carson place and knocked on the side door. Inside, the home was everything you might imagine the home of a country superstar to be. There were warm pine hardwoods, comfy leather chairs and sofas, and coffee tables you could put your boots up on. Gold and platinum records hung on the walls, award trophys littered the mantle over the big fireplace in the great room, and acoustic guitars could be seen tucked away in several nooks. Overall, the house had an air of casual messiness. It was easy to see that four children lived here, and that their house was a home. It was lived in and loved.

Keith led us to a secluded media room that I think was over the four-car garage. The house was large and I got twisted around. We each grabbed a club chair and Keith set the footage on go. There were actually two sets of video footage. The first was from the unpersonable Fitch and the company that had been hired to shoot the music video. It included take after boring take of each scene from each camera.

While I knew I was going to look at footage of my friend, I hadn't thought the idea through. Melody was so young and alive and vibrant on the screen that I felt I could reach out and touch her. To know that her body now lay in a box in the ground on top of Pinnacle Hill, well it was like learning anew that she had been killed. Jon and Keith both handed me a Kleenex box at the same time.

We fast-forwarded through most of the Fitch footage, as almost all of it was solely of Keith and Melody. I certainly didn't see anything in there that indicated that Keith had killed his duet partner and Jon later said that he didn't either.

The video company also had concert footage of Keith and Melody on stage and then it was my turn to hand a box of Kleenex back to Keith. The final scene from this company had been filmed at the riding center. But, it was all close-ups of the program's riders and horses, with a few glimpses of leaders and sidewalkers—nothing that showed anything other than staged interactions.

Then we looked closely at the music video itself. The shot of Keith and Melody cantering across the steeplechase grounds on Bob and Sally with the rich drape of fall foliage behind them was stunning. This was followed by the two stars walking hand in hand, leading their horses. The videographer had reached deep to capture an array of moving expressions that played across each of their faces.

I'd actually had to compromise on that shot. For the two stars to walk hand in hand, Melody had to lead Sally from the right side, rather than the traditional left. Only a horse person would catch that, though. The video next showed Melody and Keith helping a child with a disability get on her horse. Lots of smiles and high fives all around.

Keith paused the video and leaned over to talk to Jon and me. "That footage came from my personal videographer. He filmed with a hand held, rather than with a tripod, so the footage has a raw feel. It's also grainier because it was indoors and there wasn't as much light as we should have had. But I think it works, don't you?"

The next shot was also at the center and showed Melody and Keith shaking the hands of adults in wheelchairs, one of whom was dressed in military garb. Then the concert footage kicked back in.

"Soundcheck," said Keith.

"The rehearsal place," I added to Jon. Jon nodded. The horrendous Nashville flood of 2010 had put Soundcheck under about ten feet of water. Many top artists lost stage sets, memorabilia, instruments, and costumes. But, the facility had rebounded nicely and was back in full swing.

The video closed with another shot of Melody, Keith, and the horses cantering across the field, but this time they stopped for a kiss. I didn't know much about award-winning videos, but if I had ever seen one, this was it. It was full of color and emotion, and was sure to tug on the heartstrings of each and every viewer.

For our purposes, the raw footage from Keith's personal videographer was far more interesting than Fitch's footage had been. At craft services, a morning shot found Buffy and Davis in a heated argument. As the shot was from a distance we could not hear the words, but quick movements of his head and jabs with his arms punctuated Davis's body language. Buffy's arms spread wide several times before she turned and walked toward the camera. Her face was grim.

In a dressing room at Soundcheck, there were Buffy and Davis again, rifling through a row of clothes that were hanging on a portable metal clothing rack. By the look of them, the clothes were for Melody. Neither person wore a happy expression. At the riding center, in another long shot, Ruthie was vivaciously interacting with some of the riders and their families. But then she straightened and stared in the direction of the barn. The look on her face was pensive. We backed up the video several times to try to figure out what, or who, Ruthie was looking at, but it was impossible.

Also at the riding center was a happy Rowan Harding, swinging between the arms of her parents, Allen and Emily. Emily was full of doting looks toward her daughter, but Allen was not so happy. In fact, his face was set in stone as he looked past the camera.

There was some footage of Keith and Melody talking quietly, their bodies relaxed, as they waited for a shot to be set up. Robert Griggs hurried past in several of the shots, clipboard in hand. One time he stopped to talk to Fitch, the director, who waved him away. Robert walked off, then stopped to turn back to look at Fitch. Robert's expression was cold.

A number of Mighty Happy volunteers in long sleeved gold t-shirts with the center logo on them mingled in and out of the shots. Once, Sandy Sweet spoke with Ruthie and Emily, but the conversation seemed pleasant enough.

The last bit of footage found Allen and Ruthie off in a corner of the arena. The area was not well lit, but one could easily see the family resemblance. Both were stocky with heavy thighs, although Allen was much taller than Ruthie's five-foot-four. They had the same hooked nose, blue eyes, and crooked smile, but Ruthie's posture was casual, while Allen's was all business. His shoulders were square and his arms were folded as he listened to his sister.

I wished there had been better sound, but most of the shots were not taken close in and it seemed as if most of the subjects were not even aware that they were being filmed. All in all, it made me want more than ever to go to the volunteer training at the riding center that evening. I also wanted to speak with Buffy and Davis. Something was definitely going on between those two, something that might even lead to finding Melody's killer.

Before we left, I asked Keith about the looks Annie saw he and Buffy share at the funeral.

"Was it that obvious?" he laughed. "Buffy is not my publicist, but we see each other frequently, because she worked with Melody. That woman is after me all the time. I keep telling her I am a happily married man, but she never gives up."

Keith must have seen the disbelieving expression on my face.

"Oh, she's subtle. She'd never say or do anything that anyone else would notice, but gosh darn she makes me uncomfortable."

So Buffy also had a crush on Keith Carson. Maybe hers was not as platonic as mine. As Jon and I walked back to the barn I wondered if Buffy's feelings were strong enough for her to kill someone she thought might steal away his potential affections. Someone like Melody Cross?

14

THERE WERE ABOUT A DOZEN people at the Mighty Happy Therapeutic Riding Center's new volunteer orientation, including Darcy and me. After this afternoon's encounter, I didn't have the strength to call Hill to ask if Bubba could come along. Besides, Hill had just gotten home. He and Bubba needed some father/son bonding time. I hoped part of that time would be spent cleaning up their house.

All of the prospective volunteers gathered at one end of the arena, where a dozen or so chairs had been set up around a power point screen and projector. The other new volunteers seemed to come from a cross section of the community. A few sported windbreakers stamped with the church logo, and combined, the group ranged in age from high school students to retirees.

After a mighty happy welcome, Emily led the training with Robert's help. We started by filling out a lot of paperwork that absolved the center of liability should anyone happen to fall underneath a horse, be bitten, or break an ankle stepping on or off the mounting ramp. We then watched a promotional video about the center before Emily got down to business.

First off was a tour, where we were shown the tack and feed rooms, and the large, cork bulletin board where instructions were left for volunteers. Then, by flashlight, we toured the pasture and paddocks.

"We have a 'no treat' rule for the horses, so leave those carrots and peppermints at home," Emily said. "The horses sometimes are given treats by staff, but you can imagine what would happen if all of our volunteers brought treats whenever they came out. Our horses would be on sugar overload and develop dental problems."

"The horses also might start to look for treats and nuzzle your pocket, or the pocket of a participant," Robert added. "Some of our people have poor balance, so if a horse bumps them with their nose, the person could fall over."

Point taken. We next were shown where the first aid kit and telephones were, on the off chance there was an emergency. We also learned that the tack room doubled as an official storm shelter, and where the water shut off valve and the electric breaker box were located. I got the feeling that Emily was so organized that an emergency would never be allowed to happen in her presence, but we were shown where to go and what to do, just in case a rogue disaster dared to sneak in.

Emily's mood here was quite different than I had seen in her before. With Rowan she had been a kind and loving mom. In lessons she was a fun teacher who knew just how much to challenge her students. Here she was so businesslike she was almost clinical in her delivery. It made me wonder if she could turn her moods off and on, much as I had seen Pastor Ruthie flick the switch on her charisma.

Next, we were given instruction on how to relate to the program participants. Some of their "riders" didn't actually ride, but instead did obstacle courses and other leading exercises with their horse, so "participant" was the center's catch-all word. We were taught how to shake hands with a locked elbow and upper arm, so the participant who did not understand boundaries would not get too up close and personal, and how to gracefully avoid a hug, if one was not welcomed. Hot dog! I could put this stuff to use if I ever hit the dating pool again.

I also learned that when it came to the world of therapeutic riding, I knew nothing. In fact, the correct terminology was EAAT, equine assisted activities and therapies. Therapy horses at this center were trained to respond correctly to the least experienced human handler, so consistent horse handling practices were firmly in place. We all needed to follow their horse handling rules, even if we interacted with our own horses differently.

After learning the specific steps they took to groom, saddle, and otherwise tack their horses (most of the horses were led, and ridden, in a halter, rather than a bridle), we went to the wooden mounting ramp. This was a structure of about twenty feet in length with a ramp at one end and a platform of about three feet in height at the other. The ramp was wide enough for a wheelchair to be pushed up it.

"The mount is the most dangerous part of the lesson," said Emily. "If the rider does not end up in the center of the horse's back, they could slip off. An uncentered rider will also cause the horse pain, so the horse could scoot forward or back. A sidewalker or the instructor could trip, fall, and be stepped on. The possibilities are endless.

"Our instructors and volunteers know all of this, and sometimes are tense during the mounting process. Especially with a heavier rider. The horse then picks up on the stress and becomes tense, too. That's why we all like to take a moment for a few deep breaths right before the mount."

We all breathed in and out several times, and our demonstration horse, the brown Saddlebred cross named Cinnamon, sighed, too.

Robert and Sandy, who was also there to help, demonstrated the proper position for a leader and sidewalker during the mount, while Emily and another volunteer, a short, slim young woman whose name I didn't catch, demonstrated the usual mounting positions for the rider and instructor.

And on we went through a pretend lesson. We learned the three basic ways a sidewalker "holds" the rider. One was to drape an arm over the rider's thigh, the second was to put the sidewalker's hand on the back of the calf, and the third was to place the hand on the back of the heel.

Emily spoke at length about the importance of the movement of the horse. "Movement improves the focus of riders, especially those with autism. I feel it helps those with ADD (attention deficit disorder) and ADHD (attention deficit hyper activity disorder), too," she said. "That's why if a rider is coming undone, we might break into a trot. The extra movement helps the brain focus.

"We might also put an unfocused rider on a horse with a lot of movement at the walk and a bouncy trot. A physically fragile rider, on the other hand, might need a horse with less movement and smoother gaits. A lot goes into developing the right horse herd when it comes to the height, width, and movement of each horse. Then we add in the horse's temperament, training, and personality to match a horse with each rider."

Finally, we learned how to pull the rider off the horse in case the emergency that would never dare show up in Emily's presence actually arrived.

"Questions?" Emily asked when she had finished.

Almost every one raised a hand. Emily looked as if she didn't know whether to be ticked off because we didn't absorb everything she said, or to be pleased that her new volunteers were taking such an interest. I watched the varied expressions in her face and was glad when she chose to morph into the role of fun, intelligent instructor. Darcy gave me a nudge, and I knew she had seen exactly what I had. Still waters certainly ran deep in Emily Harding. I would have to find a way to get to know her better. I raised my hand.

Most of the other questions had been about specific circumstances that might happen during a lesson. What should a volunteer do if the horse fell down? Fell asleep? If the saddle slipped? If they slipped? I needed my question to be different.

When Emily had answered all of the other questions and finally pointed at me I asked, "How is the program funded?"

Her eyes narrowed. "What do you mean?"

I took another tack. "How do you get your hay, for example? Is it donated, or do you purchase it out of donated funds? The same for the tack, and the horses, too."

Emily looked at me as if she did not quite know if she should trust me. "A little of both," she said finally. "If you want more information you should talk to Allen. He's our financial person. Or Ruthie, our pastor. Either could help you with that more than I."

It was a brush off, but a soft one. I thought I'd follow up on her suggestion, though. It would give me an excuse to talk to both Allen and Ruthie. Melody, I thought, had lived a very large life. I wasn't sure if I should be looking for clues here at the church and riding center, or with people involved in her career. If it was a random fan, well, then we may never know who had killed her.

Martin and his team of law enforcement professionals did their jobs very well. They might even find the murderer. But I had an edge into her personal life that they did not. I knew Melody. I knew her likes and dislikes, as well as her quirks. In talking to the many different people who circled around her busy life, I might spot something out of the ordinary that the police would gloss over. *Melody*, I thought, *we'll find the dirtbag, and I promise that I will not rest until we do.*

On the way home, I turned on WSM-AM. Johnny Paycheck was telling us to "Take This Job and Shove it." We listened for a bit, then I asked Darcy if she wanted to choose the center as her senior service project.

"It's better than being a pre-school aide," she said. The lights from the truck's dashboard let me see a new piece of purple bubblegum form a balloon outside her mouth, and then pop.

"You need a better reason than that," I said. "If you volunteer someplace, you need to care about what the organization does."

"I care," she said. "I don't know if I want to make a center like that my life's work, but I care. I think it's cool that horses can help people. And it's fun. Emily is a bit intense, though, if you ask me."

"She seems like a good instructor," I said.

"Probably," answered Darcy, "but I wouldn't want her job either. Way too much responsibility. What if a kid who can't walk fell off a horse? I'd feel awful."

"Falling off is part of riding, and it seems like they have good safety precautions in place. I bet that doesn't happen very often." I turned left onto Sam's Creek Road and my truck hesitated before it started the long climb up the hill. "You've mentioned a few things you don't want to do with your life. Any idea what you do want to do?"

"Be a lawyer, maybe. Then I could get involved in politics. I could make a difference there."

I glanced in my rearview mirror. "You'd be a great lawyer," I said, "and I'll help you any way I can. Your grades are going to have to go up a bit if you plan to go to law school, though."

Darcy made a face. "Maybe I'll just be a lobbyist."

By this time David Allan Coe was singing "The Ride." It was a spooky song for a foggy night and I was concerned about the car behind us. One light was yellower than the other. I had first noticed it at the three way stop near the Sonic in Kingston Springs. It wasn't unusual for two consecutive vehicles to travel from Kingston Springs to Sam's Creek Road. What bothered me was that this was not the first time this car had been behind me. I also noticed the same unusual lights behind us Friday evening, after Melody had been found.

Darkness falls early in Tennessee in November. After our visit to the center last Friday, by the time Bubba, Jon, Darcy, and I left the riding center it had been dark. The car with the strange lights had been behind my truck on Sam's Creek Road then, too. I shrugged. It was probably someone who worked in Kingston Springs—or who had family there—and lived in Ashland City. No worries.

I should have been more concerned.

Cat's Horse Tip #10

"A good therapy horse can be a horse of any breed, but must be patient, tolerant, kind, nurturing, smart, intuitive, reliable, healthy, and strong."

15

I HAD JUST TAKEN THE first sip of my morning hot chocolate when my landline rang. I looked at the called ID and groaned.

"Good morning, Agnes," I said, taking a big gulp of chocolate to fortify myself. I needed fortification before a conversation with Agnes.

"Cat, my dearest lovely darling. How are you?"

Agnes tended to go overboard on her adjectives and adverbs.

"Good, Agnes. We're all good."

"Oh, my. I am quite relieved," she said. "Did you get the tarot cards?"

"Ah, no. Not yet."

"Rest assured that they will arrive soon."

Oh goodie.

"Cat, dear, I was happily communing with Ira, one of my husbands, you know, at our local little ashram here in beautiful Louisville yesterday and you know what? My dear, shy Ira sensed that you were troubled. Of course I knew that, because of your friend. Oh, that poor girl. Why, I—"

I knew if I didn't jump in here soon that it would be another fifteen minutes before Agnes slowed down for a breath. I also wasn't sure that Agnes ever got it right when she communed with Ira, because he had passed on about twenty years ago. I knew she still felt close to him, but that was because she carried his ashes around in her purse. You'd think it would be a little crowded, what with her other two husbands also bouncing around in there, but Agnes said they all got along just fine.

"Agnes—"

"—am so sorry about that poor little thing—"

"Agnes, Sally Blue has a new friend."

I said the words as fast as I could and it did the trick. Agnes stopped talking.

"A new friend? Oh, I am just thrilled." Agnes cooed. "Who is it? A new fan? Oh, I bet it's that wonderful friend of Keith's that I met the other night. Brad? Yes. Brad Paisley. Is he Sally's new friend? You know Brad is an accomplished singer. Not like Keith, but—"

"Agnes, stop. It's not Brad."

"But—"

I felt her deflate. "I'm sure Brad would love Sally if he ever has the chance to meet her. Sally's new friend is named Ringo."

Too late, I realized that Agnes would jump to the conclusion that Sally's new friend Ringo was Ringo Starr, of The Beatles. Ugh. I was right. In frustration with myself I banged my forehead into the wall of my kitchen. Several times.

It took me another twenty minutes to settle Agnes down and rectify my faux pas, and by that time Hank had thumped on the kitchen door twice in an effort to show me his latest stick. Finally, I was able to disengage myself from Agnes's call, admire the stick, and head to the barn.

I found Petey in the cross ties, and Jon double checking the fit of Petey's driving harness. Jon also had "the look" on his face, the one he got when he felt I was getting distracted from my barn duties.

"Agnes," was all I usually had to say to get his expression to change. This time it didn't work. I tried again. "I know. I'm distracted by Melody's murder. But wouldn't you be, too, if it was your best friend?"

I wondered, not for the first time, if Jon even had a best friend. Then my mind again jumped to the phone call. The one where he had told someone he loved them. Who had that been?

"I just don't want you getting hurt," said Jon.

I started to protest, then realized he had a point. In the past nine months I had been kidnapped, left for dead, had a near miss in a potentially fatal car accident, and was drugged and thrown into a dumpster. I'd also had my upper arm and a few ribs broken. Fortunately, I recovered quickly from all that.

"I know," I finally said. "But I just have to help. Melody had her whole life in front of her. She was talented, funny, and kind . . . and I miss her."

The look faded from Jon's face as he gave Petey a pat. "Who do you think did it?" he asked.

"I have no idea. I've been thinking about motive, but I can't figure out why anyone would want to kill her."

"For one of the usual reasons," Jon said. "Secrets, jealousy, rage, passion, blackmail, money."

"Well that narrows it down. I'm going to give the police any information that I can either remember or find. But I also don't want to leave too much for you to do here. In the past I've done that, and I want to be sure it doesn't happen again."

Jon looked at me, and then nodded. "Do you still want to do an eval on Ringo today?"

"I do. How about four o'clock?"

Jon nodded again, unhooked Petey, and we took him into the arena.

After another good driving session, Hank and I walked back to the house. Hank often stayed in the barn with Jon, but whenever I was troubled he seemed to stay closer to me. He too, had been kidnapped—or should I say, dognapped—recently, so I wasn't sure if the closeness had to do with him protecting me, or me protecting him. Either way, I enjoyed his company.

After filling another mug with hot chocolate, I called Brent to fill him in. He seemed distant, but that could have been because he was surrounded by what sounded like a thousand yapping dogs. He must be in the back of the clinic, I thought. We made a dinner date for that evening.

"But let's stay in," I said. "Pizza and a movie at my place? My treat, although Jon and Darcy may join us for the pizza."

"Great." he said. "Maybe we can watch an old movie on one of those off-beat channels that you have."

That sounded perfect.

Next I called Buffy, fully aware that she could have killed Melody. We decided to meet for an early lunch, and she suggested Provence, a trendy bakery and café in Hillsboro Village.

The location was great, as I wanted to pop into Davis's office after, and Hillsboro Village was Music Row adjacent.

"Park around the corner on Acklen," suggested Buffy. "There's usually parking there in front of the post office."

I was grateful for the suggestion, as parking could be a nightmare in the village. My closet was filled with horse clothes and little else, so I changed into a fresh pair of Wranglers, a clean pair of Ariat paddock boots, a green long-sleeved tee with the Cat Enright Stables logo on it, and shrugged into a matching green goose down vest. The vest also had my logo on it. My years on the show circuit had taught me never to waste a good opportunity to advertise. The weather was balmy today, in the mid-fifties with lots of sun, so I wouldn't need my heavy jacket.

When I got to Provence, Buffy was already seated, so I went to the counter and ordered the chop salad, which the waitress told me came loaded with roast corn, peppers, grilled onions, chicken, salami, feta, olives, chickpeas, romaine, and sunflower seeds, and was tossed in a tomato-tahini dressing. I didn't know what half that stuff was, but it sounded good. I also decided to stick with water, having already had several cups of chocolate that morning.

When the meal came, the waitress deposited a plate of smoked salmon crepes in front of Buffy. I should have ordered that, I thought. Not that the salad wasn't great, but whenever I ate out nothing I ordered ever looked as good as what other people chose.

"Melody's will is being read tomorrow," Buffy said between tiny bites of her food. Ah. She was one of those people who moved food around on their plate rather than eating it. I dug into my salad.

"They're bringing all of the beneficiaries in for the reading," she continued.

"Do they still do that?" I asked. "I thought everyone was notified by mail these days."

"I think that's usually the case, but the sheriff asked them to do it this way. Guess they wanted to see everyone's reactions when they learn who gets all the money."

"Is there a lot?" I asked.

"I assume so." Buffy put a morsel of salmon onto her fork and brought it to her mouth. I looked down at my plate. My big bowl of salad was almost gone. "Melody had three number one singles last year and her debut album was also number one. The label will charge back every cent they spent on the album, and on her," she continued, "but there should be some profit there. She had major numbers in digital downloads. She had that big tour last year, too, and she opened for Brad in the spring, then for Jason Aldean in the fall."

I studied Buffy as she picked at her food. Could she have killed Melody? There was the Keith crush to consider, but it was hard for me to imagine that Buffy felt passionate enough to actually kill a possible rival. She had always seemed so superficial. She grew up with bucket loads of money, but was nice enough, as potential murderers go. When she worked as a reporter for the *Ashland City Times* she had always treated me fairly. I'd have to give the idea more thought.

"Who is on the list of invitees for the will reading?" I asked. I'd give three of my left toes to be there. Well, maybe just two.

"Not sure. Scott said everyone would be notified."

I made a strong mental note to call Martin. Would he be there? Buffy said the sheriff had requested the will be read with everyone in attendance. Maybe I could tag along, be another set of eyes for him.

As we finished up, I asked Buffy about a young man who was sitting at a rectangular table against the far wall. He kept looking our way, yet whenever I tried to make eye contact, he busied himself with his phone.

"Which guy?" she asked, looking around. The restaurant had filled up while we had been talking. "The preppy looking guy with the short brown hair?"

I nodded.

"No clue," she said. "Never seen him before. But if you like him, you should walk over and introduce yourself."

"No, it's not that. I'm actually seeing someone. I just thought I'd seen him somewhere before. Can't put my finger on where, though."

"No clue," Buffy said again, gathering her things.

Buffy and I parted ways on the sidewalk in front of the eclectic BookManBookWoman store, and I walked back to my truck. I knew Davis's office was on 16th Avenue, just a stone's throw away, and I watched the house numbers carefully as I drove slowly down the street.

The upper end of 16th was still largely made up of rambling, old brick houses, and many music businesses had offices there. North of 16th and Edgehill, however, most of the homes had been torn down and replaced with modern office buildings. I liked the old houses better, and hoped this part of Music Row would stay the same for some time to come.

I found Davis in a house on the left side of the street, halfway between Horton and Edgehill, and snagged a parking spot off the alley in back. His office, and the entire home, was well done. Rich, dark wood floors that looked original, and lush oriental rugs topped with furniture that screamed expensive antique dominated the rooms. I was so busy looking at the furniture that I almost missed all of the gold and platinum records hanging on the walls. Wouldn't want that to happen. The display was impressive.

"Cat," Davis said, getting up from his desk. "We didn't have a meeting, did we? I didn't have you on my calendar and I have to head out in a few minutes."

I was surprised I had gotten past his gatekeeper, a formidable battle-axe of a woman with short, steel-gray hair and a British accent who sat at a desk outside Davis's office door.

"I just wanted to ask two quick questions and hoped you'd be in," I said. Of course, I could have called and I am sure that thought was on his mind. But I had wanted to see him, see the space where he worked, to get a better feel for him. Could he be the one? Could he have strangled Melody? He had a good poker face, so I had a hard time knowing his thoughts.

"I hoped you could tell me if Melody's family was still in town," I said. With the reading of the will not until tomorrow, I was betting that they were. "I'd like to see them, to give them my condolences."

In reality, I'd like nothing less. Brandyne was obviously the kind of person who could start an argument in an empty house, and if her mother continued to wail, I am sure that my visit would be very short. But, I wanted to get a better idea of them, too. Melody had practically disowned her family. Certainly, nothing she ever said about them showed them in a positive light. Maybe they took offense to her lack of interest and decided to take her out.

"They are," said Davis, consulting something on his iPad. "They're at the Y'all Come Inn. The place is an extended stay motel on Old Hickory Boulevard, just before Hwy. 70 in Bellevue. Room 217."

Good that he added "in Bellevue," as Old Hickory snaked around the entire city of Nashville, stopping seemingly at will, then picking up inexplicably several blocks away. Bellevue was a nice community not too far from Pegram, where Melody had lived. But this hotel, I knew, was home to a lot of transient workers and was the kind of place where ten people might crowd into a single room, each drinking a six-pack for dinner. Guess Claudine and Brandyne would fit right in.

"They're not at Melody's house?" I asked.

"No, they wanted to be there, fought me pretty hard about that in fact, but the police are still poking through it. Do you want me to call Claudine, to see if they're there?" He looked pointedly at me.

I smiled. "No. Thanks, Davis. I really don't make a habit of dropping in unannounced. You were a last minute thought after I had lunch with Buffy at Provence." I didn't think one white lie would hurt in the greater scheme of things. "But in light of Brandyne's behavior at the reception, I don't want to give them time to get all worked up. If they're not there, I'll stop back by another time."

Davis's face almost changed expression. "Can't blame you there. We all hoped to get through the funeral without one of them going off. I thought it would be Bodine. He's a loose cannon, and not much brighter. It almost took an act of God to get him released for the funeral. You saw the guards. He's got another six years on an aggravated robbery. Tried to rob a Walmart in Springfield, Tennessee about eighteen months ago. He walked out the door with a shopping cart full of Melody's CDs and a flat screen TV."

Davis said the odd thing was, Bodine might have gotten away with it if not for the TV. A Walmart staffer asked him for his receipt, like they sometimes do when you have a large ticket item in your cart, and Bodine made a run for it.

"Security surrounded him in the parking lot and Bodine decided to shoot his way out," Davis said. "He didn't hit anyone, but he did nail a tire or two—and a windshield. The boy doesn't have the sense of a sidewalk."

"One more question," I said. "Keith Carson asked me over to look at the b-roll and outtakes from the video shoot. His videographer caught you and Buffy in an argument, although you were far enough away that your voices didn't pick up."

The only muscle that moved in Davis's face was one on the left side of his jaw. Finally he said, "Not that it's any of your business, but because you were such a good friend of Melody's, I'll be honest. I was telling Buffy that I had a problem with the publicist I hired for my artist throwing herself at Keith Carson when she should be doing her job."

The face I made must have told Davis that I knew all about that little problem. "Keith told me," I confirmed.

Davis stood up; our time was clearly over. As I drove toward Bellevue, I wondered about Melody's manager. His manner had been stern, but I didn't get any sense that he was nervous about me being there, or about me asking questions. Cold blooded and guilty, or poker faced and innocent?

As I turned on Old Hickory Boulevard from I-40, I put Davis aside and steeled myself for the encounter with Melody's mother and sister. As a precaution, I texted Darcy to let her know where I would be, and asked her to call Martin if I hadn't gotten back in touch by three-thirty. I had no idea what I was going to find in room 217.

16

AT THE HOTEL, I PARKED my truck among a series of rusted out sedans with cracked windshields and duct tape that held heavy plastic in place instead of glass windows. I looked for a car without a dent and did not find one. I should have brought Hank to act as a security guard, I thought.

My truck had some tears in and stains on the upholstery, and it hiccupped going up the occasional hill, but it had over two hundred thousand miles on it, so it was entitled. Okay, it sometimes didn't want to start unless I held the driver's side door open, and it had rust, but you almost couldn't see it unless you knew where to look. I really wanted to keep it dent-free.

I gave my truck a final glance, found room 217, held my breath, and knocked on the door. After a moment Brandyne opened it.

"You," she said.

"May I come in?"

The expression on her face said she'd rather walk barefoot through a field of doggie doo, but she widened the opening in the door. Inside, the room was much as I had expected: stained carpet, dingy bedspread, a wall with streaks running down it from a past leak, and a smell that made me want to clamp a clothespin over my nose. There was a dorm sized fridge, and a microwave on top of a shelf that also held a coffeemaker, which I guessed allowed hotel management to advertise that their rooms came complete with a kitchenette. I didn't look into the bathroom. Some things are best left to the imagination.

Claudine was sitting at a crooked little table near the window smoking a cigarette. She'd been at it a while, because the room was blue with stale smoke. Well that simplified things. My visit would definitely be short.

"Mrs. Potts, Brandyne," I nodded to each of them and decided to ignore the fiasco that had happened at the reception. "I'm Cat Enright. We didn't get to speak properly at the funeral, but I wanted to say how sorry I am about Melody. She was well-liked here in Nashville and had many friends. I was proud to call myself one of them."

A "humpf," was all I got from Claudine. Brandyne stood in the center of the room with her arms folded. I stared at her and finally her posture relaxed.

"Can't say as I agree with you 'bout Raylene havin' all those friends you're talkin' about, as you're the only one's come to call," said Brandyne.

At first I didn't know who she was talking about, then it dawned on me that Melody's family must still have called her by her birth name. Raylene.

"We been sittin' here for two days, waitin' on the will, an' not one person come to say boo to us," she continued.

"Except me," I reminded her. I was trying to hold my breath while I spoke. The smoke in the room was so thick I was certain that I could feel cancer cells multiplying in my lungs.

"'Cept you," she conceded. "Look, I'm sorry about the other day. I was outta my mind with grief. If I ever get my hands on the slimeball who kilt Raylene I'll kick his ass right on into next Tuesday."

"Humpf," commented Claudine.

At least it was better than her wailing.

"Apology accepted," I said. It was another little white lie. By golly I was racking them up. I'm not sure I ever would forgive Brandyne, though. My head still hurt where she had pulled my hair. "Melody was special and I will really miss her."

"I never could cotton to people callin' my baby Melody," Claudine said. "Her name was Raylene Claudette Potts."

"Don't matter what people called her, Momma," said Brandyne. "She's dead."

At that, Claudine started to wail.

"Now look what you gone and done," she said to me.

Me? Brandyne was the passive aggressive one here.

"Thank God this will all be over and done tomorrow and we can get outta Dodge," Brandyne said, offering no comfort whatsoever to her mother. "Soon as we collect our money, we're gone."

I couldn't help myself, even if it meant staying longer so I could grow a few hundred thousand more cancer cells. "What money is that, Brandyne?"

"From Raylene's estate, stupid. My sister was a rich little girl, and we're her family. That money is ours now, mine and

Momma's and Bodine's. Well, it'll be Bodine's when he gets outta prison. I'll take care of it for him until then."

I just bet she would. I was just as sure that Bodine would never see a red cent of his sister's estate.

"If she was gonna change her name, why'd she choose somethin' as awful as Melody Cross?" This from Claudine, whose brain was apparently stuck on broken. I looked around and saw a trash can overflowing with beer bottles. Quart sized ones. Ah. That explained it.

"She wanted to get away from us, Momma. To 'distance' herself." Brandyne made quote marks with her fingers when she said "distance." "That's why she changed her name. We weren't good enough for the little princess." This last part Brandyne said with a sneer.

"You know, I probably should go," I said edging my way toward the door. But Claudine got there before me, blocking my way on her unsteady feet.

"I couldn't help it if I wanted to have a little fun, could I?" she asked, waving a cigarette so close to my face I almost gagged. I don't begrudge people the right to smoke. I just normally don't choose to be around them when they do.

"I had them kids, Brandyne and Bodine, when I was just a kid. I was thirty when Raylene came along. Same daddy, in case you're askin.'"

I wasn't.

"By the time Raylene arrived I'd been a momma most half my life. When she got in kindy-garden, I was more than ready to party. This one," she said, now waving her cigarette at Brandyne, "already had two young 'uns of her own by then, and Bodine had got hisself into prison—for the first time. You can't blame me none for wantin' to have a little fun, but I'll never forgive them social service people who came and took my little Raylene from me. Not ever. Look where that got her. My baby's done been kilt."

With that, Claudine wavered, then slumped into a nearby chair. Looked to me as if she'd be out for a while. I should have picked Claudine's burning cigarette up off the floor, but I couldn't quite bring myself to do it. Instead, I said my goodbyes to Brandyne, and got the heck out of there.

I couldn't believe that smart, sweet Melody had come from those people. No wonder she wanted to distance herself. The older church-going couple that had raised her had done an incredible job. I wondered what Melody had been like when they first welcomed her into their home, what she had been like when she was six.

Melody had worked hard to make a better life for herself, and it made me mad all over again to realize that someone had stolen that life from her. Brandyne, I thought, as I got into the truck, could have killed Melody in a heartbeat. There was no love lost there. I wondered where she had been last week. Maybe Martin would know.

Before I started up the truck I texted Darcy that I was safe, then rolled down the windows. The smell of Claudine's cigarettes had gotten into my hair and clothes and I couldn't stand to smell myself. First thing on the agenda when I got home was a shower.

I drove back down Old Hickory Boulevard and wove my way up Charlotte Pike and onto River Road. All the time I was trying to come up with a Plan B, just in case Martin wouldn't let me be his shadow at the will reading the next day. I felt as dumb as Bodine, as I couldn't come up with a thing.

I also wondered about the furniture that Melody had promised me. Not that it was a big deal. But Davis knew about it, and there was the note Melody had put on the table for the movers. I'd like to have the furniture for the sole reason that the pieces had meant something to my friend.

I kicked myself for not asking Davis about the furniture when I was in his office. But maybe that could be my excuse to pop in at the will reading tomorrow. I could arrive on the pretense of asking about the furniture. I didn't know the time of the reading, but if I parked myself outside Scott Donelson's office until I saw familiar faces . . . It was weak, I knew, but it was all I had. Hopefully Martin would agree with my Plan A.

On River Road, with a Keith Carson song blasting through my radio, Jon called.

"You close?" he asked.

"Ten minutes max. What's up?"

"Sally's acting weird again. Or I should say, weirder."

"What now?"

"She was in the pasture and was facing the road, holding her right foreleg in front of her and waving it around."

"Is she lame?"

"Nothing like that. She trotted out fine. I noticed it because Gigi was running circles around Sally while Sally stood with her foreleg like that."

"I guess they should come in, then."

"Already done. Sally walked in just fine."

"I'll be back in a few to do Ringo's evaluation," I said. "We can watch Sally for colic, but I'm thinking this is just Sally, and that she's not really hurt."

"We might get her a massage, or a chiropractic adjustment," said Jon. "She's been lying in such a strange position that she might have soreness, even though she isn't lame."

I asked Jon to schedule a massage first, and we'd evaluate after. I drove into my driveway a few minutes later and hustled upstairs for a shower. After, I filled Darcy in and asked if she wanted to check out Ringo with Jon and me.

"No. I thought I'd ride Petey in the front pasture, if that's okay. I just saw Jon those horses in."

"Sounds like a plan."

Out in the barn, Sally was holding her leg up in her stall. I slid the stall door open and palpated the limb from the top of her shoulder to the sole of her hoof. There was no soreness that I could find. When Jon came by with a flake of hay, Sally put her foot down on the ground and ate like a normal horse. Or, as normal as a horse like Sally could be.

Cat's Horse Tip #11

"Horses easily recognize the emotions of other horses, as well as the emotions of humans, dogs, cats, and other animals."

17

JON AND I STARTED RINGO'S eval by taking photos. Front, back, and sides, with close-ups of his legs. The photos would help us measure changes in his body as he progressed through training, and would serve as documentation that he arrived with certain blemishes on his body, such as the small scar on the fetlock of his right front leg.

We then filmed him moving, with side views of his walk and trot, and views of him walking and trotting straight to and away from the camera. If he ever developed lameness, these videos would help us see a normal gait for this horse. We could also slow the video down in the next few days to look for any existing gait abnormalities.

Next, we looked at Ringo's body. We noted wide set eyes that allowed him to see far around himself. This was good, as his peripheral vision would be greater than a horse whose eyes were set on a narrow face. Those horses often were spooky, because their range of vision was not as good.

Ringo's ears were a little large as compared to breed standard, but not overly so. He had large nostrils, which helped him bring air into his body and scent into his sinus cavities. His wither to shoulder angle, and hip to point of buttock angles matched, and his front pastern matched his shoulder angle. This was a well-balanced horse who should be athletic.

Other than the scar on his fetlock, his legs were clean. His back, loin, and croup were of even length, and standing from behind, we could see that his hips were even. The number of horses who went around with one hip higher than the other was amazing. Then owners wondered why their horses could not perform well. Ringo also carried his tail flat between his butt cheeks, an indication that he did not have major issues with his hips, pelvis, or lower spine.

Jon and I then turned our hands into claw-like shapes, and ran them over Ringo's body to check for soreness. Ringo was touchy where the girth attached to the saddle on both the left and right sides of his body. This was a common place to find soreness, even with the light race and exercise saddles Ringo had worn. Jon made a note to do liniment rubs and light massage in those areas.

The last part of the ground evaluation involved stretches to test for flexibility. Ringo was more flexible in his neck going to the left than to the right, and we would be sure to pay special attention to that area.

I had not ridden Ringo before I agreed to take him on. That was unusual, but when Gusher and I had talked, Ringo was finishing up his race career. When Gusher approached me he had photos, video of his horse running at the track, and testimonials about the horse's personality from his race trainer and groom. Then I'd done a little Internet research (more on Gusher than on Ringo) before I agreed to take the horse. Owners could be the bane of a trainer's existence. Once I realized Gusher would stay out of my hair as long as I delivered the results he expected, I decided to give the horse a go.

Before I got on, Ringo and I did some round pen work. This is a matter of turning a horse loose in a pen that is round and sixty feet across. The sixty feet is important because the outer edge of a horse's personal space is about thirty feet, which is the distance between the horse on the perimeter of the pen and the human in the center.

Today I wanted to establish leadership. In a horse's mind, when two beings are together it creates a herd, and one of them must be the leader. By turning Ringo loose in the pen, I was showing him that I was responsible enough to be his leader, that he could trust me to keep him safe, and that I wanted the job.

I showed all of this to Ringo by controlling his movement. I got behind his center of gravity and urged him forward with my voice, arms, facial expression, and body. When he had gone around the pen a few times, and when his ear nearest to me was pointed toward me, I stepped in front of his center of gravity, and with my voice and body, asked him to turn around and go the other way.

This is how horses control each other. A dominant horse controls the movement of a more submissive one. Soon, I had Ringo stopping, going, and turning easily, and his ear, which is an indication of where the horse's attention is focused, was pointed consistently at me.

I asked Ringo to stop and left the pen. Jon had videotaped the session, which we would later use to further analyze his movement. Together, we went to the tack room to select a few different saddles, and a snaffle bridle. I also grabbed my riding helmet.

Back at the round pen Jon and I brought in all the tack, along with half a bucket of water, in case Ringo wanted to drink. He had not worked hard and was quite fit, but too much water after exercise is not good for any horse. I was glad to see that Ringo was more interested in me than in the water.

"Let's try Petey's hunt seat saddle on him," I said. "They are close in build."

Good saddle fit was a pet peeve of mine. It used to be that people saw a saddle and bought it because it was pretty, or because it felt good when they sat in it. Thank goodness those days were long gone. Today, people were smart enough to know that a saddle had to fit the horse, too. Poor saddle fit was probably the number one cause of soreness in horses.

Jon gently placed the saddle on Ringo's back, and I checked to be sure it was not too tight in the shoulders, had enough clearance in the wither, the seat sat level on Ringo's back, and that the saddle provided even contact where it touched the horse.

"Looks like a winner," said Jon.

I was surprised. With some horses I went through a dozen or more saddles before I found a good fit. I was also glad we found a hunt saddle that worked, because the style of that saddle was the closest thing I had to a racing saddle, which was what Ringo was used to.

I didn't have a mounting block in the round pen, so Jon gave me a leg up. Recent studies showed that mounting a horse from the ground caused torque on a horse's back that created soreness, so I rarely did that anymore, either.

Ringo moved off easily, and after checking his eagerness to turn and stop when I asked, I put him through his paces. Like many race horses, Ringo had only been taught the basics. His job on the track had been to run fast and the finer points of being ridden weren't needed. I would have to teach him collection, balance, leg yields, and to give to the bit, rather than to push into it. I'd do most of that from the ground by long lining and ground driving him, then get back on him in a month or so to see where we were.

After I dismounted, Jon and I did a brief desensitizing session with Ringo. We introduced a large beach ball into the round pen to get Ringo's reaction, and were pleased when he showed interest in the rolling object, rather than fear. We gently tossed small stuffed toys along his body, and slowly rang bells as we stood next to him. We'd do much more in the weeks to come, especially with the bells, as they were the only thing that made Ringo mildly anxious.

"Not surprising," said Jon as he gathered the equipment and put it into a wheelbarrow to take back to the tack room. "A loud bell rings in the starting gate at the track. Ringo probably thought he was supposed to run like the dickens when he heard it, even though our bells sound much different."

Jon was right. We'd also have our local equine veterinarian run baseline blood work, check for worms, and weigh in on Ringo's quality of sight and hearing. Doc Tucker, who was one of Gigi's favorite people, was scheduled to come in a week or so. He was a veterinarian who specialized in equine dentistry, and who took care of horses up and down the entire east coast. He'd give us a report on the state of Ringo's teeth.

I turned Ringo into a paddock, then caught Jon looking at me when we were putting the tack away.

"What?" I asked.

"You needed that," he said.

"Needed what?"

"The session with Ringo. It took your mind off Melody. It was the first time in a while that you seemed like you."

I considered his thought and conceded that he might be right. "It did feel good. Ringo's got a big trot, so I think we're looking at English classes. Gusher doesn't care what performance class Ringo wins or leads the nation in points, so we'll see how he does in training."

Darcy had finished with her ride and had started to bring in horses from pastures and paddocks before the daylight faded to darkness. The house, barn, driveway, arena, parking area, and round pen took up a few acres, which meant we had at least sixteen acres for the horses to roam. In the warmer seasons, Jon cut hay on the eight-acre front pasture, which left another four or so acres for paddocks, along with a four-acre field. Today, Sally came in with her face dripping wet.

"She was blowing bubbles in the water trough," said Darcy reaching for a barn towel. Sally was soaked up past her eyeballs. The mare looked brightly at me, as if to telepathically impart some important bit of information. My human brain was too dense to receive, however, so I gave Sally a hug instead. She sighed.

Jon came in next with a bouncy Gigi. At a few months shy of her second birthday, she was starting to fill into her body. I didn't think she was going to be an overly tall horse, maybe 15.2 hands, possibly an inch taller. If she topped 16 hands she might like jumping, if her body didn't end up stocky, as Sally's was.

Many of the good, young halter horses ended up with lots of muscles. Time would tell.

I left Jon and Darcy to do the feeding and went to the house to see what we had on hand to go with the pizza for my dinner with Brent. I had just finished placing a call for pizza delivery when Agnes rang.

"Isn't it exciting?" she said with exhilaration. There was an odd, breathless tone to her voice. I hoped she wasn't stuck in one of her yoga positions again. Maybe Lars was around and could untangle her. I certainly was not going to drive to Louisville to do that, as she had asked me the last time.

"What's exciting, Agnes?" I concentrated on balancing the phone and the few salad makings I had found in the refrigerator, leftovers from Annie and Tony's visit. Someone needed to eat them before they went bad.

"Why the single, dear! Keith and Melody's single. Haven't you heard?"

"I've been busy with the horses this afternoon."

"Of course you have, dear. But it's all over the news. Keith and Melody's single, that 'Do Good' song has gone number one—and so has the video. My darling Sally Blue is a star! Oh, my goodness, do you think they will ask Sally to be at the number one party? I hope they have it in a place that lets horses in."

"Ahhh . . . not sure about that Agnes. Sally might have to stay home."

"Really? Why, that's so sad! She'll miss out on all the fun."

"Sally is a big girl, Agnes. I think she'll be able to handle the disappointment. But, I will ask about the party. I can probably wrangle invitations for you and Lars."

"Would you ask? Oh, I really want to go."

"I know. I'll see what I can do."

Actually, if there was a number one party, I wanted to be there, especially if Melody's killer had not yet been caught. The more I could mingle with people who knew her, the better chance I might pick up on something.

I tuned into WSM-AM on the kitchen radio just in time for the six o'clock news. They had the "Do Good" story as a part of the ongoing murder investigation, but what was most interesting was that the label had decided to donate all of their proceeds from digital downloads of the single to the therapeutic riding center. Bet that made Ruthie and Allen mighty happy. Sorry. I couldn't help myself.

A few minutes later there was a knock on my front door. Strange that Brent would come in that way, I thought. He and everyone else I knew used my kitchen door. I glanced at my reflection as I passed an oval mirror that hung in the hall. By the time my right hand reached out to open the door, my left had smoothed my hair several times.

The welcoming grin on my face faded as I looked at the man who stood on my front porch. He was fifty-ish, and dressed in navy dress pants and a dark, warm jacket with HARPETH COURIER embroidered over the left breast pocket.

"Mary Catherine Enright?"

I hated when people called me by my full name. It almost always involved something bad.

"Yes?" I watched as a set of headlights turned into my driveway. It had to be either the pizza delivery or Brent.

"Delivery for you. Sign here."

The man held out a portable electronic device that had an x on the screen that showed me where to sign.

"Uh, what is it? Can I refuse to sign?" I hadn't ordered anything and I was always suspicious of unexpected deliveries.

"Most people just sign, ma'am." Was that the hint of a grin? Was I the one difficult customer he was going to talk about when he had dinner that night with his wife and kids? "Great day honey, except for this one person."

Nope. Wasn't going to be me. I signed the thing and took the envelope. Then I wished him a nice evening and closed the door. That would teach him not to discuss me with his family.

The envelope was a standard 9" x 12" manila and came from a downtown law firm that I did not recognize. Fabulous, I thought as another knock sounded on my front door, someone is suing me. I opened the door for the second time in five minutes to find Frog Berry on the other side. Frog was an interesting friend, of sorts, of Bubba's, who lived in a trailer up the road. At sixteen, he had already maxed out all the places he could possibly pierce his body and had started in with the tattoos. As soon as he opened his mouth I also saw that he hadn't yet fixed his missing front tooth. Pity.

"You order pizza, Miz Cat?"

"You're delivering pizzas now, Frog?"

"My PO, my probation officer, he said I had to get a job. It's not too bad though, 'cuz I can spit into the pizzas I'm deliverin' to people that haven't shown me any respect."

He must have seen the look of horror on my face.

"But not yours Miz Cat. You've always been nice to me, even that time you found me sleepin' in one a your horse stalls. 'Sides, I wouldn't a told you about the spittin' if I'd done it to these pizzas here."

He had a point. I paid him and added a far more generous tip than was necessary. I hoped he'd see the tip for what it was: insurance that my pizzas would never, ever be spit upon. Too bad Frog worked at the only pizza restaurant that delivered as far out as my stables, otherwise I'd make a point to order from another place in the future.

I put the two large pizzas on the kitchen table, found plastic cups, paper plates, and napkins; and pulled a jug of sweet tea and some sliced lemons from the refrigerator. With the salad, we'd have all of the major food groups. Then I went back to the envelope in the hall.

There is something safe about an unopened envelope. Whatever bad information it held was contained inside until it was opened. I had been looking forward to this evening with Brent and tried to talk myself into holding off on opening the envelope. But, the only person I could think of right now who was mad enough to sue me was Hill Henley, and I doubted he had gotten his act together fast enough to result in this envelope. So maybe it wasn't a lawsuit.

I flipped the metal clasp on the back of the envelope to the open position and lifted the flap. One sheet of paper lay inside and I slowly slid it out. I didn't have to read it now, I told myself. I could lay the paper down and read it after Brent left. Or tomorrow. But of course I couldn't do that. The paper was already in my hands. Slowly, I turned the page over.

> YOUR PRESENCE IS REQUESTED THIS THURSDAY MORNING AT ELEVEN A.M. AT THE LAW OFFICES OF PEETE, BARWELL, AND PEETE FOR THE READING OF THE LAST WILL AND TESTAMENT OF MELODY RAY CROSS. PLEASE CONTACT OUR OFFICE BEFORE THAT TIME IF YOU ARE UNABLE TO ATTEND.

The letter gave a downtown address and instructions for parking. My first thought was: I wouldn't have to ask Martin if

I could tag along. My second was: why had I been asked to be there? I didn't have time to ponder either thought, as the next thing I knew the kitchen door flew open, and Jon, Darcy, and Brent all piled in. I was swept up in the commotion and almost forgot about the letter. Almost.

Later, lying in bed, I picked up the letter again and read it. I was glad for the parking instructions. Without them I could be driving around downtown for hours searching for a spot. I also wondered who else would be there, and what I could wear. I'd worn my one good outfit to the funeral.

I also thought back to this evening. It had been nice to sit around the table with people I cared about. Early on, Brent made a rule for the evening. No talk about work or Melody Cross. So, we talked about Frog Berry, and made up hilarious uses for the twin condo towers that had been built on the edge of Ashland City that no wanted to move into. We'd all eaten more than we should have, then Brent and I snuggled on the couch with a Hunger Games movie, while Jon checked on the horses and Darcy went upstairs, supposedly to study. I had a feeling, however, that she was on Snapchat or another of the social media sites that she spent too much time on.

It was nice not to talk about anything stressful or sad for an entire evening. As I drifted off to sleep I thought that maybe Jon was right. Maybe, despite the ongoing questions that surrounded Melody's murder, I was over the worst of the shock and life was getting back to normal.

I couldn't have been more wrong.

18

THE NEXT MORNING I WOKE up exhausted. My dreams had been filled with Melody, who popped out from behind an endless series of trees and doors, pleading with me to bring her back to life. I felt wrung out as I fed the horses. Sally, I was glad to see, was acting like a normal horse, and Ringo had cleaned up the huge pile of hay Jon had left for him last night. We'd start him on grain tomorrow. After a horse had traveled a long distance, or if he or she was new, I liked to feed hay for a few days. For such big animals, horses had delicate digestive systems and grain could cause tummy troubles.

Before I left the barn, I wrote a note for Jon and tacked it onto the bulletin board on the office door. Just in case something unforeseen happened, I wanted him to know where I was going. True to Brent's command to forego the topics of work or murder, last night I had not told a soul about the letter, or today's reading of the will.

Back at the house, I got Darcy up and out the door to school, then perused my closet for all of half a second before I called Carole, who was still in Indiana. What did one wear to a will reading?

"I have jeans and sweaters, t-shirts, long sleeved t-shirts, riding breeches . . . let's see, and a skirt, but no shoes or boots to go with it," I told her. "Any ideas?"

"I can have Keith pull something out of my closet for you," she offered.

The offer was nice, extraordinary actually, but Carole was four inches taller and a size smaller than I was. I tried to picture how her clothes might look on me and stifled a laugh.

"Darcy?" asked Carole. Yes, technically I could borrow something from Darcy, but she was three inches shorter and a size larger. I continued to rummage through my closet while Carole offered suggestions.

"Oohhh! A new pair of black Wranglers," I cried, pulling them from the black hole that was the back of my wardrobe.

"Good start," said Carole. "Do you have a scarf?"

"I think so." I rummaged some more and came up with a silver scarf with rust swirls.

"Dress boots?"

"Yes. I have lots of boots that I wear in the show ring."

"Any black ones?"

"Yep. Oh, and here's a rust colored sweater that matches the scarf."

"Then just do up your hair and you're set," Carole said.

It was wonderful at times like these to have a former model as a next door neighbor.

"Thanks, Carole," I said, then lowered my voice. "Any more near misses for Keith?"

"No, but he's being very careful, and extra security is still around."

I was glad to hear that. Maybe the security guards would deter any future attempts on Keith's life—if that's what the incidents had been.

Downtown I found a spot in the parking garage not too far from the elevator, then meandered my way through a maze of hallways until I got to the law office. Before I could enter, though, I had to give my ID to a young woman, who examined it closely before she checked my name off a list. Then she put my ID in a drawer, along with my cell phone.

"You'll get them back on the way out," she said. "We've already had two media outlets try to slip a reporter in, so we can't be too careful."

Next, I walked through a metal detector while an armed guard checked my purse. Finally, I arrived in a room with a long table at the far end and about twenty chairs set up in front of it. Even though I was ten minutes early, a lot of people were there ahead of me. Sliding into a seat in the last of the three rows of chairs, I looked around. Claudine and Brandyne were there, of course, front and center, and I wasn't surprised to see Ruthie and Allen. Melody had generously given to the church and the riding center during her life, and I suspected she had left them something in her will.

I hadn't had time to give more thought about why I was there. I assumed it was about the furniture, but Melody would not have had time to put the specific pieces I had chosen in her will. Maybe Davis, who also sat in the back row, but on the other end, told her attorney about it. Satisfied, I relaxed—some. Buffy and Augie whispered in seats in front of Davis. Martin and the red-headed Bobby Lee arrived a few minutes after I did and sat down next to me. In front of me were two people I did not know, two men in their forties who looked as clean cut as Howdy Doody. The other person I did not know was a blond, heavy-set woman in a gray pantsuit who sat on the right side of the front row. At the last minute Bill Vandiver sailed in. He waved his fingers at the room and sat down near Buffy, who by way of hand motions near her hair, looked like she had quickly pulled Bill into a hair consultation.

Other than the new, whispered talk between Buffy and Bill, no one said a word. There was an expectant hush to the room and my stomach started doing uncomfortable little flip-flops.

At the stroke of eleven, three people carrying thick files walked into the room through a side door that I had not noticed. One was Scott Donelson, Melody's attorney. The other two were a tall, thin woman with short red hair, and a short, balding man in an expensive suit. I had never seen either before. All sat behind the long desk and opened their files.

"We'll go ahead and get started," said the short man. "My name is Frank Barwell and I am the attorney for the estate of Melody Ray Cross. To my left is Scott Donelson, Miss Cross's entertainment attorney and general counsel. To my right is Cindy Johnson, a California attorney who consults for my office here in Nashville."

People in the room began to stir, as everyone, myself included, paid close attention to Frank Barwell's words. Next to me, Martin and Bobby Lee watched the crowd.

"As background, Miss Cross updated her will on September thirty of this year. The year or so previous to that had shown a quite a large spike in her career, and she wanted to be sure her assets were distributed exactly according to her wishes." The attorney scanned the room and his eyes seemed to make contact with every person in it.

"One of Miss Cross's wishes was that no one contest her will. She selected her beneficiaries only after long and careful thought, and was quite sure that this is what she wanted to do. If," he paused, "any beneficiary wishes to contest any part of Miss Cross's will, then he or she will forfeit their portion of the assets, and those assets will be distributed proportionally to the other beneficiaries.

"In addition, before any beneficiary receives their portion of Miss Cross's estate, he or she will have to sign an agreement regarding the non-contest clause. Is that clear?"

The stirring turned into full-fledged rustling and I had a sense that some people would not be mighty happy when they walked out of here. Who those people would be, I hadn't a clue. But I didn't have to wait long to find out.

"Here is the list of disbursements that Miss Cross wished to make," continued Frank. "First, to the Country Music Hall of Fame, six stage, video, or red-carpet outfits of their choice, along with accessories and two of her stage guitars."

The woman in the gray suit started writing and I assumed she was with the Hall of Fame, especially as Frank addressed his next words to her. "Please get with my staff to make arrangements to choose the outfits, the sooner the better."

I saw her nod.

Claudine addressed the lawyer in dismay, "But what if she takes somethin' I want to remember my little girl by? Raylene was my baby. Her clothes and them guitars ought to belong to me."

"Hush, Momma," said Brandyne. "Let's hear the man out."

"To Davis Young, Buffy Thorndyke, and Augie Freemont, Miss Cross wanted each of you to have four months of commissions or retainers, with those commissions or retainers being averaged out over the past twelve months. There is also a personal letter from Miss Cross to each of you, and a bequest to Mr. Young giving him all of her musical equipment, including the rest of her guitars. Mr. Young is also to serve as executor and will manage Miss Cross's song catalog, and future licensing, merchandising, and royalties."

I glanced to my left. Buffy looked happy, Augie looked disgruntled, and Davis had an impassive look on his poker face.

"Four months!" exclaimed Claudine. "What was my baby thinking? That's money should have gone to her family."

"Momma," warned Brandyne. "Hush up."

"Mrs. Potts, I suggest that you listen to your daughter." Cindy Johnson spoke for the first time. "In fact, let's have no further comment on the disbursements until Mr. Barwell is finished. Thank you." She went back to reading her file.

Martin shifted beside me and I watched as he pointed his chin at Davis. Bobby Lee nodded.

"To the Fellowship of Christ Church, whose representatives drove in from Arkansas earlier this morning, Miss Cross leaves ten thousand dollars, her car, and a letter from her to the congregation thanking them for encouraging her music dreams when she was young."

The two men in front of me smiled and nodded at each other. I heard a "humpf," from the front row, but a look from Cindy Johnson ensured that the outburst occurred only once.

"To William Vandiver," Frank paused as Bill straightened in attention, "Miss Cross leaves fifty thousand dollars toward the sports car of his dreams, along with a personal letter."

All eyes were on Bill as he put his face in his hands. Buffy reached over to rub his back.

"To Mary Catherine Enright." Without thinking I reached out to grab Martin's hand. He squeezed it tightly. "Miss Cross leaves one hundred thousand dollars, a letter, and all of her journals, songwriting notebooks, and other handwritten materials. She also leaves Miss Enright her computers, iPad, phone, and other electronic equipment."

"One hundred thou—," cried Claudine.

"Mrs. Potts!" This was from Scott Donelson, who had yet to say anything.

"But—"

"Shhh." This was from Brandyne, who I thought was showing remarkable restraint.

The flip-flops in my stomach went into overtime. One hundred thousand dollars! I had to remind myself to breathe. I couldn't even fathom her other gifts to me.

"To her siblings, Brandyne and Bodine Potts, Miss Cross leaves each of them the sum of fifteen thousand dollars."

"Fifteen—" An indignant Brandyne started to rise, then sat back down after looking at Cindy Johnson.

"To her mother, Mrs. Claudine Potts, fifteen thousand dollars, and the balance of her clothes and household goods."

I could see that both Claudine and Brandyne were agitated to the point of explosion. Hopefully Frank was about done. I wasn't sure how long the two could contain themselves.

"To the Holy Church of the Mighty Happy, and to the Mighty Happy Therapeutic Riding Center, Miss Cross leaves the balance of her finances, which after probate, should amount to about six hundred fifty thousand dollars."

Brandyne clamped her hand over her mother's mouth as Ruthie sagged into her brother's arms.

"In addition, there are royalties, copyrights, and other intellectual properties to consider," said Frank, eyeing Claudine cautiously. "Any future advances or royalties from record sales or songwriting, or sums from merchandise sales or licensing, or any other such income including the entire rest of her estate, will be divided as follows. Twelve percent each to Davis Young, the Fellowship of Christ Church, William Vandiver, and Mary Catherine Enright. Four percent to Claudine Potts, four percent to Brandyne Potts, and four percent to Bodine Potts, with forty percent to the Holy Church of the Mighty Happy.

"Regarding the notebooks and journals bequeathed to Miss Enright," Frank continued, "the physical materials belong only to her. But, advances, royalties, and copyrights from unrecorded or unpublished lyrics within the notebooks that later become published or recorded will be split by the group of beneficiaries named earlier. Davis Young is appointed sole administrator."

Brandyne by this time was holding her mother down in her chair. Guess I now knew who the unhappy people were. The small crowd began to murmur, but Frank quickly took control before he finished.

"Those of you who have received letters from Miss Cross, you can pick them up on your way out, but you will have to sign for them first. Miss Cross's last mention is of her father, Cletus Bodine Billy Joe Potts, and she has specifically excluded him from receiving any portion of her estate."

It was then that a tornado broke loose in the form of Cletus and Claudine's daughter, Brandyne.

19

WHEN ALL WAS SORTED OUT, Cindy Johnson had a firm grip on the arm of a wailing Claudine, and Brandyne had been taken into custody for assault. Brandyne had first taken a swing at Scott Donelson and connected solidly with the side of his head. She then lit into Martin when he tried to calm her down.

Cindy handed Claudine off to Frank Barwell with a strong admonition to behave herself, then dusted her hands off on a napkin, picked up her files, and left the room.

"Her house," I heard Claudine say to Frank. "What about my baby's house?"

"It was rented, Mrs. Potts," Frank said. "Your daughter had not yet closed on the home she was purchasing. Miss Cross wanted you to have the fifteen thousand and all of her personal property, after her bequests to others. I suggest you be satisfied with that, as the intent of her will is clear. If you contest her wishes, you will forfeit your daughter's bequest to you."

I had to feel the teensiest bit sorry for Claudine. After all, she had every expectation that she or Brandyne would inherit the bulk of Melody's estate. The news she received had to be a huge disappointment. On the other hand, if Claudine had not abandoned Melody for the party life when Melody was still a child, then Claudine might have had a very different morning.

"But if she had bought her new house, I would'a gotten that, too?" Claudine asked through her tears.

"Not necessarily. That would have been something called real property," said Frank. "I can't speculate on what your daughter might or might not have done with it, or about the terms of her purchase."

Claudine sat, defeated, until the young woman who had checked my ID at the door came to escort her out. Just about everyone else was in the hallway by now and I followed Claudine out the door. We picked up our IDs, cell phones and other electronic devices, and signed for our letters. My hand shook as I reached out to take mine. What had Melody written to me? I'd have to wait to find out, because whatever it was, I wanted to read it in private. While we all waited for an unusually slow elevator I tucked the letter into my purse, then drifted toward Ruthie and Allen. They had been the big winners today, if you could call it that.

"I am stunned, just stunned," Ruthie said, shaking her head. Her body posture was respectful of those of us who had not just walked off with more than half a million dollars, but standing next to her, I could tell that she was as happy as a pig in sunshine. "Many of our people leave us a little something when they pass on to glory, but nothing like this. You've seen our cemetery, Cat. There's only a few dozen souls there. We haven't had much experience with large bequests."

"We will have to pray about how to put Melody's gift to its highest purpose," said Allen. "Praise God."

"Praise Melody," said Ruthie. "Of course we would so much rather have her bright spirit here with us. There was so much good she could have done."

Ruthie was beginning to get emotional so I patted her on her shoulder, and moved away. What was I supposed to do? Congratulate her? "Gee, Ruthie, I'm so glad my best friend got whacked so your church could get a pile of cash?" Or maybe I should have commiserated with her. She did seem genuinely rattled about Melody. I am never good with overt displays of emotion and avoid them when I can. Like now.

I found myself next to Bill Vandiver, who was leaning on the wall next to the elevator. "Whenever she came in to get her hair done we'd talk about the sports car I was going to buy someday," he said, tears glistening in his eyes. "I've always wanted a silver 1963 Corvette Sting Ray with a split window, and now that I can afford to indulge myself and get one, I'll never be able to take her for a ride in it."

I absolutely understood his feelings. I was a bit overwhelmed myself. One hundred thousand dollars! Not to mention all of the intellectual property stuff, which I didn't even come close to understanding. I smiled ruefully, though, as I thought of all the electronic devices that Melody had left me. She certainly had a sense of humor, because she knew how technologically challenged I was.

I pictured my friend on her back porch, glass of her signature iced tea in hand, as she decided who would get which of her assets. In my mind's eye, I could see her writing down names and bequests, then crossing them out and writing in new names and numbers. Certainly, Frank Barwell had been correct when he said Melody had only finalized her will after a lot of careful thought and deliberation. I wasn't yet sure what I would do with the money, but whatever it was, I'd be sure to do something that Melody would have approved of.

"Cat?" I realized that most of the people had already gone down in the elevator, and just Bill, Martin, and Bobby Lee were still here with me. "I asked if you wanted to go get some tea or something."

I looked at Bill as if I had never seen him before. My head was clearly someplace else. "Um, sure." What the heck. I didn't know Bill well and hopefully he wouldn't feel the need to comment on my hair, but we had both been good friends of Melody's. It was fitting that we spend some time together. Melody would have liked that.

"Martin, Bobby Lee?" I asked. "Do you want to come with us? There must be a coffee shop or a deli somewhere close by."

Martin was rubbing his shoulder where Brandyne had connected. I wondered what her hand looked like. Martin was a beefy guy.

"No thanks, Miz Cat. We'd better get on back," said Martin. "We've both got reports to write and I've got a meeting this afternoon. Bobby Lee needs to get back out on patrol."

He gave me a look that I knew meant he'd be by later to fill me in on whatever was running through his head. Martin was a lot like his brother, and by now I could read those Giles boys like a book. The elevator arrived and we all rode down in silence, lost in our own thoughts. At the lobby level I asked at the information desk and was directed to a small café a half block away.

Bill and I walked the short distance and after scanning a menu that was written on the wall behind the counter I ordered hot chocolate with extra whipped cream and a huge, luscious brownie. Bill got a bowl of homemade chicken soup, two large slices of lemon cake, and a water. We took our food to a table in the corner, and I snagged napkins and silverware on the way.

My brownie was warm and melt-in-my-mouth delicious and I tried to eat it, rather than inhale it. While I was busy with my brownie, I studied Bill. Tall, thin, gray haired and goateed, he was fashionably chic in dark dress pants, light dress shirt with the sleeves rolled up, and unbuttoned suit vest. There was something inexplicably Nashville about him.

"That," he said after eating his first slice of cake, "was quite the little scene in the lawyer's office. Can you believe her family? I mean, Melody told me about them and why she stayed away, but I really wasn't prepared for that."

"It was interesting," I agreed.

"So here's what I think," he said starting in on the other slice of cake. He noticed me staring at his untouched soup. "It's hot. I'm waiting for it to cool off."

Of course. Even if that wasn't the case, I'd go for the cake first, too.

"I think," he continued, "that Brandyne killed her sister."

My thought processes about who had killed Melody were still so muddled that I stopped eating my brownie to listen.

"Cat, here's what I saw at the lawyer's office. Brandyne and her mother were fully expecting to inherit most of Melody's money. Fully expecting to. There was no love lost between them and Melody. They didn't care about her, and that Brandyne is a schemer. She saw the money, and she also saw the fame attached to being the sister of the tragically killed Melody

Cross. Remember Nicole Brown Simpson's sister, Denise? She was all over the news for years after Nicole was killed. Years. I think Brandyne wanted that kind of fame, and her sister's money, for herself."

I went back to my brownie while I thought.

"You could be right," I admitted. "But what about Davis Young? I was sitting next to the detectives from Cheatham County and I think they are interested in him."

"Davis?" Bill asked. "Maybe, but Melody's career was brand new. He could have managed her into being the next Taylor Swift. Melody had that kind of talent and appeal. Davis could have made a lot more money with Melody over the years than he got today."

"But what if he needed the money now?" I asked. "As her manager, would he have had any knowledge that he was a beneficiary in her will?"

"Possibly. I will say this. Melody trusted Davis, and as you know, she didn't trust many people. If Davis killed her, that would be a big abuse of trust."

"I can't imagine it being anyone," I said. Suddenly I had a huge flash of anger toward whoever had killed Melody, and my entire body filled with tension. Annie told me that grief comes in stages and that anger was one of them. Guess I had reached that point. Sometimes when I was mad I said things I didn't mean and I didn't want to do that here. I took a deep breath and measured my words.

"I feel like I have been robbed of a life-long friendship." I took another deep breath. "And Melody was robbed too, of a long and full life. And you, Bill, whoever killed Melody robbed you, too. You'd been friends for a long time. I swear that one day I will punch her killer in the face and spit in his eye.

I realized I was too worked up. My upper body had been swaying back and forth in my chair, and my arms had been flying all over the place. I was even in danger of knocking over my hot chocolate. Couldn't have that. I took another breath.

"Sorry," I said. "Probably, I wouldn't spit."

"Don't be sorry," Bill said. "All the people who loved her feel just like you do. Besides, I see you have a little fire in you. Melody needed that in a friend."

Bill moved his cake plates away and pulled the soup bowl closer. "On another note, what do you think of those church people? Melody spent a lot of time there."

Hmmm. What did I think?

"Allen is pompous and patronizing, but a hard read," I finally said. "Emily seems to compartmentalize her life and be different people within her boundaries. Does that make sense?"

Bill nodded, and I continued.

"Ruthie is kind of drab until she turns on the charm. I've heard her preach, though, and she is moving. Did any of them kill Melody? I don't know. I've always heard you should follow the money and they got most of it. Did they know they were getting it? Impossible to tell. But maybe we're looking at this the wrong way. Did Melody seem off to you recently? Nervous?"

"No," said Bill. "If anything, she was excited about the single and the tour. You know what's interesting, though. You know who wasn't there today?"

I didn't understand what he was getting at.

"Chas Chadwick. The label head. Not that you'd expect anyone to write their label head into their will, but he is a person I could picture killing someone. He's got that dark, thoughtful look, and as insecure as label jobs are these days, you have to know that whatever decision he makes is going to be for the good of the label, not the artist. Maybe Melody had something on him and was going to blow the whistle."

My reply got stuck in my throat when I spotted a man trying not to look in our direction. It was the same clean-cut guy I had seen in the restaurant with Buffy. What were the chances of that? Especially when this downtown café was not all that close to Hillsboro Village, where Buffy and I had eaten. Bill saw the look on my face.

"What?" he asked.

"Don't turn around now," I said, "but in a minute, casually check out the guy in the blue shirt sitting near the far wall. Brown hair, young, clean cut, reading a paper."

Bill gave me a quizzical look, then knocked his fork off the table and bent down to get it.

"Never seen him before," he said, straightening up.

"This is the second time I've seen him. The first time was yesterday in Provence, in Hillsboro Village with Buffy. The coincidence just strikes me as odd."

"What, that a nice looking guy would look your way in a restaurant?"

"No," I smiled in spite of myself. "There's just something about him that I don't trust."

"How about I go over and talk to him," Bill said.

"No!" I hissed.

"Seriously, I can pretend to mistake him for someone else, start a conversation."

Before I could protest, Bill was out of his chair and walking toward the man. That's when Mr. Clean Cut put down his paper and bolted from the café.

20

I WAS SUPPOSED TO RIDE Sally that afternoon, but my excitement about the will and my nervous energy about the mysterious Mr. Clean Cut ruled that out. Horses are intuitive and pick up on human emotion quickly. As herd animals, they need their people partners to be the herd leaders. When a horse knows the human is not capable, trouble arises in the form of poor behavior from the horse. In addition, most horse related accidents are due to human error. I knew that this afternoon I could neither earn respect from a horse nor make good judgments.

Jon needed to know of the change of plans, and rather than text him, I decided to tell him in person. We'd been talking more lately and I wanted him to know that I would be fine by tomorrow.

He was standing at the gate to the arena, sending a text. That in itself was unusual, as Jon rarely texted, but the big smile on his face was even more uncommon. Not that it was any of my business, but I wanted to grab the phone from his hands to see who he was texting. I restrained myself, however. Jon was allowed to have a life. I just didn't like mysteries.

When Jon saw me, he quickly stuck the phone in his pocket, and turned his gaze to Gigi, who was trotting around the pen with her tail up over her back. A raised tail was a sure sign of a horse in good spirits. With Gigi, though, that was her natural state of being.

"News?" Jon asked as he scanned my face.

"Yes, but I'm not ready to share. I, uh, need some time to process. Can you longe Sally over some ground poles?" Cavaletti, or ground poles, helped a horse develop cadence and balance.

Jon nodded. "Maybe try some low risers?"

"Sure. Four to six inches off the ground will make her use some different muscles. See how she does."

Jon didn't ask what, specifically, I needed to process, and that was one thing I liked about him. He respected a person's space.

"Will you come for dinner?" I asked. "Brent and Darcy will be there and I can fill everyone in at once."

"Wouldn't miss it," he said, fingering the phone in his pocket.

I should have gotten caught up on paperwork that afternoon, but I took a nap instead. Some of my best thinking is done when I am asleep. At five o'clock I awoke, refreshed and with a plan.

A while back I'd tasked Darcy with cooking one night a week and tonight was the night. While I didn't have to worry about making dinner, eating it could be an adventure. When she lived at home with her dad, they had a cook who handled all of the kitchen details. But in less than a year Darcy was going to be a college student. She needed to know how to fend for herself.

When Brent, Jon, Darcy and I sat down to dinner I looked at my plate with some trepidation.

"So. Chopped frozen spinach nuked with butter, salt, and parmesan," said Darcy. "Frozen broccoli, nuked with butter, salt, and parmesan. And, ground turkey meatloaf that I, like, made all by myself with bread crumbs, onion, ketchup—"

"And let me guess," said Jon. "Butter, salt, and parmesan."

"You must have a hankering for those three ingredients," said Brent, digging in. He was a brave man.

"Not really," Darcy said. "That's all we had in the refrigerator." This last part was said with a pointed look in my direction.

"Grocery run tomorrow," I replied, looking dubiously at a bite of meatloaf on my fork. I soon discovered that Darcy's meal wasn't half bad.

During dinner I filled them in on the morning's events, although I left out the part about Mr. Clean Cut. I didn't want anyone to worry. Brandyne's behavior and the various bequests stunned my friends into silence.

"That's a lot of money," Jon finally offered after eating a full helping of seconds. He tended to consume all of his daily calories in one meal.

"And the intellectual property rights. Cat, that could make you a rich woman," Brent said.

I hadn't considered that, and because I still didn't understand it, I put it out of my mind. For now.

"So what are you going to do with it?" Darcy asked.

"OMG! You could go on a cruise! Of course, you'd need someone to go with you. I'd volunteer for that. Lots of sun, water, good-looking guys. We could go over Christmas break!"

As a wealthy teen who would eventually have access to her trust fund, money was less important to her than it was to most other people. I had more practical plans. Initially, I had been going to wait until I actually got the money, which would not be until the estate was settled some months from now, to decide what to do with it. But while I slept, a plan had bounced around in my brain.

"Good idea, Darce. But first, I want to do things around here that Melody would have approved of," I said.

"What, like give it to the riding center?" Darcy asked.

"No, I think they got enough today to last them a while. Every time Melody came out here, she mentioned that she didn't like to see the horses in stalls. She understood that show horses have to be kept in more than other horses, but she also understood that horses are herd animals. Jon, I'd like you to start looking at wire mesh stalls, like the ones they have at the riding center. We'll also need to figure in the cost of taking the existing stalls out."

Jon's eyes lit up. "I like that idea," he said. "When it's time, I can round up guys to pull out the old stalls. It'll take just a day or two. Maybe do the left side on the first day, and the right side the next. That way the horses aren't displaced for too long. I can save the wood we pull out for other projects."

"I like your idea, too. What other plans do you have for your windfall?" Brent asked.

"Melody never had much growing up, but what she had, she took care of. She had to, because she needed to make what little she had last. We need to make our barn last and the biggest problem we have with it right now is the roof."

I turned to Jon again. "I don't want to put too much on you, but will you get some bids on replacing the entire roof? Not with metal. I want shingles." Jon nodded. "When the rain comes down on a metal roof," I explained, "the sound is amplified and horses can't hear potential predators, so they don't rest as well."

"Also speaking of roofs," I said. "I think Melody would want us to put a cover over the round pen. She was a natural blond with fair skin and needed to be protected from the sun. The same goes for some of our horses. A roofed round pen also means that we could use it when it's raining—or really hot."

Jon gave me a thumbs up.

"What else?" Darcy asked. I could tell she was still hoping for something fun.

"Well, those two things will eat up a big chunk, but I think there will still be enough for a new, or newer, truck."

"'Bout time," she said, standing to clear the dishes away.

"Jon, you've already been looking," I said. "Send me your info and I'll pick it up from there. Then you and I can go over the projected costs of everything in a few weeks. We'll know more then. But I also want to upgrade your apartment."

Jon started to protest, but I held up my hand. "Keeping the apartment up is an investment. It's cheaper in the long run to have a good, new energy efficient refrigerator in there than the old one you have now, which doesn't even work all that well.

Plus, we need to change out the flooring, put in some nice tile. The linoleum is getting worn.

"Lastly," I said, "and Jon, this is one more thing for your list, is one of those big, horse-sized vibration plates that we used at the all-breed invitational show last summer."

"Yes!" Jon rarely showed over the top emotion, so I could tell he was very pleased with this last addition to the list. The vibration plate was really a vibrating floor that horses stood on that stimulated blood circulation and acted like a deep massage. It had settled Gigi down at the show, and I admit to using it myself. I was sure we could put it to lots of good use—horses, dogs, and people alike.

"We'll have to budget well," I added. "One hundred thousand is a lot of money, but we have a lot to do, so it will go quickly. I think it's all doable, though."

"What's all doable?" asked Martin, coming through the door that Darcy had opened for him. He carried a square, cardboard box that he placed on the counter. "Mama sent over one of her apple pies."

Brent updated Martin on our conversation while Darcy and I got out plates and forks. We looked in the freezer for ice cream, but everyone would have to settle for whipped cream. Even though I had eaten a bigger dinner than I had planned, my mouth watered. Mama Giles was an excellent cook.

It was an issue that bothered me when I had time to think about it, which fortunately was not all that often. I could never begin to compete with Mama in the kitchen. If Brent and I stayed a couple, the issue of cooking would sooner or later come up. He was pretty good with a grill, but that was the extent of his skill. My cooking skills weren't even up to Darcy's level. Everything I made was either boiled or microwaved.

Mama Giles would not think I was taking good care of her son if I didn't give him a good home cooked dinner every night—and she'd be vocal about letting me know her thoughts.

"Tell your mom thanks for the pie," I said when Martin sat down across the table from me. "Apple is one of my favorites." It was an olive branch to Mama, but one that rang true.

I had met Martin before I met Brent. Martin had responded to a 911 call I made last February when Bubba had gone missing. Then the sheriff, who had recently been voted out of office, suspected me of murdering my neighbor. Martin had the good sense to realize that I was innocent, and involved me as much as he could in the investigation. Which, come to think of it, he hadn't done so much this time around.

When Glenda's murderer had bashed in my shoulder, Martin called Brent to sit with me at the hospital while he chased after the culprit. Martin later told me he had not trusted anyone else to keep me safe. That was the start and here we were in November. It was one of the longest relationships I'd ever had.

"You went to the reading of the will, didn't you?" Brent asked Martin.

"I did," Martin said.

"You have thoughts about it?" Brent asked.

"I do," said Martin.

"What about Augie Freemont, Melody's agent?" I asked. "He's got these weird rolls of fat on the back of his head," I explained to Darcy.

"Totally untrustworthy," she agreed.

"If you ladies are done," Martin said. "I'll give you some news."

Darcy and I closed our mouths.

"I still can't share a lot of what we know, but we are makin' progress in the case," he said. "First off, we're goin' through all the computers and electronic stuff that was willed to you, Miz Cat. Maybe we'll find a lead in there somewhere. I'll let you and Davis Young know when we're through."

I nodded.

"Then," he continued, "the guy who found Miz Cross in the water was a Vanderbilt student who kept a cheap phone for when he went canoeing, as he didn't want to chance that his good phone might get wet. He panicked after he called. But, he was in a chemistry lab until midnight Wednesday night, then hit the tail end of a frat party where he crashed on the couch in the living room and was seen by others as early as five Thursday morning.

"We still aren't sure of the time of death, so solid alibis for many people are hard to determine—assuming they killed Melody and didn't pay someone else to. Chas Chadwick and your fat roll friend Augie Fremont were both in Dallas at a music conference from Wednesday afternoon to Friday morning. We've checked with the airlines and they did not get back in town until noon. They are not high on our list."

"What about someone from the film crew?" Darcy asked. "Maybe someone was like obsessed with Melody. Maybe—"

Martin jumped in before Darcy got too wound up in her maybes. "Most were editing all week, but we haven't had time to check where all of them were from Wednesday night until early Thursday—with the exception of Homer Bugg, who has been cleared."

"Homer Bugg?" I asked.

"You know him as Fitch, the director."

"What were his parents thinking?" Brent asked.

"Maybe it's a family name," said Jon.

"Anyway," said Martin, bringing us back on topic. "Davis Young was supposedly home alone Wednesday night and Thursday morning. His wife and kids were visitin' relatives out of town and he says he had car trouble on his way to work. We're waitin' on verification of a service call."

Martin then said that Claudine Potts was in a bar in Toad Suck, Arkansas Wednesday evening until someone poured her out the door at closing time. "Accordin' to several people, she was still out cold at noon on Thursday. Allen and Emily Harding were at church with Ruthie Wednesday night. Then they all went back to the Harding home until about midnight. Allen and Ruthie were back at the church by eight and were there all day. Emily home schooled Rowan until noon, then dropped her off at her mom's and came out to the therapy center."

The police, he said, were still verifying the locations of a number of people during the time in question. "Keep in mind," he said, "that just because we can't verify where they were, doesn't mean they did it."

I nodded. "Find any clues on the b-roll?"

"Nothin' you haven't already mentioned to us after you reviewed it."

"And Keith Carson?" I was full of questions.

"We think the accidents were just that, accidents. His wife says he was home Wednesday, and all that night. Thursday mornin' he had that interview that Miz Cross missed. We're pretty sure she was dead by then, as she also never showed up for the lunch, or to close on her house or check into the Lowe's." He paused. "I can also tell you a few things that will be on the ten o'clock news tonight."

All eyes were on the detective and my stomach went into flip-flop mode, which didn't sit well with Mama Giles's pie.

There was something about the way Martin delivered his words. I knew I wasn't going to like what came next.

"As we suspected," he said to me, "your friend was held under water by her throat."

I stopped breathing. Brent rubbed my back.

"The cause of death was drowning, and the circle of bruises around her neck were caused by someone's palms, fingers, and thumbs. In addition, she had no skin or unusual fibers under her fingernails. We think she was wearing gloves of some sort when she was killed. That, plus the fact she was in the river, means there is no DNA from the killer on her body."

Cat's Horse Tip #12

"Safety is found in numbers. Humans can never fully understand how important the protection of a herd is to a horse."

21

I COULDN'T SLEEP. INSTEAD, MY mind kept asking how Melody ended up naked in the Harpeth River. Did she start out near the church and riding center, or farther upstream? The Harpeth curved around, but she was found down stream from the Mighty Happy complex.

And when did it happen? Melody attended the church service Wednesday evening. She would have left about seven-thirty to drive from Kingston Springs back to her rented house in Pegram, a distance of less than six miles. Then she didn't show up at her radio interview at ten o'clock Thursday morning. What had happened to my friend between those hours?

According to other information from Martin last night, no one saw her car by her house either Wednesday night or Thursday morning. But that wasn't unusual. Melody often pulled around behind the house and entered from the porch door in the back. Shrubbery in front provided a partial screen from the little road, so if she were home, it would have been hard to see her lights on after dark.

And that was the other thing. Melody lived on a one-lane road. There were no houses directly across from her and only two houses farther down before the lane ended in a tiny turn around. She didn't have very many neighbors.

Martin said the autopsy found she had not had breakfast or even coffee Thursday morning, as she had no recent food in her stomach. That's why they thought she hadn't made it home Wednesday night. But Melody never ate breakfast, and her "coffee" would have been from the pot of tea in her refrigerator, either iced or heated in the microwave. Either would have been poured into her "to go" mug.

My mind turned to the questions surrounding Melody's royalties and intellectual property. It was supposed to be a significant thing, but I didn't understand it. I lay there for another minute, then threw off the covers and padded downstairs to my office. Clicking on to Google's search engine, I typed in INTELLECTUAL PROPERTY and scanned the results. A Nashville lawyer had some info on his website, so I clicked through to that and began to read.

Basically, intellectual property meant creations of the mind. Patents, copyrights, songs, articles, books, music, and other artistic work. The owner of those works then had the right to sell, license, or produce the work for monetary gain. If I understood that correctly, Melody wanted me to have twelve percent of all the songs she had written, along with future advances and royalties from her record sales, merchandising, licensing, or any film or television projects about her.

I closed out of the browser, stunned. I wasn't sure how much all of that was, but I knew that in less than a year of "big star" status Melody had been able to purchase her dream home for cash. Of course, a lot of that money had come from touring. Melody had told me that record and songwriting royalties were often delayed up to a year—or longer.

Holy cow, Brent was right. Melody's bequest might not make me a wealthy woman, but I also might not have to shop at the thrift store anymore. I tiptoed back up the stairs, cautious of the two squeaky steps. When they were stepped on they gave off a sound much like a screech owl, and I didn't want to wake Darcy. Maybe I could get the steps fixed, too.

I knew I had to stop thinking and get some sleep, but it was hard to turn my brain off. Our vet was coming in the morning to do a full exam on Ringo: soundness, vision, x-rays, the whole kaboodle. Next week Ringo would have a massage to establish baseline soreness, if any, and after that the equine chiropractor would come. Gusher Black had assured me that when it came to his horse I was to spare no expense. I was taking him on his word. And his signed contract, of course.

Our vet didn't see any reason Ringo couldn't jump right into training, I hadn't been breathing much during the exam, and air rushed into my lungs at the news. I needed Ringo, or a horse like him. If Ringo hadn't cleared his vet check, I would have had to start another nationwide search for a top horse to show next year. It was late for that, as other trainers had already snapped up the best horses. I'd still like to get another horse or two to campaign, and already had some potentials there.

As Doc loaded his equipment back into his truck, a question popped into my mind. "Don't you take care of the horses at the Mighty Happy center in Kingston Springs?" I asked.

"I do," he said, slotting a portable x-ray machine into a cubby in the vet box on the back of his truck.

"You know, my friend Melody Cross was a volunteer there. She was the country music star who was killed."

"Really? I'm sorry. I didn't realize you were close."

I nodded. "The police haven't figured out who did it yet and I was wondering... did anything ever strike you as strange when you were out there? Anything odd?"

He raised his eyebrows. "Strange? No. Emily Harding is the horse person there. The center was her idea. Most of the horses are older, but they're well cared for." He took time to think. "There is something, though."

"What?"

"They put their back fence too close to the river. That's my opinion. As soon as the next big flood comes, that whole line of fencing will be taken out." He smiled. "They're good people, Cat, and they're doing good work."

With that, he was in his truck and headed down my drive. Ringo had earned some free time, so I put him in the arena, and when I turned around I spotted Sally pinning her ears in her paddock. I followed her angry gaze to find a car parked next door at Fairbanks. That was strange. Since Glenda Dupree's death her elderly mother, Opal, had mostly kept the house closed.

I couldn't help myself. Wearing the guise of a concerned neighbor I jogged across the property and up the antebellum mansion's front steps. Turned out a cleaning crew was inside. The house was going to be put on the market and I knew that must have been a hard decision for Opal to make. Her now deceased daughter had owned the home and the place held a lot of memories. Of course, many of the memories were tragic. Maybe some of those sad recollections had played into her decision.

I debated calling Opal to get the full scoop, or even popping in at her assisted living place for a visit. But the less I had to do with the Duprees, the better. They were distant cousins of the Giles family, though. That meant if Brent and I ever married (which was a topic that had not even remotely been discussed), then I'd be a cousin, too. Distasteful thought, that.

Slipping back between the fence rails I felt my phone buzz in my jeans pocket. I had turned the ringer off during Ringo's vet check, so as not to disturb the process. When I pulled the phone out of my pocket I saw that a text had come in from an unknown number. I flicked the screen from locked to unlocked to better read the message, then all the air whooshed right back out of me.

BACK OFF OR YOU WILL END UP LIKE MELODY

Oh boy. This was so not good. Jon took most of the farm calls so only a few people had my cell number. I could count them off in my head: Jon, Brent, and Martin; Annie, Tony, and Agnes, Darcy, Darcy's Dad, and Bubba; Hill (unfortunately), my college friend Noah Gregory, Bob's owner Doc Williams, our vet and farrier, Gusher Black, and Melody.

Who else had gotten hold of my cell number? Mr. Clean Cut maybe? And just who was he anyway? My hands began to shake as the full meaning of the text slowly dawned on me. Whoever killed Melody, had my number.

My legs suddenly didn't seem to want to hold me and I plopped down in the dry grass, smack between my house and the Fairbanks fence line. Breathe, I told myself. Just breathe. It took a few minutes to calm myself, and when I did, I called Martin.

Fortunately, my favorite detective was not too far away and arrived a few minutes later. By that time I had gotten myself into my house.

"I'll need to take your phone," he said. "I can either get a warrant for it, or—"

I slid the phone across my kitchen table to him.

"Our forensics team can maybe get some info from it. They hook it up to a do-hickey and get all kinds of data," he said. Then he paused, folding his hands and placing them on the table. "I 'spose I should tell you that we found Melody's car."

"And?" It took a conscious will of effort to stop the shrieking inside my head.

"It was behind the church, behind that thick screen of trees between the playground and the river."

The church again. Allen, Emily, Ruthie, and Robert. Did one of them kill my friend? The shrieking in my brain morphed into a rage-like anger and I grabbed the table to keep myself from getting into my truck and driving to the church. That would not have ended well. One day I'll do something about my anger issues. But not today. Martin reached across the table to hold one of my shaking hands.

"Do you want to hear the rest?"

I nodded.

"According to several people at the church, the only time people go behind that screen of trees is to walk down to the river to be baptized, or to sit peacefully near the water to pray." He looked into my eyes. "You with me?"

I nodded again. I didn't trust myself with words.

"There's a little, paved parkin' spot there behind the trees. People park, walk the several hundred yards to the river. The church couldn't put a longer road in to get closer to the river 'cause it floods there sometimes, mostly in the spring. Now, Miz Cross drove a five-year-old gray Toyota Camry. 'Cept when we looked back there behind the trees a few days ago, the car wasn't there."

"How did you find it, then?"

"Churchgoer went back there and parked. Was going to sit by the river, then realized the car prob'ly belonged to Miz Cross and called us."

"But," I processed, "just because the car is there doesn't necessarily mean someone from the church is involved."

"No, it doesn't," he said.

"Could Melody's body have been moved?" I asked. "Could she have been killed somewhere else?"

"Possibly." He loosened his grip on my hand as he explained. "The water in her lungs was river water. Harpeth River water. Could she have been drowned somewhere in the Harpeth other than behind the church? Maybe. We've got an expert working on weather conditions—temperature and wind and such all—matching it to the water depth and flow. She can maybe help us know, given the time frame from seven-thirty Wednesday night to eight a.m. Thursday morning, where and when Miz Cross entered the river. Pathology says she probably died more toward Thursday morning, but water and the cold night temperatures make that difficult to pinpoint."

It was all so complicated. I wished for the thousandth time that none of this was happening, that I didn't have to sit across my kitchen table with a police detective and have him explain the details of my friend's death.

"There's somethin' else," Martin said.

There always was something else.

"We recovered her car, but not her purse, so you are right. Whoever killed Miz Cross has her phone—and your number."

Cat's Horse Tip #13

"A pre-purchase or pre-training vet check can uncover important and hidden health problems."

22

AFTER MARTIN LEFT WITH MY phone I realized that the recent emotional events called for major hot chocolate. I took out some of my special dark chocolate blend, heated two cups of water to boiling, mixed in the chocolate, added a splash of whole milk and a tablespoon of sugar, then poured it all into a thermal to go mug and topped it with a generous amount of whipped cream. I'd be on sugar overload for the next week and a half, but I didn't care.

Before I walked out the door, I took the letter Melody had left me out of my purse and tucked it into my jacket pocket. Then I wrote a note for Jon, left it on the kitchen table, and headed for the riverbank. That was where I went whenever I needed to think, to wash away my emotions, or to pound my fists into the ground.

My favorite place on the steep, wooded bank was in the crook of the trunk of a large maple tree that hung diagonally out over the water. The tree was near the top of the bank, and when I was there, I was hidden from the world. As soon as I got comfortable I realized that Hank had followed me. The tree-filled riverbank was a treasure trove of sticks, and I watched as he nosed around, first choosing one, then discarding it when he found another that was more suitable. Then he settled on the ground a few feet below me at the base of the tree. His gnawing presence was soothing, and I was glad that he chose to spend this time with me. There's nothing like the comforting presence of a loyal hound dog.

I thought of other emotional times when I had sat in this tree. I'd run here after I discovered Glenda Dupree's body, and after my first serious boyfriend told me the only redeeming thing about me was my green eyes. Today, the remains of the fall foliage was beautiful. November is typically the most colorful month in Middle Tennessee, and I saw a swirl of red, orange and yellow, backed with the brilliant blues of river and sky.

I leaned my head against the rough bark of the maple and watched a series of dark clouds descend over the river. I had decisions to make. The first was contact with other people. Melody's killer had my phone number, but I no longer had to worry about that because the police had my phone. I'd have no worries that the next call or text would scare me to death.

I'd unplug my landline, then email my clients and friends (and Melody's team) that the best way to reach me during the next few days would be through email. All I'd have to do was check my email more than once a week. Then I'd run up to Walmart and get one of those pre-paid disposable phones for emergencies. I'd give the number only to Brent, Martin, Darcy, and Jon.

My second decision was who to tell about the threatening text. I'd have to tell Jon. He always knew when I was holding out, and in the spirit of our newly regained cooperation, he needed to know. And Darcy. I took a sip of the hot chocolate and felt it's warmth spread through me, and the sugar rush to my brain.

Brent? I'd have to tell him, because Martin knew. I dreaded that little conversation. Brent liked life simple and smooth. He was different from his younger brother in that way. Martin loved tackling a complex puzzle, and reasoning through people's bad choices.

My third decision was safety, and my eventual decisions here were based on one of two main choices. I could back off, as the text suggested, or I could continue to nose around Melody's life to see if I could come up with anything the police couldn't. I had already been able to tell them a lot about Melody's daily habits, and about her personality. As her closest friend, I could see life through her eyes better than anyone else could.

I turned the thought sideways. What would Melody want? She'd want me to be safe, but she was never one to back down from something she believed in. She believed in the mission of her church and the riding center so strongly that she had worked hard to carve out time to spend there. She certainly would not have been as successful so early in her music career had she been a shrinking violet. No. Melody would not have let this text scare her, and I wouldn't either.

So, how to stay safe? At horse shows I made the younger kids who showed with me use the buddy system. When they were in my care, they could not go anywhere past our immediate barn aisle without someone else being with them. I could do that. I could buddy up.

Decisions made, I relaxed. I took another sip of chocolate, then fingered the letter in my pocket. Part of me couldn't wait to open it, but the other part of me never wanted to read it. If I read the letter, it meant that Melody was really and truly gone. Somehow the envelope ended up in my lap. It was just a plain number ten business envelope with my name written on it in Melody's handwriting. What was Melody thinking when she wrote the letter? Did she sit at her kitchen table? Or was she on her back porch? It made me sad to think that I'd never know.

Cautiously, I opened the flap, slid the letter out, and unfolded it. It was two pages, written by hand on plain white copy paper.

Dear Cat,

Well, if you're reading this then something awful happened to me. I just hope it was quick. I want to let you know that you mean the world to me. I am so very glad that we met and became such good friends. We haven't known each other long, at least we haven't at the time I am writing this, but I feel as if you are the sister I never had. Well, I do have a sister and if you are reading this then you have probably met her and know exactly what I mean.

Moving forward, I want you to remember all the fun times we had. Every one of them. Remember when we hiked up to Hidden Lake and picnicked on the old cement dance floor? We sat in a pile of fire ants and itched and laughed all the way down the hill. And the time we were asked to leave the movie theater because we were laughing so hard? It wasn't even a funny movie! I am still glad I wasn't recognized. Davis would not have been pleased.

But seriously. Cat, you are an awesome person, and I love you more than my silly words can say. I've left you a little something in my will. I hope you find it helpful. Even though I know you will do something practical with it, over time, I hope you do something fun, too. For us. I want you to do something that will make you laugh. I'm not sure how heaven works, but no matter what, I'll be right beside you for the rest of your life, laughing along with you.

Please don't let my mother or anyone else contest my will. Making out my will was like all the instructions I ever received about writing a song: keep it simple and write what you mean. I meant everything that I put into my will and I want people to respect that. I also entrusted my electronics and journals to you because I know without a doubt that you will keep my private thoughts private. Guess I should wind this up. Pastor Ruthie says our soul never dies, so know that I will be the first one to greet you whenever it is your time. Hugs and love to you, Cat, for all of your life.

Your loving sister,
Melody

It took me a long time to read the letter because I was crying so hard I couldn't see very well. I hadn't brought any Kleenex with me, so had to use the sleeve of my jacket to wipe my eyes and blow my nose. After I'd read the letter for the second time, and the third, I was so emotionally drained that I felt like I'd been sucked down a garbage disposal. Eventually I climbed down out of the tree and Hank and I made our way back to the house. I felt a hundred years old.

After I changed my jacket and splashed some cold water on my face I went out to the barn.

"Want to make a Walmart run with me?" I asked Jon.

He looked up from a spot he was rubbing on Gigi's back. Jon had been doing some basic massage on Gigi every day and it helped take the edge off her flightiness. I couldn't wait to get the vibration plate and whispered my thanks to Melody. "I've got a lot to do," he said.

"Me too, but it will give us a chance to catch up."

Jon thought about it. "West Nashville or Ashland City?" he asked.

We were located almost equal distance between the two.

"Either," I said.

"If we go to the Walmart in Ashland City we can stop at the Co-op. I was going to pick up feed tomorrow morning, but could do it today."

I got my purse, turned on the headlights to combat the increasing gloom of the day and we headed down the drive, Jerry Reed singing "East Bound and Down." Before I had a chance to make a right onto River Road Jon said, "Okay, what's up?"

I sighed, turned the radio down, and filled Jon in on the text and on my phone situation.

"So I'm your safety buddy," he said.

"For now."

Jon considered the information, and then nodded.

At Walmart, we selected a phone, and Jon put the number into his cell.

"Put it in your address book as 'Sally,'" I said on impulse. "Just in case."

"In case what?" he asked.

"In case the killer gets your phone, or taps into it somehow." I had no idea if a phone could be hacked, but I did not want to take a chance.

We then picked up a few groceries, and my eyes scanned the darkening parking lot as we walked back to the truck, Jon carrying the bags. To my great surprise, I spotted a familiar man pushing a cart several rows away. I took stock: sunglasses, ball cap, and a jacket that was too large for his frame. He looked suspiciously like Mr. Clean Cut. Without thinking I darted between two cars and began to run toward him.

Unfortunately, the man was near his car. He jumped into an older, dark green Honda and sped away. I just had time to see that when he started the car, and when the headlights came on, one light was yellower than the other.

I stopped running, placed my hands on my knees and bent over, gasping.

Jon ran up beside me. "What was that all about?"

I waved my hand at him, indicating that I'd tell him as soon as I had enough air to form words. Before long I stood up and filled him in.

"And you haven't mentioned all this before because . . ."

"I thought it was coincidence, that I was making something out of nothing. But now that I know Mr. Clean Cut drives the car that has been behind me a lot, it's probably something."

"You have to call Martin," Jon said.

"I know, but let's get the grain first."

We drove west on Hwy. 12 to the center of town, but instead of making a left on Hwy 49 toward the Co-op I kept going. Jon just raised an eyebrow.

"I forgot. I want to stop in at Mayfield's Books," I said.

John Mayfield had a great used bookstore and gave all the proceeds to local charities. Besides, I wanted to see if he had a Goosebumps book for Bubba. As I had loved the pseudo scary books when I was younger, I thought Bubba would, too. There was a copy of a classic, *Night of the Living Dummy*, on a crowded shelf so I paid John his dollar, then drove the half mile or so to the Co-op where Jim Ed rose from the bench in front of the store to greet us.

Jim Ed was a chatty member of the Giles family who held court every day from the Co-op, as a way keep his marriage intact. Since his retirement a decade or so ago, Jim Ed had wandered down to the Co-op just about every morning, and stayed most of the day.

Store management figured out early on that having Jim Ed ensconced on the bench out front was the equivalent of thousands of dollars worth of advertising each week. Fact was, Jim Ed was the town's biggest gossip and a lot of people came by just to hear what news Jim Ed had to share. Today he wore his usual white undershirt, dark blue work pants, black suspenders, white tube socks, and black lace up shoes with thick soles. He'd added a heavy, thigh-length green raincoat dotted with yellow flowers to ward off the chill. Jim Ed had a habit of borrowing his wife's coats.

His thinning hair, usually blond, had recently been dyed dark brown, and spots of the dye hadn't quite been scrubbed from his neck. When it came to his teeth, Jim Ed once joked that he used to have "summer teeth." "Some're here, some're there," he said. But he'd gotten those pulled a while back and now sported a full set of sparkling white dentures.

"Holy reintarnation, if it ain't Jon Gardner and Miz Enright," Jim Ed said, holding out his large, bony hand. Jim Ed welcomed everyone as if they were the King and Queen of England. When he stopped shaking my shoulder out of its socket he took off his hat and held it over his heart. "Miz Enright, I am truly sorry for the loss of your dear friend. You must be de-viled." I was pretty sure he meant devastated.

"Thank you Jim Ed," I said. "She left us far too soon. Life can sometimes be unfair."

"Well, expecting life to be fair is like expecting the bull not to make a run at you because you're one a them vegetarians."

I smiled. "True, Jim Ed. Very true."

"Say now—," Jim Ed could be as windy as a sack full of farts, but fortunately another truck pulled in and the occupants pulled his attention away from us. Jon and I took the opportunity to dash into the Co-op. Before I knew it, five hundred pounds of feed had been loaded into the bed of the truck and we were back at the farm by the time raindrops started to fall.

"I'll unload," Jon said when we pulled up to the barn.

I wasn't above lifting a few feedbags, but we'd called Martin as soon as we left the Co-op and his unmarked car was already in the drive. This was the second time Detective Giles had shown up in mere seconds. I was beginning to think he was related to Flash, the speedy superhero.

I told the story of Mr. Clean Cut for the second time. "Bill Vandiver saw him too, in the café after the reading of the will, and Buffy saw him when we had lunch at Provence," I added.

Martin had a long fuse, but I could tell his anger was close to bursting. He stomped around my kitchen dispelling energy right and left. "Did you ever think if you called me as soon as he drove out of the parkin' lot I could have sent someone to look for him? By this time we could've stopped him and we'd know who he was."

Darn. I hadn't thought of that.

"It's just that I like you," he said, sticking his hands into his pockets, then just as quickly pulling them back out. "My brother likes you. Even my mother likes you."

"Now that's going too far," I said. By this time I was mad and on my feet, too. "Your mother hates me. Call it for what it is, Martin. She'd rather have her son date a pig goober than me."

We were both surprised by the honesty of my words and stopped to take stock. Sometimes it was hard for me to differentiate the brother of my boyfriend from the law enforcement official. Right now I wasn't sure which hat he wore.

Martin spoke first and his words were soft. "It's not that she doesn't like you. She actually thinks highly of you."

I snorted.

"She just thinks you are not a good match for Brent." Martin held up his hands before I could protest. "She thinks Brent needs someone who is more of a homebody. That's all. Other than that, she really does like you as a person."

I didn't want to argue the point. Mama Giles might even be right. But even if she was, it wasn't any of her business.

"I have a new cell number," I said. We'd called earlier from Jon's phone. "I'm using the buddy system. I promise not to go anywhere on my own until the murderer is in custody. I promise to use caution, and to be careful." Then I drew on my fine command of language, and shut my mouth.

"Okay," he said. "But if anything, and I mean anything the slightest bit out of the ordinary comes up, you call me. Now lock all of the doors and windows after I go, and don't be stupid like you were a few months ago and open the door without first seeing who's on the other side."

I did make that teensy mistake once and ended up getting myself kidnapped. I'd learned from that experience though, and added no door opening and not getting kidnapped to the list of promises that I made to the detective.

Brent was on call that night and was staying close to home. I still had not had time to tell him all that was going on. Soon, though. I would do that soon.

Darcy had gone home with her friend Amber after school. The two had been close since kindergarten and were going to treat Amber's mom, who was going through her second divorce, to dinner and a movie.

Even though it came in spurts, sometimes Darcy's generosity and compassion amazed me. She was going to stay at Amber's that night, then in the morning head to her dad's. Mason had set up a meeting with a college prep counselor. Darcy had wrinkled her nose distastefully when she heard that news, but she walked the line with her dad pretty well. She regularly pushed his boundaries, but never too hard.

That left me with the choice of having dinner alone, or with Jon. I often ate by myself, but the day's events had made me jumpy.

"Dinner?" I asked when I called him. "Six thirty?"

Jon and I ate a jumbo lasagna that I had picked up at Walmart, along with a salad. We were just finishing up some double fudge chocolate ice cream for dessert when a knock sounded at the back door. Jon and I exchanged glances, then I called, "Who is it?"

"It's me, Bubba."

"You stay here. I'll go to the door to be sure no one else is with him," Jon said. He pulled back the blind on the window and peered out, then cracked the door open with the security chain still latched. All must have seemed secure, because Jon took the chain off the hook. Bubba trudged in with his backpack and a plastic grocery sack. Clothes spilled over the top of the sack.

"My dad, he had to go away again. Said I could stay with you," Bubba said.

I looked at Jon, my eyes full of worry for Bubba, anger at Hill, and concern that I might inadvertently put Bubba in danger. There was, after all, a killer gunning for me. Bubba, however, misinterpreted the look and dropped the plastic sack as he ran back out the door. I saw the look on his face and realized that Bubba thought he was not welcome.

Before I knew it I had jumped up to go after him, but Jon caught my arm. "You stay here," he said. "Lock the door after me. I'll find him. I promise."

Cat's Horse Tip #14

"Every day, the average horse eats a minimum of 1 percent of his body weight in forage (grass or hay), so a 1,000 pound horse would eat ten pounds of hay. Active horses in training might eat up to three times that amount."

23

I SPENT THE NEXT HOUR pacing the lower level of my house. Kitchen to living room to office and back again. So many thoughts swirled through my brain that I couldn't catch a single one of them. Never in a million years did I want Bubba to think he wasn't welcome. Twenty years ago I had been that kid who didn't have a place to go. I didn't want Bubba to ever go through what I'd had to.

When it came to Hill Henley, I understood that everyone was entitled to be stupid sometimes, but Hill abused the privilege. Why did Hill think it was okay to send Bubba over here without asking me in advance? Hill had been working for several months now with a social worker. He'd been taking parenting classes. He should have learned something. What if I had been out of town?

When I was making what seemed like the four hundredth circuit of my downstairs, my new phone finally rang. I hadn't taken time to add any phone numbers into it so it took a moment for me to look at the number and figure out who was calling. Jon.

"Found him," he said. "He was in the hay stall. He's going to bunk with me tonight."

I was surprised by the amount of relief I felt. Tomorrow I'd talk to Bubba, tell him he was always welcome here. Then Hill would come back in a day or so and I'd talk to him, too. Martin was working hard and would catch Melody's killer, and then life could get back to usual, or as usual as it would ever be without Melody.

Those were my thoughts in that moment. I'd quickly find, though, that if I imagined life was going to improve soon, I was dead wrong.

Right after I got up the next morning I checked my email. There were only two of any importance. The first was from Jenn at *Horses in the Morning*, who asked if I would talk to their listeners about Melody and her love of horses. I wanted to, I really did, but I wasn't ready.

LOTS GOING ON. AFTER THANKSGIVING OKAY?

That would buy me a few weeks time. The other important email was one from Buffy, who asked if I was interested in being on a committee to help plan Melody's public memorial service.

> WE'RE MEETING AT THE HOLY CHURCH OF THE MIGHTY HAPPY AT 3 THIS AFTERNOON. SORRY FOR THE SHORT NOTICE. THIS IS ALL COMING TOGETHER QUICKLY. WOULD REALLY LIKE YOUR INPUT.
>
> EMILY, RUTHIE, DAVIS, CHAS CHADWICK, AND I ARE ON THE COMMITTEE—AND *YOU* WE HOPE. WE'VE ASKED KEITH, TOO, BUT HAVEN'T HEARD BACK. KNOW HE IS OUT ON TOUR UNTIL THE THANKSGIVING BREAK BUT THOUGHT HE MIGHT BE ABLE TO SKYPE IN IF HE IS NOT BUSY WITH A SOUND CHECK. WE NORMALLY WOULDN'T MEET ON A WEEKEND, BUT WE'RE ALL PULLING IN EXTRA HOURS ON THIS.

I gave Buffy's email some thought before I answered. Of course I wanted to be there. Melody would want me to be involved. But would a meeting such as this seem to the killer that I was snooping? It was an excellent opportunity to get closer to the key players in Melody's life, though.

My fingers clicked on reply before I was even aware that I had made up my mind.

> LOVE TO BE INVOLVED. COUNT ME IN. CAT

While I typed, another email came in. It was from Brent saying that his schedule had changed and he was on call through the weekend. I sighed. Between Melody's murder, and the schedule at Brent's clinic, we hadn't been able to spend much time together lately.

It was still early when I went out to feed, and the air was crisp with the smell of fall. This was one of the first really cool mornings of the season, although the temperature was supposed to reach sixty later in the day.

Hank met me by the feed room, and helped me give each horse a little hay. Then I measured and ladled grain and supplements for all of the horses. Each horse had a specific mixture of feed that optimized health and performance. The result was that I fed three different formulas, plus a variety of bone and joint, and skin and hair and hoof supplements. Wheeler also took allergy meds.

After the horses finished eating, I put Reddi and Wheeler into the big pasture in the front. Reddi pranced and snorted her way around the field, while Wheeler put his nose down and got to the business of eating the brown November grass.

Gigi got to go into the round pen and she, too, took the opportunity to snort in the cool air. Ringo went into a paddock with Sally. This was his first turnout at my place with another horse. Sally was sensible, and would also teach him the rules. As a former race and halter horse, it probably had been some time since Ringo had been allowed out in a pen with other horses. He needed to be re-socialized, and hanging with Sally Blue was a great way to start.

I stayed by the fence rail for a few minutes to be sure they got along, and after a few nose to nose squeals, and a strike or two with her front foot, Sally wheeled around and kicked at Ringo twice, then they settled down companionably to graze. I noted that Sally didn't kick Ringo, but kicked at him. There was a difference. This round of kicking was a warning. If Ringo didn't follow detailed equine societal rules, then the next kick could make contact.

By the time I got back to the barn, Jon and Bubba were coming down the wooden steps from the loft. Jon gave me a thumbs up, so whatever he said to Bubba must have eased his mind. Now it was my turn.

"Breakfast?"

Jon shook his head. "No thanks. I'm good." Jon was not a breakfast person.

"Then I think Bubba and I should go to McDonalds."

Bubba's face lit up. McDonalds was, hands down, his favorite restaurant.

"Can I have one a them Egg McMuffins with hash browns and a triple berry smoothie?" he asked already running toward the truck.

I told Jon we'd be back within the hour and that I'd be very aware of our surroundings. Bubba would be my safety buddy. Then I drove west on River Road, up and over the hill and across the Cumberland River. We went through the drive-in, then I swung into Sycamore Park where we found a picnic table near the river. Even though it was a chilly morning, I mixed an orange juice and sprite together, my usual summertime drink. McDonalds did offer hot chocolate, but this morning I decided to pass.

"So," I said, "you and Jon have a good night last night?"

"Yep. Me an' him, we has us a boys night."

Oh boy, I thought. I envisioned a night of action movies and burping contests. Although, I had a hard time picturing Jon as a serial belcher.

"What, ah, what did you do during your boys night?"

"We played Go Fish, an' we drank us some root beer."

I also had a hard time seeing Jon as a Go Fish kind of guy, but life is full of surprises.

"An' he told me that you an' him, you guys wanted me to come over whenever I could."

"That's true, Bubba. I was just a little startled last night, that's all. I'd had a rough day and I was worried, because your dad usually tells me when he is going out of town."

"This was one a them last minute kind of trips," Bubba said. His Egg McMuffin was long gone, as were the hash browns.

"Well, I just want you to know that no matter what, you are always welcome at my house," I said, as I gathered up cups and wrappers. I meant the words, but I also hoped I wasn't opening the door to something that would become problematic. I had enough difficulty in my life already. Then Bubba smiled, and I thought, *what's so difficult?*

By the time we got back to the farm, Jon had Petey's harness on and Bob tacked up in western gear.

"I thought Bubba could ride Bob while we worked with Petey," Jon said.

"Can I?" Bubba asked me.

"Get a helmet first," I said. "Look in the tack room, to the left of the door."

Even though Bubba was the son of a horse trainer, Hill had neglected to teach his son how to ride. What riding experience Bubba had came from my letting him sit on a horse now and then, along with a few informal lessons. Hill had made it quite clear that he didn't want me putting my "silly girl" notions about horses into Bubba's head. He also didn't like the way I fed or trained my horses, or how I managed my pastures. The way Hill found fault with me, he must think there was some kind of reward.

Bob was gentle, and he and Bubba had spent time together in the past. Helmet on, I gave Bubba a leg up and the two began to plod around the far end of the covered arena. Jon had set out some trail obstacles, and some cones and poles, so Bubba had plenty to do down there.

On the other end, Jon led Petey while I pulled the new black cart up behind him, almost as close as it would be if Petey was pulling it. Petey showed no concern, even when we did some figure eights and trotted some. Next session, Jon and I would try hooking Petey up.

Bubba and Bob did well together, but after their ride, I cautioned Bubba not to mention Petey and the cart to Darcy.

"It's a secret, Bubba, a big secret and Jon and I want to surprise Darcy for Christmas, okay?"

Bubba nodded. "Pinky swear. I won't tell."

"Then you'll have to be here with us when we show Darcy," I said.

"If'n my dad will let me," he said.

It surprised me how much I hoped Hill would. After Bubba and I shared a lunch of milk and peanut butter and jelly sandwiches, I checked my email. Checking email twice in one day was probably a record. Twice a week was usually pushing it. Among a few junk emails was another email from Buffy.

MEETING MOVED TO MHTRC, SAME TIME. C U THEN.
BUFFY

It took me a moment to figure out that MHTRC stood for Mighty Happy Therapeutic Riding Center. It was then that I realized I had a problem, well, three problems actually. The first was Hill Henley. I had no idea where he'd gone or when he'd be back, and I had no way to find out. If Hill had not left any clues to his whereabouts the last time, he certainly wouldn't have this time, either. I also didn't want to go inside their scummy trailer. Even if Hill and Bubba had picked up the trash, I was sure they had not cleaned. For now Bubba was safe and happy. We'd see what events the next few days brought.

Problem number two was Brent. I needed to catch him up on the happenings of the past few days, but wanted to do it in person. Now, with him on call all weekend, we'd have to talk over the phone. He'd probably work until four or so, unless there was an emergency, and then who knew how late he might be at the clinic. I'd call him this evening, after dinner.

My third problem was the meeting itself. I had agreed to go, but just realized I didn't have a buddy to take with me. I didn't think it was appropriate for Bubba to go. Besides, he wanted to help Jon with the evening feeding. I put my thinking cap on, and soon my dilemma was solved.

Jon and Bubba would follow me to the riding center, then Darcy would stop by after her meeting with the career counselor and follow me home. I felt silly taking these precautions, yet the people around me seemed to feel they were necessary. I guessed that I didn't mind indulging them.

Bubba questioned the need for he and Jon to follow me, but Jon explained that my truck hadn't been working all that well, and he wanted to be sure that I arrived at the meeting safely.

"Why don't she just take your car?" he asked.

Jon, who was standing behind Bubba, grimaced and raised his hands palms up.

"Because Jon might need his car," I said quickly.

Bubba seemed to accept that and soon I was headed south on Sam's Creek Road, a man, a boy, and a hound dog with his head hanging out the window following behind. How did I ever get so lucky?

24

I YAWNED WHEN I WENT through Kingston Springs and thought I'd much rather take a Saturday afternoon nap than attend a meeting—even a meeting for Melody. I had a killer headache, too. But soon I was on West Kingston Springs Road and the church was in sight. I rolled down my window, and stuck my arm out and waved when I turned into the drive of the riding center. But, Jon pulled into the driveway anyway. He idled his ancient car while I got out of my truck and was greeted by a Mighty Happy volunteer in a gold sweatshirt. Only then did he turn his car around and left.

Even though I was a few minutes early, Buffy was there ahead of me, in the aisle, a sleek, black messenger bag draped over her shoulder. I guessed that the bag was full of her devices: tablet, computer, phone, and all the related chargers.

Whatever happened to pen and paper? But, I hadn't brought those either, so probably shouldn't voice my opinion.

"There were a few committee meetings at the church, so Ruthie suggested we meet over here," said Buffy. "There's a lesson finishing up, but no one is in the parent room, so we can meet in there."

When I drove up, several people were outside the barn, conversing at a picnic table on the thin, grassy strip between the parking lot and the covered arena. It didn't take a light bulb going off inside my head to figure out that those were the parents. It was a nice afternoon for sitting in the sun.

The parent room had a few bottles of water sitting on a table so I grabbed one and swallowed a tired-looking aspirin that I found after scrounging around in the bottom of my purse. Then I turned to the large window that looked over the arena. There was also a speaker, so anyone who was in the room could hear what was going on during the lesson.

Today Emily had more advanced riders, and two teenaged boys made up her class. One had Down syndrome, and the other was a tall, blond boy who was very interested in waving at me when he rode by. The boy with Down syndrome rode by himself, without the aid of a leader or a sidewalker. The other boy just had a leader, although I saw three volunteers spaced around the arena. Spotters, I guessed. They would quickly step in if either rider needed assistance.

"In a few minutes we are going to trot." Emily's slow, clear voice came through the speakers, along with the tiniest bit of static. "When you get to the green cone by the far wall you will ask your horse to trot, and when you get to the red cone, you will ask your horse to walk. Now Henry, can you repeat that back to me?"

The tall boy looked at Emily and smiled. "Juan, how about you? Henry, please listen to what Juan has to say."

"Green cone trot, red cone walk," said Juan.

Juan was riding Noodle the Haflinger, and Henry was on the brown Saddlebred/Quarter Horse cross, Cinnamon.

"Good explanation, Juan!" said Emily.

"Henry, can you tell me how you get Cinnamon to trot?" asked Emily.

Henry waved at me as he passed by again, then turned to Emily and shouted, "Trot."

"Very good, Henry. Yes, you will tell your horse to trot with your voice, but maybe not quite so loud. Can you say the word using more of an indoor voice?"

"Trot," Henry boomed with a little less force.

"Better. Juan, what else do you do to ask your horse to trot?"

Juan mimicked thumping his legs against his horse's sides without actually doing so. Then Emily brought both boys through the same process, but this time going from a trot to a walk. Only when both boys had practiced saying whoa and pulling back on their reins, did she actually allow the boys to trot, one at a time.

Juan did his trot mostly standing up, with his seat out of the saddle. He did a relatively good two point, except that his toes kept pointing toward the ground, which threw his upper body forward. Emily asked him to point his toes toward the sky, and he did better the second time.

Henry did a nice sitting trot both times, but was too busy waving at the spotters and me to keep his hands on his reins. During both trots, Juan had relatively good control of his horse, although I wasn't convinced he could maintain if he went around a corner. After his second trot Juan was so excited with himself that he dropped his reins to clap his hands. One of the volunteers stepped forward to grab Noodle, on the off chance the Haflinger might decide to move faster than a moseying walk. But Juan remembered himself and picked up his reins before the volunteer could get there.

I was having such a good time watching the lesson that I hadn't realized that the rest of the committee had arrived. Chas was the one I knew the least about. He arrived last, and full of impatience, which seemed to be his natural state.

Buffy took charge of the meeting, and passed around a one-page agenda. It seemed there was a consensus that the memorial event should be held next June during the CMA Festival, country music's huge fan fest held in Nashville.

"The Ryman Auditorium books out early, but if we call now, we might get a daytime slot," said Davis. "Sometimes during CMAFest they have more than one event going on within a single day there. If we had a morning event—"

"The day and time don't matter," said Chas, looking at his watch. "Let's just find an avail and snag it." I was pretty sure I didn't like Chas.

The Ryman Auditorium had once been a church, and a number of memorial services for stars of country music had been held there over the years. Melody would have liked knowing that hers would be held there, too.

"I'll see if I can book it," Davis said.

"The label will pay for the venue rental, and for the sound," said Chas.

"I'll do event PR and media credentialing," said Buffy.

Emily popped in late, having finished her lesson and having returned the kids back to their parents. After she arrived, there was some argument over whether or not Buffy should be paid for her services, with Davis finally insisting that this was not part of the four months retainer fee that was outlined in Melody's will. Davis would pay Buffy's fee out of the estate.

On and on it went. My role seemed to be to say if Melody would have liked something or not. Ruthie said she'd perform the memorial service. Davis and Chas offered to line up a few top celebrities to perform. I mentioned that Melody would want Keith to be one of those celebrities and maybe he could perform their duet, "Do Good," with another female artist. Buffy took notes. Emily didn't have much to say.

During the meeting I had been looking closely at faces. These were the faces of Melody's friends and co-workers. Had one of them killed her? If so, the murderer wore the face of innocence well. We agreed to meet again, as soon as Davis had the venue secured and we knew more about the day and time.

When we all stood, I made a point to reach out to Emily.

"You look tired," I said.

Emily eyed me as if I had a hidden motive for talking to her. Well, I did, but she didn't need to know that. I tried again. "You put a lot of thought into your lessons. I saw part of this last one. The boys did well."

That earned me a little smile. "They've come a long way," she said. Then she gave me a curious stare. "Did you ever ask Allen or Ruthie about our funding?"

"I haven't had time," I admitted.

"I didn't mean to be short with you at orientation," she said, relaxing her body a smidgen of a degree. "We had a lot to cover. It's no secret, though. Most of the horses are donated, as is some of our hay, grain, tack, and supplies. Fees from riders make up about 15 percent of our budget. Beyond all that we rely on fundraisers, grants, and donations. Now," she said looking at her watch and stiffening her body back up, "I have to pick up Rowan."

Guess our time together was over. Too bad, as I thought for a second there that she was thinking about being friendly. I had also wanted to ask why her husband had been looking so angrily past the camera on the b-roll footage from the wrap party, but that would have to wait for another time. She and Davis, both were so self-contained that it was almost impossible to see who they really were, and that bothered me. Killer, or not? I hated that I had to think this way about almost every person I saw.

When we opened the door to step into the aisle, Darcy was there talking to Robert Griggs. I'd almost forgotten she was going to follow me home.

"Robert's telling me about this new horse that's coming in," Darcy said.

"He's a former Olympic jumper," Robert added with the most animation I'd ever seen in him. "He's twenty, but will give us a few good years before he is turned out to pasture."

"And guess what? Robert said I might be able to exercise him." Darcy was almost jumping up and down with excitement. "After you've volunteered here for a couple of months you can apply to be an exercise rider."

"Sounds perfect," I said, and I meant it. Riding a variety of horses was a great way to advance one's riding skills. I wanted to ask more about the horse, but I had another question for Robert.

"Changing the subject," I said, "what did you think of the video shoot? That was the first time I'd been involved in one of those."

"Me, too," he said. "The video will be good for both the church and the center. That day, though, was more hectic than I had anticipated."

"How so?"

"Well that Fitch guy, for starters. He was just plain rude. Then he kept changing his mind about what he wanted to eat and who could stand next to him. Me? I think he's got a personality disorder or something."

Maybe that explained the murderous look that Robert had given Fitch on the video outtakes. I looked at Robert again. He, too, was quite self-contained, but I knew him to be a pacifist, and a gentle person. Killer? Probably not. The growing darkness through the open door at the end of the aisle made me look at my watch. It was already five-thirty. Long past time to head home.

Darcy and I went to our respective vehicles, and after I got in I sighed and locked my doors. Darcy followed me out of the lot. My headache had gone away during the meeting, but came thumping back on the drive home. My first yawn came at the three-way stop light in Kingston Springs, and my second when I turned north on Sam's Creek Road. I glanced in my rearview mirror to be sure Darcy was still behind me. Maybe I needed some vitamins and a few days off. I had been running pretty hard.

Up the hill and past the animal shelter my vision blurred, then sharpened. My new phone was in my purse and I had the thought that I should call Darcy. If I was engaged in a conversation I might feel better. But I couldn't find the phone, so I gave up looking. I clicked the radio on to a Toby Keith song, but couldn't make sense of the words. Around the curve and past Little Pond Creek Road I realized my eyes had been closed for a few seconds. I should pull over, but there was no shoulder here. I drove another half mile before my body reacted to my thought.

I remember rolling to a stop in the middle of the road, putting the truck in park, and reaching out to turn the ignition off. Then my world went black.

Cat's Horse Tip #15

"Like some people, some horses are claustrophobic and are not comfortable with sidewalkers walking close to them in a therapeutic riding lesson."

25

WHEN I WOKE UP, I was in a bed in the Cheatham Medical Center. I recognized the layout of the room from the times I had been there before: narrow bed, gray walls, and a window with matching gray blinds. My room was partially lit by an early morning sun. I wasn't sure how I knew the time of day by the quality of the light, but I did.

I also wasn't sure why I was there, or how long I had been there, but I didn't care. The bed was comfy and I was tired. I decided to take a nap.

The next time I woke the sunlight was brighter and there was activity in the hall. I heard the rolling of carts and the smell of what could quite possibly be lunch. As I blinked myself awake I saw Jon dozing in a chair next to the window. I studied the sharp planes of his face and the relaxed position of his body, and wondered how long he had been there. I'd never seen Jon asleep before. Most people display a softer, more vulnerable version of themselves when they are asleep, but Jon was still very much himself. Trustworthy, smart, hard-working Jon.

For some reason I wanted to reach my hand out to touch him, but he must have sensed me watching him, because before I could do that he jerked awake.

"How are you feeling?" he asked.

I pulled my hand back and considered his question. "I'm not sure." My arms and legs seemed to be free of casts, and my neck was not in a brace. I stretched my other limbs to be sure, and they all worked just fine. "Why am I here?" I finally asked.

"What do you remember?"

Vague thoughts and impressions flooded into my brain, none of them very clear. "I was tired . . . and I had a headache. I tried to call Darcy but couldn't find my phone. Then I stopped the truck."

As I spoke, I had a sense of flashing lights and distant voices, but I couldn't place them into any kind of meaning or time frame.

"You were overcome with carbon monoxide poisoning," Jon said.

I tried to make sense of his words, but my brain was sluggish.

"There was a leak in your truck, so you were breathing toxic exhaust fumes. With the windows rolled up you had no access to fresh air. That's why the headache."

And also probably the reason for the blurred vision, exhaustion, and confusion. I was glad my brain could make that connection, at least.

"So what happened?"

"As far as I know, Darcy was following you. You started to slow down and speed up," Jon said. "First, she thought you were looking for something on the road, but then you started to weave back and forth. She called your new cell, so maybe that's why you tried to call her. Maybe you heard the phone ring and tried to answer it?"

I tried to remember hearing the phone ring, but couldn't.

"Then Darcy thought someone was in the truck with you," Jon said. "She was just getting ready to call Martin when you stopped the truck in the middle of the road. She waited for you to get out, but you didn't, so she went up to the driver side window and saw that you had passed out. When she tried to get the door open she found it was locked. The truck was still running, so she called 911."

Jon went through the next set of events, step by step. "A patrol officer and an ambulance arrived, as did a fire truck. Someone had one of those lock jimmies that you slide down inside the window and that unlocked the truck door."

Jon said I arrived here about six-thirty in the evening, an hour after I left the riding center. Martin was having dinner with Mama Giles, but Mavis, the dispatcher, called him, as she knew he was working the Melody Cross case, and that I was involved.

Martin called Jon and asked him to meet me at the medical center, and Jon left the farm as soon as Darcy got back to stay with Bubba.

"You've been here all night?" I asked.

"I have."

The last time I had stayed overnight here, Brent sat with me. That was the first time I had met him.

"Brent?" I asked.

Jon's eyes clouded. "Busy with pet emergencies."

I wondered about the look in Jon's eyes, but did not have the brainpower to figure out what it meant.

Just then Martin stepped into the room.

"You're awake," he said, stating the obvious. "Can't tell you the scare you gave us."

"Sorry."

"Not your fault," he said. "Jon fill you in on what happened?"

I nodded.

"As you know," he said with a nod toward Jon, "I had the truck towed. We looked it over pretty close. Your truck is in good shape, includin' your muffler and exhaust—except for the holes someone drilled into them, and into the floor of the vehicle."

The look I gave him must have been blank because his next words were, "Miz Cat, we're treatin' this as an attempted murder. Someone tried to kill you."

After Martin told us his news, I must have looked a bit green about the gills so he called in a nurse. Soon, medical professionals surrounded me, and Jon and Martin were hustled out of the room.

After determining that my needs were not urgent, all of them left, with the exception of a short, thin doctor who looked to be about Darcy's age.

"You're doing well," he said, looking at my chart. I'd give my eyeteeth to read my chart. Doctors and nurses were always so secretive about it. I bet they wrote things like "eyes too close together, possum dung must be smarter," or "has dirty fingernails."

"You might not remember," he said, "but when you came in we pulled blood, found your carbon monoxide, your CO levels, were too high, and started you on oxygen. That's what's flowing into your nose through the tube there."

I reached up to my face discover, for the first time, that yes indeedy, I had a tube up my nose.

"Then we took you in for a CT scan, and also ran some tests on your heart. Everything was normal by the way. Whatever confusion you still have should go away over the next few days."

Good to know, I thought.

"We'll keep you another night and if your vitals are still good in the morning, you can go home. Reduced activity for you for the next ten days or so, of course."

Of course.

As soon as the doc left, a nurse rolled a cart in with some yummy yellow Jell-o, a paper cup of Sprite, and some vanilla pudding. If I hadn't been ravenous I would have sent it all back to the chef.

Lunch dispensed with, I settled back in for another nap. I assumed Jon and Martin had been shunted off somewhere and been told to leave me alone so I could rest. But maybe not, because the next person through my door was Ruthie Cosgrove. She peered around the gray metal door frame first, before she entered, as if afraid of what she might find.

"You're awake!" she said, startled.

"So I've been told."

"The girl at the front desk said you might be sleeping."

"That was the plan," I said, "but people keep coming in to check on me."

"You are so blessed to have such a strong support system. Many people don't have that."

I supposed that she was right. I *was* fortunate to have my close-knit little family of friends.

"I heard about your incident after our service this morning and thought I'd stop by," she said. "One, your car trouble came after you left us yesterday, and I always feel responsible for making sure all of our people make it home safely. Maybe that's the mother hen coming out in me. I don't have children, but I try to take care of my little flock as if each of them were mine."

Ruthie drifted in and out of focus. I hoped it was an after affect of the carbon monoxide poisoning, and not that Ruthie was turning into a shape shifter like in some of Bubba's comic books.

Something I did must have given Ruthie encouragement, because she continued on. "You were also such a dear friend of Melody's and she shared with me that you don't have a church home of your own, so I thought I'd fill in, for now."

"I sometimes go to . . ." darn, what was the name of that church? "St. Martha's. I sometimes go to St. Martha's, the Catholic church here in Ashland City. I travel a lot on Sundays," I said. My words were true, but sounded lame, even to me. The truth was, I was a person who preferred to keep her spiritual beliefs private.

"Well. I'm glad you are doing better. You know how to reach me if you need anything, anything at all. The Holy Church of the Mighty Happy is always ready to help a friend."

Before she left, Ruthie took my hands in hers and prayed. Usually that kind of thing made me feel uncomfortable, but today it was soothing. By the time she left, I was glad she had come.

My cozy hospital bed was getting harder by the minute, so I shifted around and punched my thin pillows into submission. Then I closed my eyes for all of two seconds before the phone on my bedside table rang. My hand reached out and brought the phone to my ear. Immediately I regretted the action.

"Oh, my dear Cat. You are hospitalized!" Agnes never needed to announce herself; the emotion that she sent through the phone was enough.

"I'm going to be fine, though, Agnes. I appreciate you calling." I thought maybe she'd take the hint and hang up, but no such luck.

"My goodness, I just know you weren't wearing your trench coat, were you, dear?"

"Ah, no."

When I had been on the hunt for Glenda Dupree's killer, Agnes was concerned that I wasn't dressing the part, so she had a black trench coat delivered to me. Since then she had come to believe the coat had supernatural protective powers. But who am I to say that it didn't? Maybe if I had worn the coat I would be home safe and sound right now, instead of lying here with a tube up my nose.

"I'm sorry, Agnes, I wasn't wearing the coat—but I should have been."

"I know, dear. Now, what can I send you that will be helpful? You have some sleep masks with Sally Blue's name and logo on them, don't you?" She continued without giving me a chance to answer. "I know, something to keep you safe. How about a set of golf clubs? I can send you Ira's. You could easily whack—"

"No! No, Agnes. Thank you, but no golf clubs. A club might . . ." I had to think. "Swinging a club might scare the horses."

"You are right, just as always, dearest Cat. Oh, I know! I've got it! Night vision goggles. Those will help keep you safe. If someone comes upon you in the darkness you will be ready for them."

I wasn't so sure about that, but I thought I could use them to spot coyotes in the pasture at night.

"Thanks, Agnes. I can use the night vision goggles."

"Good, now I have to get off the phone so Lars can show me how to order them online. Bye now, dear. Rest well."

When I hung up I realized that the only thing worse than having Agnes call, was not having Agnes call. I really did love her and deep down would be disappointed if she didn't make such a fuss. Golf clubs and night vision goggles. It almost made living through a murder attempt worth it.

Before I could resume my untaken nap, a nurse showed up with a big spray of balloons from Annie, Tony, and Mickey Zinner. She tied them onto the end of my bed, next to the chart that I couldn't read. Then Doc Williams, Bob's owner, stepped into the room. Doc was an orthopedic surgeon who had patched me up a number of times in exchange for training fees. I'm not sure how his office handled that with all the insurance paperwork these days, but that was his worry, not mine.

After Doc left, Darcy called. I could tell that she was filled with worry—and not just for me.

"We haven't heard at all from Hill Henley. And Bubba's upset and I don't have a clue what to tell him," she said, her bubblegum snapping through the phone. I wondered what color she was chewing today.

"Tell Bubba that if his dad doesn't show up tomorrow Jon and I will make some calls. Also, be sure to tell him that he is welcome to stay as long as he needs to."

"Okay," she said. "And Cat? I was so scared last night when I couldn't, like, get you out of the truck. Jon says you're going to be okay. Is that true? Are you, really?"

"I am, really," I said. "I just need some rest. Why don't you and Bubba order a pizza for tonight? There's some cash in the upper desk drawer."

"Jon's cooking something," Darcy said. "Something . . . green-ish," I could hear the "ick" factor in her voice.

"Save some for me," I said. "I'll be home in the morning. When you see Jon, tell him I'll call him to pick me up when I've been discharged."

The farm was less than ten minutes away. Jon could be here in a flash.

By this time I could hear the rattling of dinner trays and knew my afternoon nap would never happen. The only person I had left to hear from was Brent, and he had been ominously silent. I debated calling him, but decided to wait.

Someone eventually brought in a tray with some passable chicken noodle soup, pink Jell-o, orange juice, and more vanilla pudding. I ate every bit of it then drifted off to a troubled sleep where I had a vivid dream that Sally Blue was diligently swimming upstream against a strong current.

26

BY MORNING I HAD BEEN cleared to go home, along with strict instructions to take it easy. Odd neurological problems could develop at any moment I was told. I nodded my understanding, and then ignored the advice.

I still had not wrapped my brain around the fact that someone had tried to kill me—and nearly succeeded. If Darcy had not been following me I could have inhaled much more of the tainted air and either died or become permanently brain damaged. Or, I shuddered, another vehicle could have come up from behind and slammed into me. Then someone else would have gotten hurt, too. The buddy system had really worked.

"Do the police still have my truck?" I asked after Jon picked me up in his old sedan.

"They do," he said.

"Would you call Martin and tell him to have the shop put a new muffler or exhaust system on it? Whatever it takes to make it safe again. Then I want to sell it. I never want to drive that truck again."

The strength of my feeling surprised me, as I had loved my old green truck. We had spent many a happy mile together.

"I'll start looking for a new truck today," I said. It felt good to have a plan. "I can make payments until Melody's estate money comes in. Besides, without a truck we can't haul the trailer or pick up feed or lumber."

Jon smiled.

"What?" I asked.

"You sound great, that's all. That makes me smile."

"It makes me smile, too," I said, wondering again at Jon's recent willingness to share his feelings.

We turned into the drive just as Jon's phone chimed. He looked at the screen, frowned, then put the phone in his pocket.

"All right. Time to come clean," I said, wondering how I felt about Jon having a girlfriend. He had lived such a monastic life since moving into my barn several years ago. Something was up and I wanted to find out who and what it was.

"Come clean about what?" he asked. His dark eyes looked puzzled.

"The phone calls. The secret smiles. The frown you gave just now when you didn't answer," I said. "What is all that about?"

By this time his car was stopped near my kitchen door. Jon bit his lip as he struggled with something inside his head. When he unbuckled his seatbelt he said, "I have to return a call. There's hot chocolate and split pea-sweet potato soup on the stove. In separate pots," he added after taking a look at the horror on my face. "Fill a mug and a soup bowl and find some place comfortable. I'll be back in a few."

When Jon and Hank came back fifteen minutes later, I had folded myself into a rocking chair on the porch, and was looking at Sally and Ringo in the front pasture. There was nothing more peaceful than watching horses graze. It was another sunny November day, and I was quite comfortable with Agnes's black trench coat wrapped around me.

Hank lay down with a new stick next to me, and Jon pulled up another rocking chair and placed it in front of me. I was going to complain that he had blocked my view, but his earnest expression stopped my mouth from opening. Whatever this was, it was going to be interesting.

Jon sat, then blew out some air. "I have . . ." he started.

He had what? Cancer? A job offer? A wombat in his kitchen? A thousand possibilities ran through my mind, none of them good.

"I have," he said, "a daughter."

A daughter? Jon had a daughter? How could that be? I'd known Jon for almost four years and he'd never said a word about a little girl. I was speechless.

Jon saw my astonishment and answered the questions my brain couldn't get organized enough to ask. "She's ten and lives with her mother in Oklahoma."

I still couldn't form any words, whether as a result of the carbon monoxide poisoning or Jon's news, I didn't know.

"Her mother was a girl I knew many years ago. I was . . . well let's just say I was a troubled teen, and so was Inola."

Annie and Tony Zinner had told me some of Jon's troubled past—but not this. I wanted to ask if they knew, but thought I'd better hold the question. Now that Jon had started talking, he couldn't seem to stop.

"She wasn't even my girlfriend. It just happened one night and I learned several years later that she had gotten pregnant. Tsula was the result." He pronounced his daughter's name as Joolah.

"I didn't learn about Tsula until she was three, when Inola hit me up for child support. It got messy, mostly because I was still a jerk back then, but after a paternity test the court made sure I paid my share. Thing is, Tsula has cerebral palsy."

"Then why are you here, Jon? Why are you not in Oklahoma with Tsula—and Inola?"

"It's complicated. Inola wasn't someone I even liked. She was a party girl then, which is how I knew her. By the time I found out about Tsula, Inola was married and she and her husband had a son."

Jon then said that Oklahoma held too many temptations for him, temptations he should not face. "I'm an alcoholic, Cat. I have trouble with liquor, and I don't do well there. Here, I have a life that I love, and I am rarely tempted, even when we go on the road. When I am there, I'm a different person."

"Is that where you go for the holidays?" I asked. Jon always disappeared the last two weeks of December. It was his vacation, after all, but he returned like clockwork about dinner time on New Year's Eve.

"Yeah. I stay with various family members, a day or so with each. After the first few hours of catching up, people in my family start to drink. Even though they know I don't want to be around it, it's their way of life. I see Tsula every day I'm there and we spend Christmas week together in a hotel. I love it here, but that week with Tsula is the best week of my year."

I saw in his eyes how that was true. "Not that it's any of my business," I said. "but is that who you've been talking to on the phone?"

Jon nodded. "And not talking to Inola. Inola is an unhappy person and not all that pleasant to talk to. I avoid her calls when I can. Tsula turned ten a few months ago and I got her a phone. Now we can keep in touch better. Inola was not pleased, but the court said she had to let Tsula keep the phone. We talk every day now."

"The cerebral palsy, she's verbal?" I had learned enough at the riding center to know that there were wide degrees of disability. Some with cerebral palsy, or CP, were nonverbal and wheelchair bound, while others might talk up a storm and walk with just a slight limp.

"Yes. She uses a walker, but I hope that one day she will walk with just a cane."

On impulse I said, "Bring her here, Jon. We can figure something out and wouldn't it be great if you could see her every day?"

He smiled. "It would be great, yes. I looked into it a few years ago, but the court won't allow it. Inola is not a bad mother, and Tsula's stepfather is good to her. Tsula loves her little brother, too. She is happy where she is."

"Tony and Annie?" I finally asked. "Do they know?"

"I have not yet crossed that bridge," said Jon. "Every day I think, today is the day. But it never is. Soon though. Soon I will tell them. But right now another little girl awaits, an impatient, four-legged redhead. It's time for Gigi's massage."

Jon gave my hand a hard squeeze as he stood, and I let my head rest on the back of the chair. Why could life not be easier? I was glad Jon finally opened up. In light of his news, I wanted to regroup on some of my plans for the money Melody had left me. Jon needed a raise.

After Jon left to give Gigi her massage, with Hank tagging along happily behind, Sally wandered up toward the porch and stopped at the fence line, which was about fifty feet away. I went over to give her some love and she spent a long time smelling my face and hands. Horses determine a lot about a person by the odors he or she carries. Everything from current emotion to yesterday's lunch could be picked up by a horse's delicate sense of smell. I probably smelled like Jell-o and hospital disinfectant.

Sally often rested her chin on my shoulder to stretch out the back of her neck and I expected her to do that today. But instead, after she finished sniffing me she laid her ears flat against her neck, gave me an ugly look, and walked away. What was it about me that Sally found distasteful today?

I didn't have time to think too much about Sally because I needed to call Brent. It was almost lunchtime and I knew he'd take a break soon. Even though we didn't see each other every day, and sometimes went a day or two without talking on the phone, it wasn't like us to not touch base when major events happened in either of our lives. But, in the weeks since Melody's death, nothing had been normal.

Back inside the house I locked the doors and plugged in my landline. When I got Brent on the phone he asked if he could call me back in five minutes. He said it in such a way that I expected him not to call at all, but he did.

"I've talked to Martin," he said in lieu of greeting.

I wasn't sure if that was a good thing or bad, so I went with neutral.

"Then you know what happened," I said carefully.

"I do. I'm sorry I didn't get to the hospital to see you. My schedule has been crazy, but Cat, to be honest, I'm not sure I can do this anymore."

"You're not sure you can do what, exactly?"

"I can't live in fear any longer that you are going to be kidnapped, or held at gunpoint, or drugged and tossed into the trash. Or that your brake lines are going to be cut, or that you're smacked in the back with a heavy weapon."

Brent had a point. Hard to believe, but those were things that had actually happened to me in the nine months I had known him.

"I can't live in fear any longer that I am going to lose you," he said. "I love you, Cat, but we aren't working."

"I know." And I did. I also noted that the first time he told me he loved me was when he was breaking up with me. Oddly enough, that wasn't the first time that had happened to me. Also, oddly enough, I felt relieved. Brent was a good man. He was funny and solid and warm and stable. And, as much as I hated to admit it, Mama Giles was right. I was not right for Brent, and he was not right for me.

"Friends?" I asked.

"Always," he said. "I'm sorry we didn't work out, and I'm sorry about the timing. It's not great to break up the same day you get out of the hospital."

"No," I admitted. "But better when I am out of the hospital than when I am in."

"True, and I meant it, Cat. About being friends."

"Me, too."

People say that all the time when they break up, but I had a feeling that Brent and I would be better apart than we ever were together. I really hoped that I was right.

"Take care, Brent."

Suddenly, I had an urgent need to be the one to hang up first, and after a quick hesitation, I did.

Cat's Horse Tip #16

"Horses that are out on pasture will graze fifteen to seventeen hours a day."

27

By early Monday afternoon Hill still had not shown up, so I asked Martin if the sheriff's office could call around to see if they could find him.

"I'm really sorry," he said. I was sure he meant that because Brent and I had broken up, that our own friendship would have to end, too. That thought hurt.

"About you and Brent," he continued. "Really sorry. But I'll get someone on Hill. 'Bout time he came home and took care of that boy of his. I'll call or stop by later to let you know what we find."

So maybe the stocky detective and I were still friends after all. My conversations with Jon and Brent had emotionally drained me, so I took a nap and slept far deeper than I had in the hospital.

When I woke up, I could hear Darcy and Bubba rummaging around in the kitchen, their voices just murmurs. Then I looked at the digital clock near my bed. Four-fifteen. I yawned, stretched, and decided that I was done with recuperating. After declaring myself completely recovered, I splashed some water on my face and went down to join Bubba and Darcy. They were both doing homework at the kitchen table, so I pulled on a light jacket and headed out to the barn. On the way my new cell phone rang. It was a call from the sheriff's office.

"It's Bobby Lee, Miz Enright. Detective Giles wanted me to let you know that we found Hill Henley," he said.

This probably wasn't going to be good, I thought, as I opened the barn door. Jon looked up from raking the aisle, and I wiggled my fingers at him.

"We don't have all the info yet, but Mr. Henley was arrested early Sunday morning in Birmingham, Alabama. Turns out he'd been transporting pirated CDs, DVDs, and other stolen goods around the Southeast."

That explained the trips with the horse trailer. You could pack a lot of CDs into the space a horse occupied.

"Just a minute, Bobby Lee. I'm going to try to put you on speaker. Jon Gardner is with me and I want him to hear this." I mouthed "sheriff's office, Bobby Lee," to Jon, as I handed the phone to him and he did something that allowed Bobby Lee's voice to be broadcast out through the phone.

"Okay, Bobby Lee. We can both hear you," I said.

For Jon's benefit, Bobby Lee repeated what he had just told me, then added, "Trouble is, when Mr. Henley was stopped for a tail light that was out, he panicked and shot the toe off of an Alabama state trooper. He's got a bond of $250,000. You wouldn't want to pay that by any chance, would you?"

Jon and I exchanged amazed glances. Hill shot the toe off of an Alabama state trooper? For Bubba's sake, I wished I could pay Hill's bond. Then I realized that even if I had the money, which I currently did not, I wouldn't. If Hill was ever going to be the father Bubba needed, someone or something had to rein him in and get his attention. This might just be it.

"Ah, no, Bobby Lee. I think I'll pass." Jon nodded in agreement.

"You and everybody else. That man's about as useful as a pogo stick in quicksand," he said. "I think Mr. Henley is going to be sitting there in jail for a while. Plus, there's video from the patrol car that shows Henley shooting the trooper, so he's probably going to do some time.

"That's really why Detective Giles wanted me to call you. It's about Bubba. If the boy's only parent is in jail, the state will take custody unless someone files papers to request emergency temporary custody. He thought that person might be you."

Temporary custody? Of Bubba?

"Do it," Jon whispered. "I'll help."

"What do I have to do?" My voice sounded tentative. What was I getting myself into? What if Hill sat in jail for six months. Or a year? Three years? I would effectively become Bubba's parent and I was pretty sure I wasn't ready for that. And what about school and our show schedule? Maybe Keith and Carole would help, too. If I had custody, though, it would solve the problem of asking Hill if Bubba could volunteer at the riding center. I still thought that would be a good activity for him, and he seemed to want to get involved. This was certainly turning out to be a barn burner of a day.

Bobby Lee told us that I needed to apply to the court, and that Bubba's social worker could help me do that. "I'll make sure no action is taken regarding Bubba until you get a court hearing," Bobby Lee said. "Today's Monday. If you get emergency papers filed tomorrow, you could have a hearing on Wednesday."

My head was spinning so fast I hoped it wouldn't pop off my neck. Maybe I wasn't completely recovered. Or, maybe I'd had so much news in the past few hours that I was getting ready to self-combust.

"Thanks, Bobby Lee," Jon said as he took the phone from my hand and clicked the "end call" button. To me he said, "Let's go into the tack room. You look like you need to sit down."

Things continued to move fast. First I called Carole, and after conferencing Keith in, they said of course they'd help with Bubba, Keith's tour schedule depending, which I took to mean that they'd help when needed, just not every day. Worked for me, and Bubba adored Keith. Then I ordered pizza for dinner.

After Frog delivered it and I again over tipped him, I told Bubba about his dad. Jon and Darcy were also at the kitchen table when I broke the news, and when Bubba broke into tears, Darcy put her arm around him and said that he'd be fine staying with us. She'd even take him to visit his dad, wherever he ended up. There was hope for Darcy, yet.

The next morning I was up early to feed and to get Darcy and Bubba up. Darcy drove herself, but I borrowed Jon's car to drive Bubba to school. After dropping him off, I parked and went in to talk to the principal. I said a prayer on the way in to ward off any arts and crafts ladies who might try to rope me into their cult. The prayer must have worked, as not one person approached me to head up a project for the school. Whew.

The principal, a short, tired-looking woman who must have been near retirement, absorbed my news without surprise.

"Let us know how the court hearing goes," she said. "Any caregiver will be an improvement over Bubba's father."

With that sterling recommendation, I then headed for the office of Bubba's social worker. On the way I realized I no longer had a safety buddy and I had not even been on the lookout for Mr. Clean Cut or his little green Honda. I called Martin to let him know where I was. He assured me he'd send someone to keep an eye on the car, and me, until I got home. I was more relieved than I let on.

"Stay in the car until Bobby Lee gets there," he said. I heeded his words.

Inside the social services office the receptionist told me there was a four to six week wait for an appointment. Hmmm. I could either insist upon speaking with her supervisor, or reach over the counter and shake her until she let me speak with Bubba's social worker. I settled for the former. Using the commanding body language I used with Gigi when she was being silly, I explained the situation and demanded five minutes of the social worker's time.

To my surprise it worked, and within minutes a social worker appeared, a woman named Claire Adams. Then she invited me back to her office, produced the forms, and helped me fill them out. When I left the building I waved at Bobby Lee, who followed me to the courthouse so I could file the temporary custody request.

We were in luck. Bubba and I were scheduled to be in court bright and early the next morning. The clerk also suggested I bring a few character references along with me. That I could do. The Carsons also faxed a letter to the clerk's office and copied me in an emailed version, and Martin and Jon agreed to come with us in the morning.

Later, after Bobby Lee followed me home, I called Mason Whitcomb, Darcy's dad, to let him know that Bubba would be staying for a while in the same house as his daughter. I was pretty sure he'd be okay with that, and he was.

"Be good for her," he said between barking orders at various assistants. "Her mother and I spoiled her. Neither of us had time for parenting, so we tried to make up for it with money. You've been good for her, and that boy will do her good, too."

By the time I hung up, I realized my head was aching. So much for slowing down. I decided to take time to sit on the porch and watch Ringo. You could learn a lot by just watching a horse. Most horses were content to have their four basic needs met: food, water, shelter, and companionship. Once they had those, they could relax into being a horse.

In just a few days, Ringo had gone from pulling up grass frantically, as if he would never have another chance in his entire lifetime to graze, to a more relaxed time in the pasture. For this horse, a horse who had been stalled most of his life, continuing pasture time would be more important to his mental health than for a horse who'd had ongoing pasture time throughout his life. And, we weren't going to campaign Ringo in conformation classes, so the occasional scratch that he might get in the pasture would not be judged against him.

Wednesday morning Darcy insisted on skipping school to come with us. "I'm, like, living in the house, too," she said. "The judge might want to ask me how many times you've beaten me, or how often I go to bed hungry. Stuff like that."

I stifled the urge to comment. Darcy prided herself on provoking outrageous reactions. All I said was, "I don't think you can chew gum inside the courtroom."

Martin arranged for us to park Jon's car behind the courthouse with the patrol cars, where he'd have someone watch it. And once we got inside the courtroom, the hearing itself was quick. Claire Adams was there and gave a recommendation on my behalf, and the judge, a kind, older man, spoke quietly to Bubba. Then the judge asked me about work and travel, looked over the fax from the Carsons, and signed the order.

"We'll revisit this after Mr. Henley has his hearing in Alabama," the judge said with nods to Claire, and to Bubba.

Claire had to get back to her office, but to celebrate, the rest of us went to McDonalds. After ingesting more than our share of chemicals and food-like products Jon drove us to Bubba's house.

"What's gonna happen to my dad's horses? An' the dogs?" Bubba asked when we drove past the barn.

"I don't know," I answered truthfully. "Your dad's helper is taking care of them for now. We'll just have to see."

No one had given us any indication how long it might be before Hill had a hearing, or, if it came to that, a trial, so I asked Bubba to put a week's worth of clothes into the bags we had brought. We also gathered some of his video games and action figures. I would clear out the closet, as well as the business files and computer that were in my office/guest room. Bubba could bunk there until we learned more.

Just in case Hill's helper hadn't heard the news, when we drove back past the barn, we stopped. I hastily scrawled a note that suggested the helper call Bobby Lee at the sheriff's office for more information. Then I tacked it to the door with a push pin I'd found in my truck. My earlier note was still tucked into the doorframe, however, so I had little hope that Hill's "man" would respond to this note, either.

That afternoon Jon, Darcy, Bubba, and Hank all went out to the barn, while I locked the doors to the house and went into Bubba's new room. I booted up my laptop and checked my email. There was one from Annie, three from Agnes, and one from Buffy. Agnes and Annie were just checking on me and I sent them short, positive replies. Buffy's however, informed me of another committee meeting.

> DAVIS HAS SECURED THE RYMAN FOR THE MEMORIAL, SO WE HAVE MUCH TO DISCUSS. NOT TO BREAK UP THE WORKDAY, LET'S ALL MEET THURSDAY AT 6 PM IN PASTOR RUTHIE COSGROVE'S OFFICE. SEE YOU THEN.

I wracked my brain for schedule conflicts and, recalling none, emailed Buffy back that I'd be there. Then I took another nap. Even though I'd told myself that I was done with all this carbon monoxide stuff, my body apparently had not yet gotten the message.

About three o'clock Darcy bounced noisily into my room to wake me.

"Martin's here," she said.

It was quite possible that after breathing all the tainted fumes in my truck, I craved fresh air. I couldn't find any other explanation for my recent desire to sit on the front porch, as it was something I rarely did. In any case, that's where Martin and I ended up, I in Agnes's black trench coat, and Martin in a windbreaker emblazoned with the sheriff's office logo. The sun was out again and felt good on my face.

"This new sheriff," Martin stated, "he's a good guy. I'd been 'bout ready to quit if our previous sheriff didn't get voted out."

Sheriff "Big Jim" Burns had been petty, sexist, and a card-carrying member of the good ol' boys network. He certainly had not been a fan of mine—or vice versa.

"We got us a bunch of new rules and procedures, all for the good," he said, "and I've been discouraged about talking about cases out of turn. But durn it Cat, you were Miz Cross's best friend and you can't give me information unless you know the context in which I'm askin' it."

"What do you want to know, Martin?"

"That's just it. I don't know what I want to know. I've asked all the questions of all the people and I still haven't got one clue as to who murdered Miz Cross."

"Well, you've ruled out Fitch, Chas Chadwick, Augie Fremont, and Claudine, right? Don't they all have tight alibis?"

"They do," he said. "Unless one of them hired someone else to do it. We don't think that's the case, though. And Bodine and Cletus Potts were both in prison. They've been interviewed and no one thinks either has the intelligence to pull something like this off from inside a cell. Both of them, it's like the engine's running but nobody's driving."

"So that leaves . . ." I forced my brain to click into gear, "Brandyne—"

"Who waits tables at a truck stop near Toad Suck. She was off on Wednesday and her shift didn't start until eleven A.M. on Thursday."

"It's what, a little more than five hours from here to there? Brandyne could have done it," I said. "She still in jail?"

"No. She made bail the next day and she and her mama went back to Arkansas. She's got a court date next month. The judge so far has managed to keep the incident quiet, well, the judge and Buffy. Brandyne has been interviewed about her sister several times in the past few days. She's a fireball for sure, but I just don't know about her."

"Then Ruthie, and Allen and Emily Harding, were supposedly all together at the Harding home until about midnight," I said. "Any one of them could have gotten to Melody."

"True, and there's motive, as the church benefited big time, but I don't get a sense that any of them knew that before the will was read. And why? It'd seem that Miz Cross was more valuable to them alive. Ongoing, she gave them a lot."

"She gave time and brought them publicity, in addition to the money," I agreed.

"Keith and Carol Carson alibi each other, but unless Keith and Miz Cross had something going on the side, there's no motive there, either," Martin said. "Miz Cross was important to the promotion of that single. Seems they're getting a bang out of it now that she's gone, but accordin' to everyone we've talked to, it would have been a big single anyway."

We talked for a few minutes about the possibility of Keith and Melody having a fling.

"Not possible," I said. "I knew Melody well, and would have known if something was going on. Plus, Keith and Carole have a solid marriage."

"Then that brings up Buffy Thorndyke," said Martin. "She has a thing for Keith. If she thought Keith and Miz Cross were secretly a couple, or even just attracted to each other . . . "

I remembered Keith saying how uncomfortable Buffy made him feel with her unwanted advances.

"Buffy has no alibi to speak of," Martin continued. "Still lives in Belle Meade in her folk's home, but they were in the Bahamas. No live-in help. There were some overnight emails sent from her laptop that Wednesday night, sent from the server in her house, but they could have been written before and saved to send during the night. We're checking on that."

Sounded like there was good reason for both Brandyne and Buffy to be high on the detective's list. "Wasn't Davis home alone Wednesday night?" I asked. "He's always so stony faced. I never know what he's thinking."

"He was, but again, motive. Miz Cross would be more valuable to him alive with a long career in front of her. Agree he's a tough read, though. The only one left, then . . . is you."

"Me!" I yelped. "Martin, I didn't kill Melody, I—"

"Calm down. No one thinks you did, not even the sheriff. But, you were home with Darcy all night. You have just as weak an alibi as some of the others. That's my point. We still have too many players and I don't know where to go next."

Martin and I kicked a few other motive ideas around until it started to grow dark. I wasn't sure what it was, but something he said, or something we discussed, threw up a red flag in my brain. I just could not pinpoint what it was.

Cat's Horse Tip #17

"The United States is home to just over nine million horses."

28

I SPENT THE REST OF Wednesday and all of Thursday morning resting, but by noon, I felt pretty good. Jon and I worked with Petey after lunch, and hooked him to the black cart for the first time. He took to it like a pro and I was glad we had spent so much time doing ground work, pulling the travois, and bringing the new cart next to and behind him before we asked him to pull it. We planned to surprise Darcy the second week in December, just before Jon left to visit Tsula.

We all ate early so I could get to my committee meeting by six, and I wondered if this family-style dinner was part of my new reality. I also wondered what I felt about it. Darcy agreed to drive me to the meeting, but she had an ulterior motive. She and a friend were meeting at the McDonalds in Kingston Springs. She'd pick me up at eight, unless I texted her first.

Everyone in our memorial planning group was present at the meeting, except for Emily, who was finishing up a class at the riding center. Ruthie said she'd fill her in, and Davis started by giving us the details of the venue agreement. The Ryman held twenty-two hundred people, and we discussed ticket prices, the number of tickets to hold back for family and friends, and which charity should benefit if there was money left over. Ruthie looked like she wanted to lay claim to it, but she'd already gotten the lion's share of the estate, so she had the good sense to keep her mouth shut. We also discussed which artists would be invited to perform.

"Keith Carson has already agreed, as has Brad Paisley," said Davis. His expression revealed nothing and I wished he'd let his guard down, just for a second.

Despite all we had to discuss, the meeting only lasted about forty-five minutes. By the time our little committee broke up, it had been full dark for over an hour, but the parking lot was lit, and through the window I could see a few people who'd had meetings in other parts of the church walking toward their cars.

I pulled my phone out of my purse, ready to text Darcy, when Ruthie asked me to stay for a minute. She saw my hesitation, then added, "I won't keep you long. I'm waiting for Emily, Sandy Sweet, and a few others who are finishing up at the riding center. I just wanted to talk about Melody."

I put my phone back in my purse, watched Melody's team get into their cars, and sat stiffly back down.

"Being a pastor is a blessing, Cat, but it has limitations," said Ruthie, sitting down behind her desk. "I have to be the wall that absorbs the pain of everyone else in the church. I don't have many people to talk to about my friendship with

Melody. I thought since we both knew her well, we might have stories to share."

I relaxed a little. In my book, sitting in a pastor's office was something akin to sitting in a principal's office. If I didn't sit up straight enough, or give the right answers, I might be criticized. But Ruthie was easy to talk to and as the minutes wore on, I found myself enjoying the time. That is, I enjoyed myself until I spotted Mr. Clean Cut walking through the parking lot. All of a sudden the Holy Church of the Mighty Happy seemed neither holy nor happy.

Ruthie saw me looking out the window and an expression that I can only describe as regret crossed her face. Before I had time to think, Ruthie stood up from her desk, stretched out her right arm, and sprayed what I later learned was a strong concentration of pepper spray into my eyes.

The pain was tremendous, and of course I did the exact opposite of what I should have done. I cried out, and brought my hands up to my face to rub the spray away, which only served to spread the residue into my nose and mouth. Then I reached out, nearly blind, searching for the door. I needed to find a bathroom, anything with water, so I could wash off the burning spray.

My outreached hands, however, only helped Ruthie grab my wrists and pull them behind me. Before I knew it, she had secured them. Tears were pouring from my eyes, and drainage poured from my nose.

"What are you doing?" I cried. I kicked out, hoping to connect with Ruthie, but instead smacked my foot into her desk. Then I swung my upper body around, also trying to connect, but with no luck. I was taller and thinner than she was, but she had the advantage of clear vision and use of her arms. Before

I knew it, she had clubbed me on the side of my head with a heavy, hardcover version of the Bible, and it stunned me enough to knock me to the ground. While I was catching my breath she wound duct tape around my ankles, then slapped some tape across my mouth. Her last move was to drag me into a closet, and close and lock the door.

Ruthie! All along it had been Ruthie. But why? I should have wondered what Ruthie's next plans for me were and how was I going to get out of the closet, but all I could think was, as a pastor, Ruthie was the one who had ultimately betrayed Melody's deepest trust. Damn her.

Then I remembered what had bothered me in my conversation with Martin. Allen and Emily could alibi each other for the time period of midnight Wednesday night to eight A.M. Thursday morning, but there was no one to back up Ruthie's whereabouts.

The closet was warm and I had trouble breathing, what with my nose running so badly and all. But after a while my eyes and nose dried up some. I was trying to formulate a plan, when Ruthie started to speak to me through the door.

"Sorry about this Cat, but you didn't take my warning. I sent you a text. You should have listened to me. Then, when Garrett Ross, the young man who screens our new parishioners, saw the detective on your porch yesterday, I knew you would have to be eliminated."

Garrett Ross. Did she mean Mr. Clean Cut? Either that, or Ruthie had gone over the edge and was speaking gibberish. While Ruthie had been talking I had silently scooted to the edge of the dark closet and was running my cheek and the back of my hands along what wall space I could reach. I hoped to find a jagged edge or a nail head, something I could use to peel the tape off my face or tear it off my wrists. So far, no luck. I also wondered what time it was. Darcy was due at eight. I desperately hoped she would not barge in and be caught by Ruthie, too.

There was no light coming in underneath the closet door. Maybe Ruthie had all of the church lights turned off. If so, that might spook Darcy into calling Martin or Bobby Lee.

"Of course, I wasn't waiting for Emily and Sandy," said Ruthie. "Everyone at the center has already left for the day. But Cat, the Holy Church of the Mighty Happy is not financially sound. Our books look it to be, but that's because Allen is a financial genius—on paper. I laughed when the police took our ledger. To them, we will look to be in excellent shape, but only because Allen vastly minimized our expenses. Truthfully, and I always want to be truthful, our happy little church is mighty broke right now."

Come on Darcy, I thought. *Get over here. See that something is wrong. Call 911.*

"When Melody updated her will," Ruthie continued, "she told me what she had done. She wanted to be sure we knew if anything happened to her that we'd be taken care of. But she didn't realize two things. One was that we were so destitute, and two, the terms of her will gave us cash, but not property. If she had closed on the new house she was paying cash for, we'd have received a lot less than we did, and Cat, we needed every single cent. Melody had to go before she closed on that house."

Just then I felt one soft thump through the floor. Ruthie went on talking, so maybe the vibration had escaped her.

"My original plan was for you to follow in your good friend's footsteps. Melody came early that Thursday morning to be re-baptized. I had convinced her that she should do this to purify herself for her new life in her new house. She parked behind the trees at six in the morning and walked down to the river. I held up a sheet while she changed into a baptismal robe, then tied heavy plastic bags around themselves over her hands. She'd just had a manicure and didn't want to mess up her nails. Of course the plastic kept me from being scratched, and kept my DNA from getting under her fingernails."

Ruthie Cosgrove was a monster. I had worked my way all the way around the closet and finally found the tiniest edge of a board that didn't quite meet up flush with its neighbor. As I listened to Ruthie's tale of horror, I began to frantically scrape the duct tape on my wrists against the edge of the board. My scraping made no sound, but I heard the teensiest scrape of a footfall somewhere close by. I shuffled around some to create noise to cover whoever was out there. I hoped it wasn't Mr. Clean Cut. What had Ruthie called him? Garrett Ross. I hoped it wasn't him. I also hoped it wasn't Darcy.

"When I dipped Melody back in the name of our Lord and Savior, I just held her under," said Ruthie. "Melody fought like a bearcat, but she was tiny. It was easy enough to do. Then I pulled the baptismal robe away, pulled the plastic bags off her hands and set her body off downriver. After, I wrapped the robe and plastic bags in a trash bag and put it all into our dumpster. Our service comes Thursday mornings to haul the trash off."

Nearby I heard a click, so I moved around some more. Anything to create noise.

"Then I drove Melody's car into the woods up the road. Later, after the back parking lot had been searched, I moved the car back. Hardly anyone goes past that screen of trees this time of year. And that, dear Cat, is what I had planned for you. Except you had the misfortune of seeing Garrett Ross in the parking lot and you panicked. Now I have to figure out what to do with you."

By this time I had made some headway on the tape on my wrists, but not enough. Not nearly enough. Suddenly there was a crash, and voices and light filled the room. Furniture was turned over and Ruthie began to scream.

I heard Martin call my name just as Bobby Lee began to read Ruthie her rights. I banged my feet against the locked closet door and Martin flipped the latch from the outside and opened the door. I am not sure what he expected to see, but me trussed up like a Thanksgiving turkey was obviously not it.

After, Darcy told me that she drove to the church about ten minutes to eight, only to find it completely dark. She then called Martin, who told her to drive the half mile back into Kingston Springs, to safety, which she did. The initial thump I heard had been a cop who had been nearby. As soon as he let himself into the building he heard Ruthie's voice and began to record it on his phone. Next was Bobby Lee, and then Martin, along with several other first responders. As soon as they had the team assembled and enough evidence on tape, they broke through the locked door to her office.

An EMT checked me out and declared me healthy enough to give a statement. After, I called Buffy so she could share the news with Melody's team. I knew everyone would want to know. Then I drove home with Darcy and, in the dark, went to my tree on the riverbank and cried.

The tears let out all the stress and emotion of the past few days. I cried for my relationship with Brent, and because I was scared to death to serve as Bubba's pseudo-parent. I knew nothing about raising a child. I cried because Ruthie had tried to kill me twice, and because she had ruined, for me, my affection for my beloved truck. I cried with gratitude for Melody who had left me so much money, and for the loss of our lifelong friendship, which hadn't been all that long. I cried because I loved horses so much I sometimes could barely breathe. I even cried for Jon, and for Inola and Tsula, whom I had never met, but hoped to one day.

My tears were cleansing, and after they stopped, I felt the cool night wind in my hair and on my face. I would always remember Melody with love and hoped someday to have another friendship as strong as ours had been. But maybe not with someone so famous. That had been the problem all along. Money, plus talent, success, passion, and vulnerability equaled fame. My friend's talent, passion, and success brought her money. But she was vulnerable when it came to matters of trust. Ultimately it was the fame equation that caused Melody's demise.

Eventually I disengaged myself from the tree and climbed the few feet up to the top of the bank. There, I was startled to see Jon, Darcy, Bubba, and Hank waiting for me, flashlights in hand.

"We thought you might decide to throw yourself in the river," exclaimed Bubba.

"No, nothing like that," I said. "I just needed some time. Thank you though, all of you. I'm sure that if I had ended up in the river, the three of you would have pulled me right out. Hank, too."

"Absolutely," Jon said, and with that he stretched out his hand. I hesitated, then took it. Bubba took my other hand and Darcy joined hands with him. Hank picked up a new stick and ran ahead, as together, we walked back to my little farmhouse.

Epilogue

ON A FROSTY SATURDAY MORNING, two weeks before Christmas, Bubba and I lured Darcy into the barn. There, in the far corner of the arena, was Petey, groomed to perfection with long red ribbons braided into his short mane, and a rosette of red flowers attached to the top of his tail. He was hitched to the new black, two-seater cart and Jon, dressed in a rented white tuxedo with top hat and tails, sat in the driver's seat. I had never seen Jon dressed up before, and I had to admit that he looked finer than frog hair, as my grandmother would have said.

Bubba flipped on Frank Sinatra's version of "Come Fly With Me" and Jon and Petey smartly pulled the cart up to where Darcy was standing. It was worth all of the time Jon and I had spent just to see Darcy's jaw drop.

"Your carriage awaits, milady," said Jon. "Hop in."

Darcy had to take her hands away from her face to climb in, but by the third circuit of the arena, Darcy was driving. Finally she stopped, handed the reins back to Jon, and jumped out of the cart.

"I can't believe you guys did this!" she cried, running up to me. She landed against me with a whoosh and it took a bit to disentangle her arms from around my neck. "Can we enter him in driving classes?" Darcy asked. "Oh, I want to! Can we?"

"Definitely. You'll have to drive Petey a lot this winter, though. Better to do it with a helper. Maybe someone like Bubba here. He helped, too."

And he had. Several times he had sat in the driver's seat while Jon led Petey, who was hitched to the cart. I drove from the ground.

I left Jon, Darcy, and Bubba to unhook Petey and wandered down to Sally's stall. After the news about Ruthie broke and Agnes called for the umpteenth time, she told me that Sally had telepathically sent her information about the clues she had been giving us.

"Sally was blowing bubbles because she knew Melody had been drowned in the river," Agnes said. "Well, we all found that out early on, but Sally knew it first."

Agnes was right in that Sally had blown bubbles before any of us knew about Melody. And, when I asked about Sally rolling onto her back with her feet up in the air, Agnes said that Sally was trying to tell us that Melody was going to be killed.

"Her head hanging, dear Cat, that was true mourning. Sally Blue loved Melody and was devastated by her loss, still is. Horses have a good sense of people, you know, and Sally knew that Melody was good, good people."

Melody sure was.

"And the waving of the foreleg in the pasture, the crossed legs, and weird positions when she was lying down?" I asked.

"Why, Sally was pointing you toward the church," Agnes said. "That should be obvious. The church is south of your place, Sally waved her leg in a southerly direction. And, the symbol of Christian churches is a cross. Sally crossed her legs."

"Uh, huh," I said. "We thought that was in honor of Melody. Melody *Cross*."

"Well," said Agnes, "maybe it was that, too. Next time our spirits commune I'll ask her."

Right, I thought.

"And Cat, Sally said to tell you she pinned her ears at you after you got out of the hospital because she knew Ruthie had been to see you. Sally knew that Ruthie person was bad news."

How, I wondered, had Agnes known about that? That was one detail I had kept to myself. I shook my head now, as I remembered all of Sally's odd behavior. Just then Bubba ran up and tugged on my hand. "Darcy's going to take us all out to lunch," he said.

"McDonalds?" I asked.

"No," he said. "The Riverside!"

The Riverside was on the river, just before the bridge over the Cumberland that led to Ashland City. My mouth watered as I envisioned fried catfish, hushpuppies, sweet potato fries, and caramel cake.

"Yum," I said, and ruffled his hair. "Let's go."

After lunch Hank and I sat on my front porch. The day had warmed up and I enjoyed watching Sally and Ringo, who were out in the pasture. As I watched, a large horse trailer pulled into the Henley place. Hill Henley had a preliminary hearing a week or so ago and was set for trial in the spring. Everyone was pretty certain that he'd get some prison time, so Bubba was going to be with me for a while. Hill's horses were apparently going to other trainers, and Claire Adams was working with the court to make my temporary custody more permanent. I still wasn't sure how I felt about that, except I absolutely knew it was the right thing to do.

As for Ruthie, she'd been charged with Melody's murder, my kidnapping and attempted murder, and a bunch of other charges. She was awaiting her own trial. The only thing they had on Garrett Ross, the man I'd thought of as Mr. Clean Cut, was drilling the exhaust system on my truck, which was serious, but he was testifying against Ruthie, so who knows what would happen to him. At Ruthie's request, the young man had regularly followed prospective new church members, and that's what he thought he was doing with me. Ruthie had told him it was the church's way of vetting new members, to be sure they were worthy of joining. Some people will believe anything.

Allen had not yet been arrested but was under investigation. I'm not sure what the official term is for financial "book cooking," but that's what the sheriff's office was looking into. For now, Allen was on official leave. Until everyone knew exactly how involved he was, he was asked to stay home. The same with Emily. Fortunately, the riding center had been able to hire several other therapeutic riding instructors part-time.

As for the church, the elders got together and immediately removed Ruthie from her position as pastor, even though she was the church's founder. They had not yet found a new pastor, but visiting pastors preached on Sundays while elders spoke during the Wednesday and Saturday services.

There was a big story in the Sunday edition of *The Tennessean* that the church elders were going to try to keep the church and riding center afloat. There was also a great deal of controversy over whether the church would get to keep the money that Melody left them. That question (and the status of the furniture that Melody promised me) would be sure to keep the lawyers tied up for some time, especially as Claudine and Brandyne were making a stink about the fact that the beneficiary that got the most money also caused Melody's death. Not exactly true, as Ruthie and the church were separate legal entities, but I had to admit that I understood Claudine's point.

I was thinking about a nap when my landline rang. I debated answering it and almost let it go to voice mail. But, I got up and went inside to look at the caller ID. When I saw that it read UNKNOWN, I realized it might be Gusher Black. His ID always came up that way, so I picked up.

"Merry Cat?"

"Dad?" I needn't have asked. My dad was the only person in the world who called me Merry Cat. It was his quirky, shortened version of my full name.

"Daughter, it's grand to be speaking with ya." My dad was born in Ireland, but came to the United States when he was twelve. He always played up the accent more than he needed to. "Merry Cat, I'd love to chat, but I'm in a spot of bother. Could ya possibly find it in your heart to help your old dad?"

"I'll try," I said, but what I thought was, *here we go again.* My dad never contacted me unless he wanted something. "What can I do for you?"

"That's the thing. I don't rightly know. I think someone's trying to kill me."

—THE END—

MELODY'S SWEET TEA RECIPE

Ingredients
12 cups water
1-1/2 cups of white sugar (or less, according to taste)
10 tea bags. Melody preferred Luzianne, but Lipton works, too
One pinch baking soda
Lemon juice or slices to taste
Mint leaves
Ice cubes

Instructions
1. In a small pot on the stove bring water to a boil.
2. Stir sugar and baking soda into boiling water. Keep stirring until dissolved.
3. Remove pot from heat.
4. Add tea bags to water, steep 25 minutes.
5. Squeeze tea bags against side of pot, then remove bags and discard. Melody put hers in her compost pile.
6. Pour tea into ice-filled glasses, add lemon to taste, serve with a sprig of mint.

GLOSSARY

Barrel: A horse's trunk or midsection.

Bitless bridle: *See sidepull*

Cavaletti: A series of very low jumps used to school horses, usually less than one foot in height; also used to describe ground poles without risers.

Cinch: A wide strap attached to a western saddle that runs under the horse's barrel and is used to keep the saddle on the horse.

Clean: Refers to the leg of a horse that has no blemish, scar, injury, or other deviation from normal.

Collection: Occurs when a horse carries more weight on his hind legs than on the front. His back raises as he tightens stomach muscles and flexes at the poll to carry himself lightly. This makes impulsion from the hindquarters greater; the horse is more easily maneuvered, and can carry a rider with greater ease. The horse also reaches farther underneath his body with his hind legs to make more precise stops and turns.

Colic: Abdominal pain that encompasses all forms of gastrointestinal conditions, as well as other causes of abdominal pain not involving the gastrointestinal tract. Because horses cannot vomit, it can be deadly.

Coming: In fall, a horse is spoken of as "coming" the age she will be in the next year. A four-year-old horse in the fall is "coming five."

Cross tie: A means of tying a horse where a rope from each side of an aisle is attached to the side rings of the horse's halter. Technically, the horse is tied "across" the aisle.

Croup: The muscular topline area of the horse's hindquarters beginning at the top of the hip and stopping at the top of the tail.

Desensitize: The process of accustoming horses to potentially frightening situations by gently introducing them to unusual sights, smells, sounds, and movements.

Drive from the ground: *See ground driving*

Fetlock: The lowest joint on a horse's leg. It corresponds to the human instep joint. Can also refer to the tuft of hair on the back of the horse's leg above the hoof

Girth: A wide strap attached to an English saddle that runs under the horse's barrel and is used to keep the saddle on the horse.

Ground drive: The art of asking a horse to move forward while a person walks behind with long reins to control the horse's motion, speed, and direction. Often a precursor to harness driving and carrying a mounted rider.

Ground poles: Poles of eight to ten feet in length spaced equal distances apart to help the horse develop cadence and balance at various gaits. Also a pole on the ground in front of a jump to help the horse and rider judge the take-off point.

Hands: The height of the horse from ground to the top of her withers. One hand is four inches, so a horse 61 inches tall is 15.1 hands.

Junior: A horse four years of age or under.

Loin: The area on the topline of the horse between the back and the croup.

Long lining: Similar to ground driving, but the human directs the horse's movement using long reins while standing in the center of a circle. The technique also develops balance and collection. Sometimes used interchangeably with ground driving.

Mounting ramp: A wooden or metal ramp wide enough for a wheelchair that ends in a platform of about three feet in height. The height of the platform helps a person with a physically disability get on a horse.

Narrow: A term used to describe the width between the horse's front legs, and thus, the width of the horse's barrel. People with some disabilities, such as cerebral palsy, have an easier time riding a narrow horse than a wide one.

Pastern: The part of the horse's lower leg that is between the fetlock and the top of the hoof.

Point of buttock: The outermost part of the rounded edge of the horse's rump, when viewing from the side.

Polo wraps: Fleece or other stretchy bandage material that is wrapped around a horse's leg below the knee. Typically used for protection during riding, longeing, driving, trailering, and turnout.

Round pen: A sixty-foot "round pen," often made of pipe or wood, used for training horses on the ground and under saddle.

Senior: For the purposes of most competitions, any horse over the age of four.

Sidepull: A general term for headgear that controls a horse without the use of a bit.

Snaffle: A simple bit with a joint in the center and large rings to attach reins to.

Split reins: Reins with unconnected ends. Usually a long, thin style of rein in the western discipline.

Spooky: Easily startled, skittish.

Surcingle: A belt that passes around the belly of a horse with metal rings to pass reins through.

Trunk exercise: An exercise that strengthen a rider's core, such as truck twists; or leaning forward or back, or from side-to-side, then returning to center.

Two point: Also known as the half seat, it is achieved by bending forward at the hips, lifting the fanny out of the saddle, and taking weight in the rider's ankles and heels. The two-point helps balance a rider, as it cannot be achieved if the rider is ahead of or behind the horse's center of balance.

Weanling: A current year foal who has been weaned from her mother.

Wither: The top of the shoulder where the neck joins the body; the tallest part of the horse's back, located at the base of the neck.

ACKNOWLEDGEMENTS

Huge thanks to my publishers, Neville and Cindy Johnson at Cool Titles, for taking another stab at Cat and me. Their commitment to this series has made me strive harder to deliver. Thanks too, to the people of Cheatham County and the cities of Ashland City and Kingston Springs. Local residents will recognize that I removed the railroad tracks from the Kingston Springs city center. Other than that, and the fact that The Holy Church of the Mighty Happy and the accompanying therapeutic riding center exist only in Cat's world, the town is depicted pretty much as it exists in real life.

Thanks to Jamie, Glenn, and Jenn of the *Horses in the Morning* crew (horsesinthemorning.com) for again being such good sports about allowing themselves to be part of Cat Enright's story. And, thanks to real-life music journalist Chuck Dauphin. Both are making their second appearance in the series.

Kudos also go to Bill Vandiver at The Edge Salon in Brentwood, Tennessee. (theedgesalon.com). He has been a tremendous supporter of Cat Enright from the moment she was first published, and his talent with hair is genuine in both Cat's worlds and ours. I appreciate his willingness to be part of *The Fame Equation*.

Thanks too, to Jane Muir who confirmed my suspicions regarding the cart versus buggy debate.

Many thanks also go to Mike Breedlove, the real sheriff of Cheatham County and an all around good guy, who lent his considerable time and talents to make this book better. I have known Mike a long time and he has always been a supporter of mystery authors. He was with the Tennessee Bureau of Investigation for many years, and has been a panelist at a number of mystery writing conferences, including Killer Nashville. If I got any of the local law enforcement details wrong, the fault is entirely mine.

Publisher Cindy Johnson requested a small role in the book, and I always think it is a good sign when your publisher wants to be written into the story. I hope I did her justice. She is an amazing woman.

SheilAnne Smith at the Appaloosa Horse Club helped with specific questions regarding show rules, points, and the medallion system, and the character of Sandy Sweet, the sidewalker, is named in honor of Sandy Sweet Lovato. Sandy founded the Stampede of Dreams Therapeutic Riding Program, but passed away after a tragic car accident in 2014. She was a huge fan of Cat Enright and I hope she would be pleased with her namesake here in the book.

To those of you who have not yet discovered therapeutic riding, please check it out. There are nearly eight hundred PATH (Professional Association of Therapeutic Horsemanship) centers across the United States, as well as a number of EAGALA (Equine Assisted Growth and Learning Association), E3A (Equine Experiential Education Association) AHA (American Hippotherapy Association) and many other centers. There is sure to be one near you.

To you, the reader, Cat and I so appreciate you picking up *The Fame Equation*, as well as the earlier Cat Enright books. I hope you enjoy Cat's latest mystery. If you do, please tell others about it, and her. Many adventures lie ahead for Cat, but she has told me that public demand is the only reason she will agree to share them with you. So, tell your friends what you think. In the meantime, please visit Cat and me at LisaWysocky.com or at CatEnrightStables.blogspot.com.

READER QUESTIONS

1. What draws Cat to horses?
2. Which character would you most like to spend time with, and why?
3. Why do you think Jon took four years to let Cat know his secret?
4. Do you know anyone like Agnes? If so, how do you relate to that person?
5. Do you think celebrities carry any special burdens? If yes, what are they?
6. How does the setting impact the story?
7. In what ways are Cat's friends important to her?
8. What professional field do you think Darcy should go into? Would she make a better lawyer, lobbyist, or social worker? Or, should she do something else?
9. How ready is Cat to take on Bubba full time? Do you think he will be better off with her than with his father?
10. How do you explain Sally Blue's continued odd behavior? Is she really psychic?

ABOUT THE AUTHOR

Lisa Wysocky is an award-winning author, clinician, riding instructor, and horsewoman who helps humans grow through horses. She is a PATH International instructor who trains horses for therapeutic riding and other equine assisted activities and therapies. In addition, Lisa is the executive director of the nonprofit organization Colby's Army (ColbysArmy.org) formed in memory of her son. Colby's Army helps people, animals, and the environment. Lisa splits her time between Tennessee and Minnesota, and you can find her online at:

Facebook.com/ThePowerofaWhisper

on Twitter @LisaWysocky, or at:

LisaWysocky.com or CatEnrightStables.blogspot.com.

Author photo on back cover by Monica Powell, wardrobe by Wrangler/VF Jeanswear, hair by Bill Vandiver at The Edge Salon.

IF YOU ENJOYED *THE FAME EQUATION*, YOU MAY ALSO ENJOY THESE, AND OTHER, AWARD-WINNING BOOKS FROM COOL TITLES.
Learn more at CoolTitles.com

From award-winning author Jonathan Miller: The Rattlesnake Lawyer, Dan Shepard, finally popped the question to his girlfriend, former judge Luna Cruz. Unfortunately, the father of Luna's child is back in the picture and Dan is representing him on a felony. But, Dan doesn't know if he wants to win the case. Worse, he finds Luna and himself on opposite sides. *Rattlesnake Wedding* is the seventh in Miller's award-winning series.

Mom's Choice Medalist! IBPA Benjamin Franklin Book of the Year Award Medalist! *ForeWord* **Book of the Year Finalist!** Human reason tells her she's crazy; the voice she hears tells otherwise. Emerald McGintay experiences dreams and visions and is diagnosed with schizophrenia. When she stumbles upon a trail of hidden secrets, her father decides to send her away to a special clinic. She flees her luxurious home in Philadephia to a safe haven in the Colorado Rockies where she meets a rancher who suggests he recognizes the voice she hears. Battered by a relentless storm of strange encounters, Emerald struggles to discover her reality.

An American Horse Publications, IBPA Book of the Year, and Mom's Choice Silver Medalist; and National Indie Excellence Finalist! When retired movie star Glenda Dupree was murdered in her antebellum mansion in Tennessee, there was much speculation. Prior to leaving life on earth, Glenda had offended everyone, including her neighbor, a (mostly) law-abiding horse trainer named Cat Enright. Cat finds Glenda's body, is implicated in the murder, and also in the disappearance of a ten-year-old neighbor, Bubba Henley. An unpopular sheriff and upcoming election mean the pressure to close the case is on. With the help of her riding students, a (possibly) psychic horse, a local cop, a kid named Frog, and an eccentric client of a certain age with electric blue hair, Cat takes time from her horse training business to try to solve the case and keep herself out of prison.

Winner of Best Equine-related Book at the American Horse Publications Awards. A horse trainer, juvenile delinquent, eccentric client of a certain age with electric blue hair, and a (possibly) psychic horse lead this Southern equestrian mystery into a fast paced, lightly comic read. Join Cat Enright and her crew as she tries to solve murder and mayhem at a prestigious all-breed horse show. When horses become ill and a show-goer's last hurrah is in the port-a-potty, Cat decides to find the cause of the trouble. *The Magnum Equation* is the second in the award-winning Cat Enright series.

Raves for the Cat Enright Equestrian Mystery Series

"From the first page to the last *The Opium Equation* will keep you engaged and wanting more, horse lover or not."
—Glenn the Geek, founder, Horse Radio Network

"A murder, a mystery, and a psychic horse. What's not to love?"
—*Horsemen's Yankee Pedlar*

"Wysocky puts out an excellent product. Readers will be waiting to lap up more Cat Enright adventures. And there is that hunky country singer."
—*Midwest Book Review*

"This quick and entertaining read will amuse fans of Carolyn Banks's equine mysteries."
—*Library Journal*

"I couldn't put *The Fame Equation* down. A great read and a great ride! I loved it!"
—Robin Hutton, author of the *New York TImes* Bestseller *Sgt. Reckless: America's War Horse*

"The mark of a storyteller is when the reader begins to genuinely care about the characters in the story. Such is the case in *The Fame Equation*. Lisa Wysocky captures the culture of the South—both people and horses—with deep insight, and as the plot deepens, the suspense tightens its grip."
—Jean Abernethy, author, cartoonist, creator of Fergus the Horse